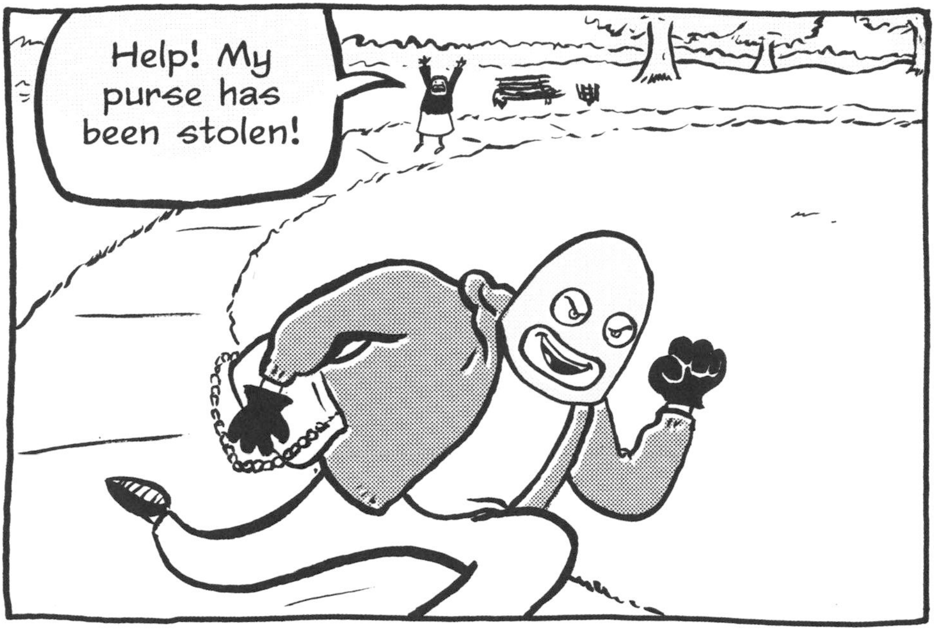
Help! My purse has been stolen!

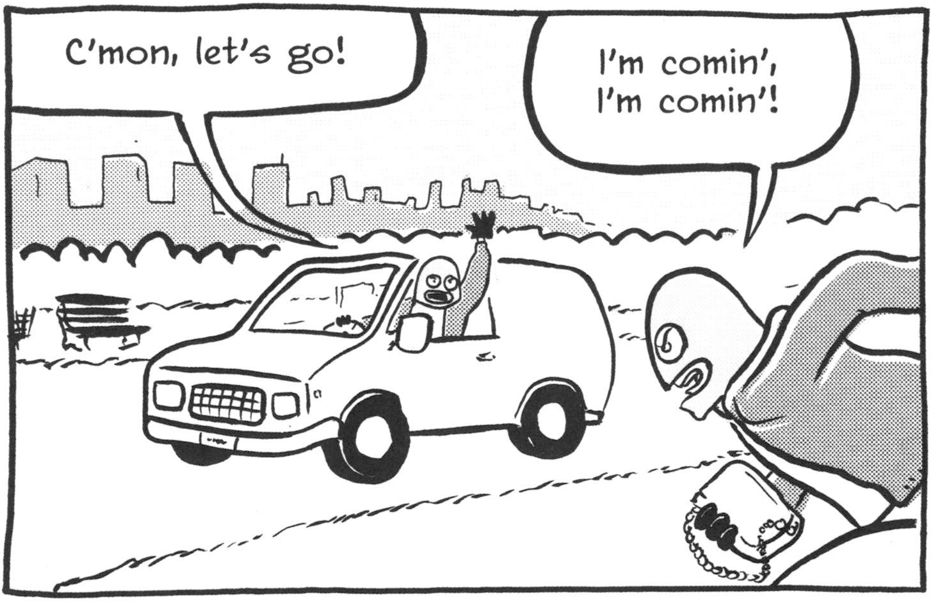
C'mon, let's go!
I'm comin', I'm comin'!

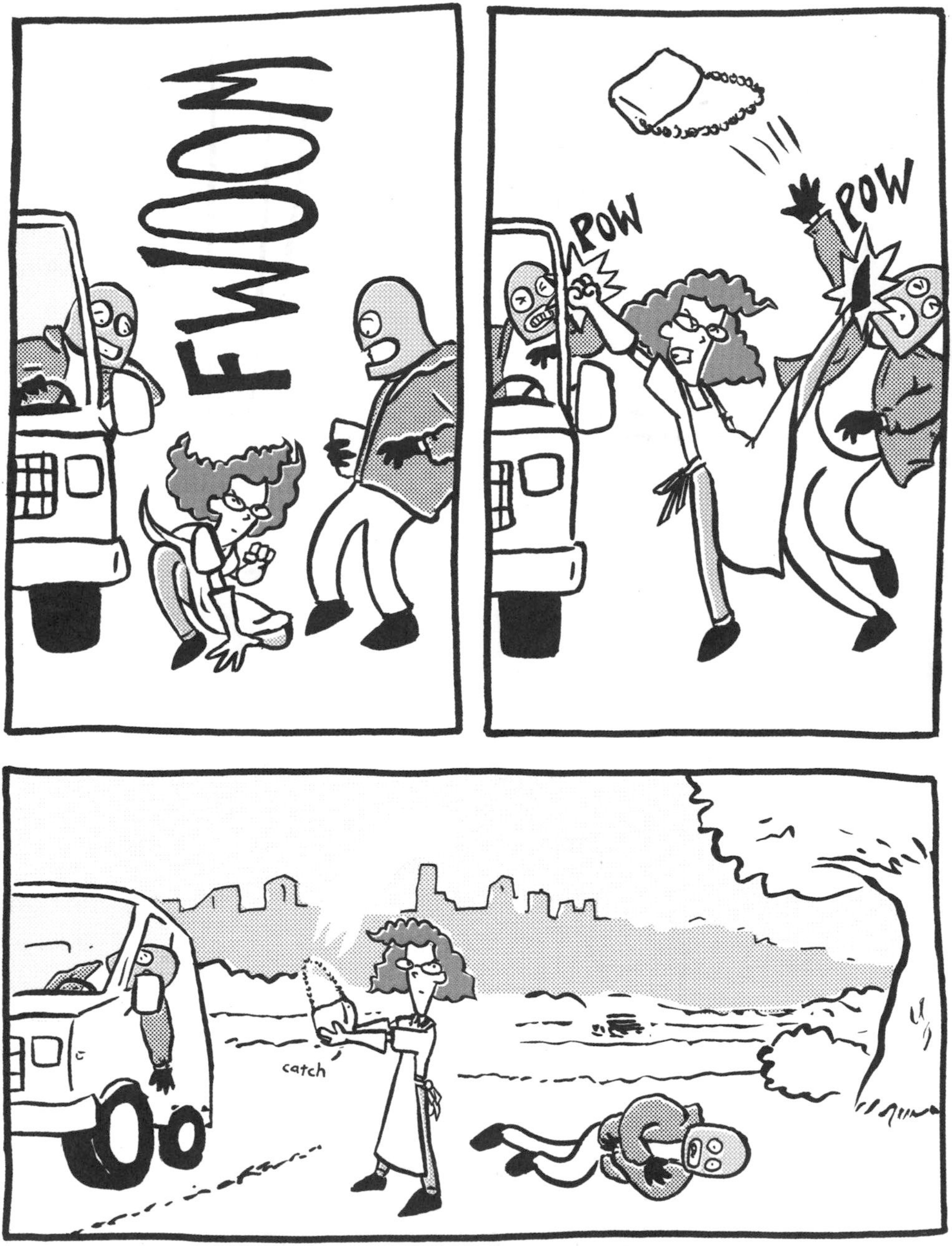
FWOOM
POW
POW
catch

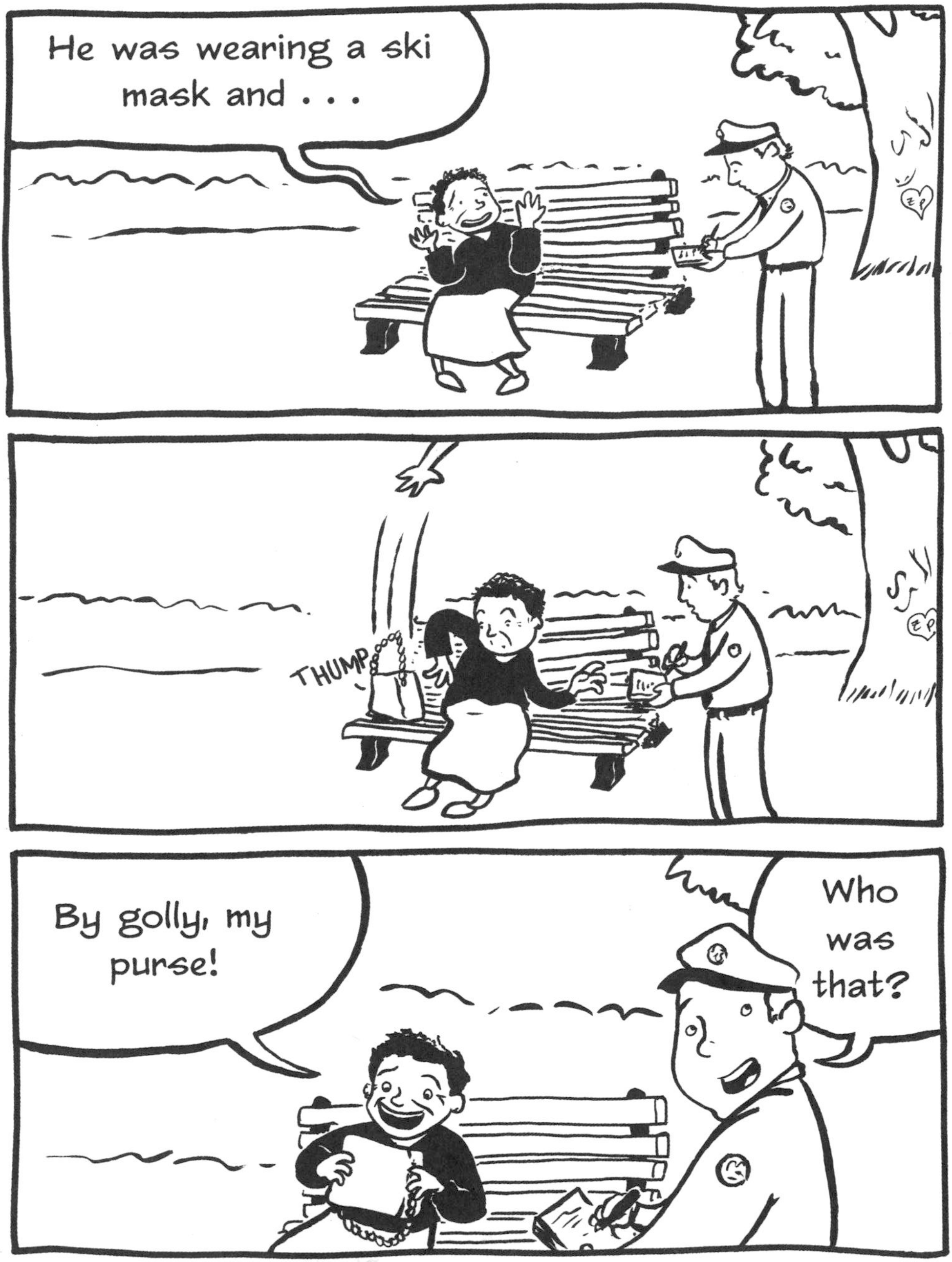
He was wearing a ski mask and . . .
THUMP
By golly, my purse!
Who was that?

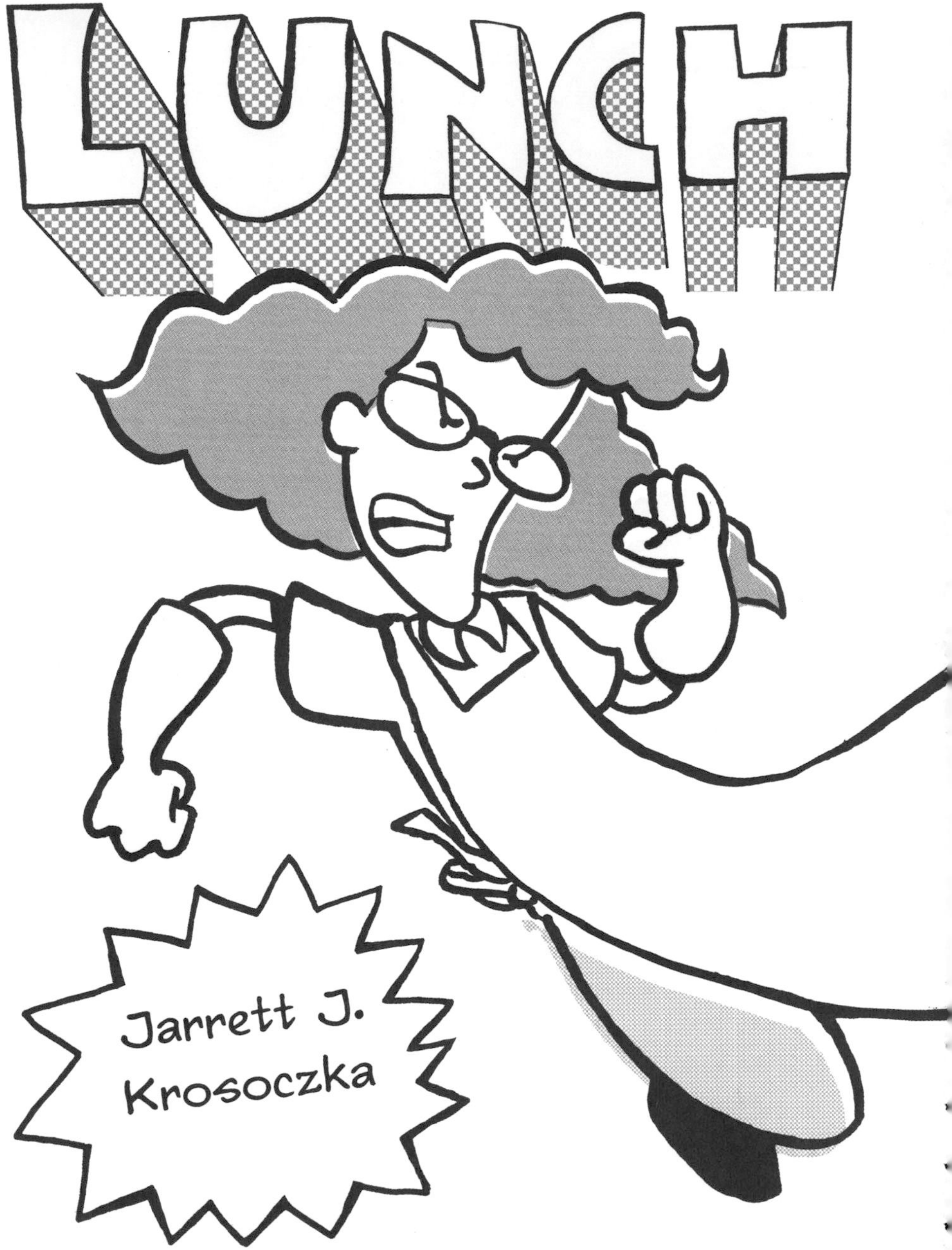
LUNCH
Jarrett J. Krosoczka

LADY

and the League of Librarians

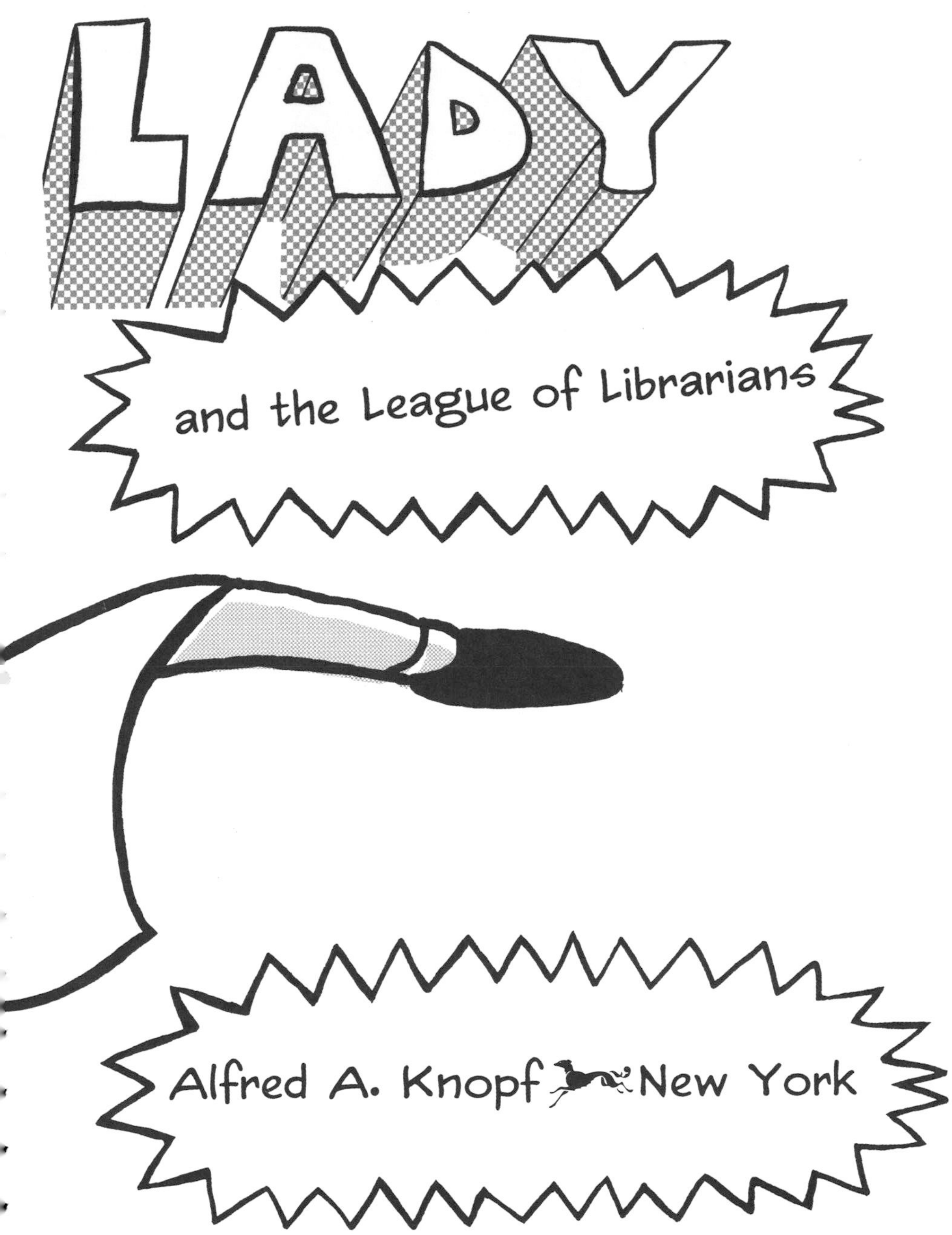

Alfred A. Knopf New York

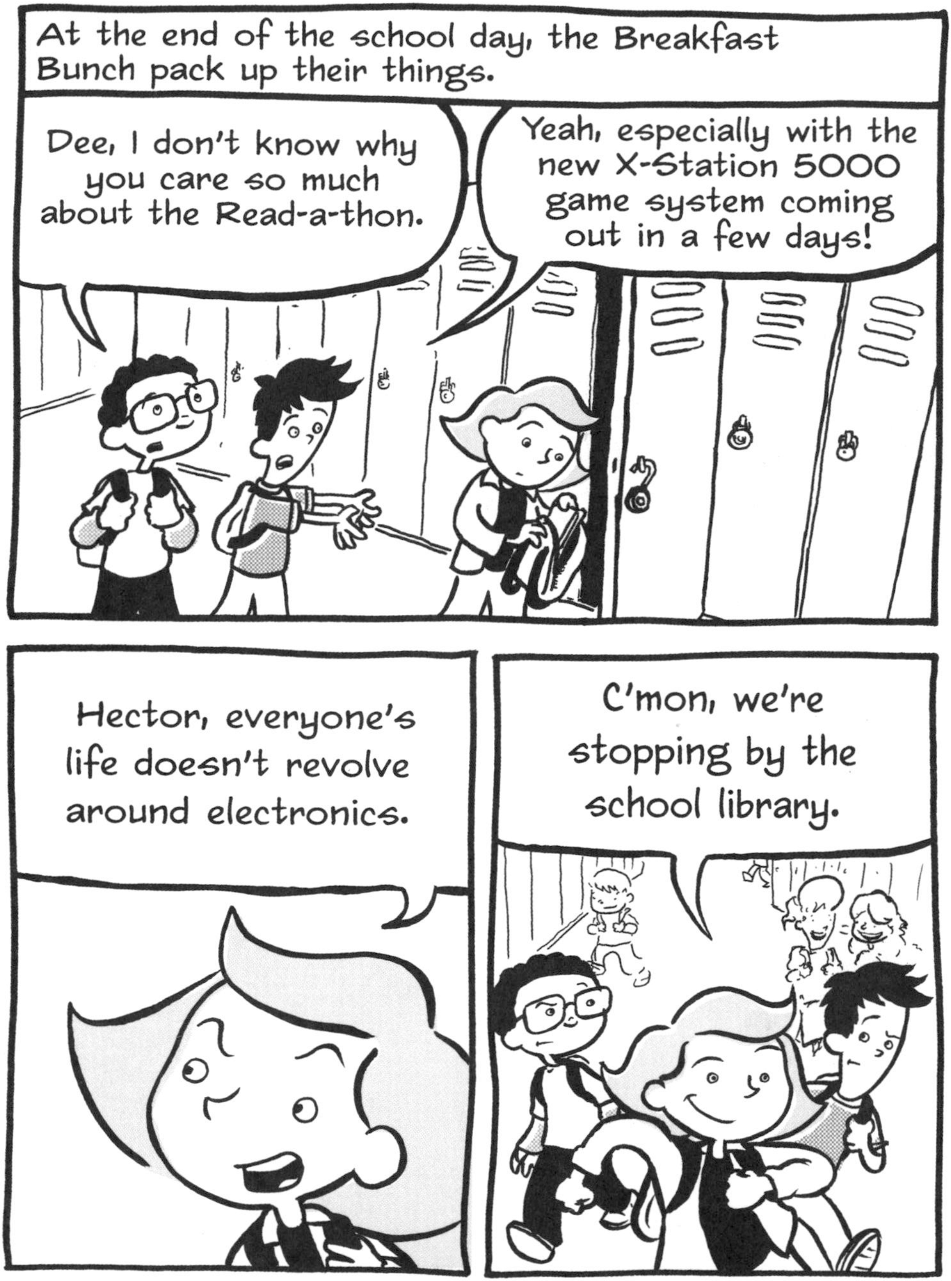
At the end of the school day, the Breakfast Bunch pack up their things.
Dee, I don't know why you care so much about the Read-a-thon.
Yeah, especially with the new X-Station 5000 game system coming out in a few days!
Hector, everyone's life doesn't revolve around electronics.
C'mon, we're stopping by the school library.

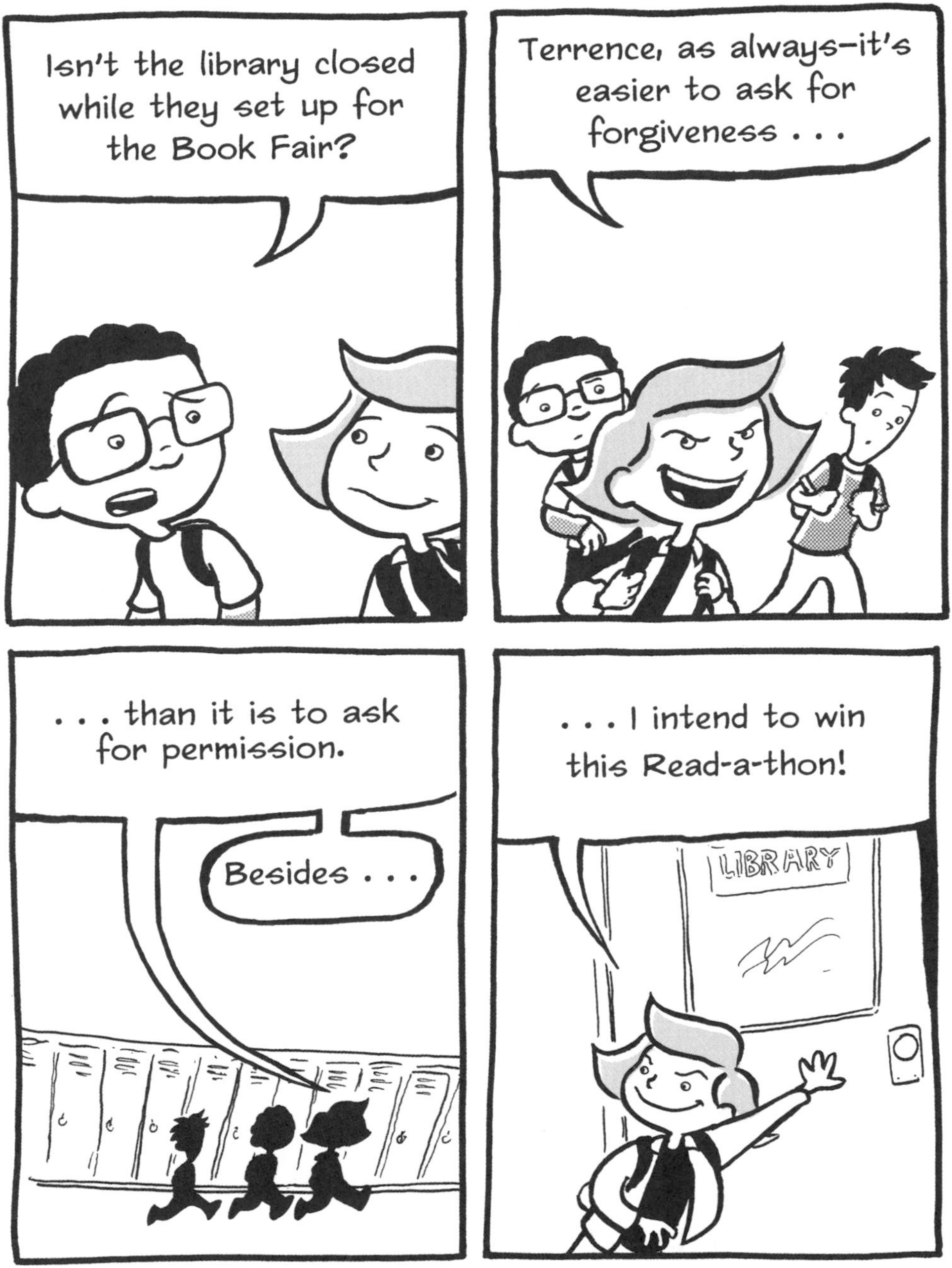
Isn't the library closed while they set up for the Book Fair?
Terrence, as always—it's easier to ask for forgiveness . . .
. . . than it is to ask for permission.
Besides . . .
. . . I intend to win this Read-a-thon!
LIBRARY

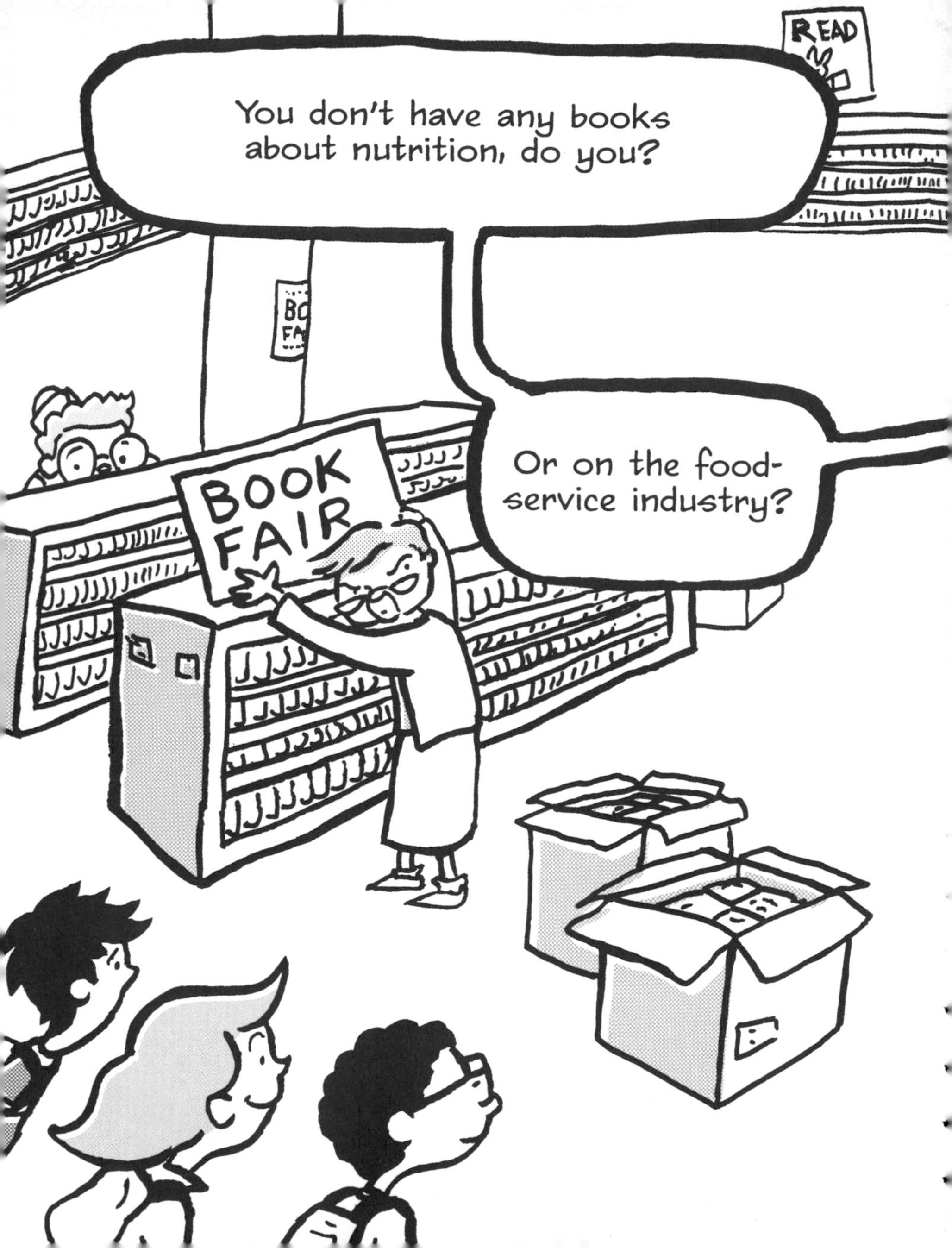
You don't have any books about nutrition, do you?
Or on the food-service industry?
READ
BOOK FAIR

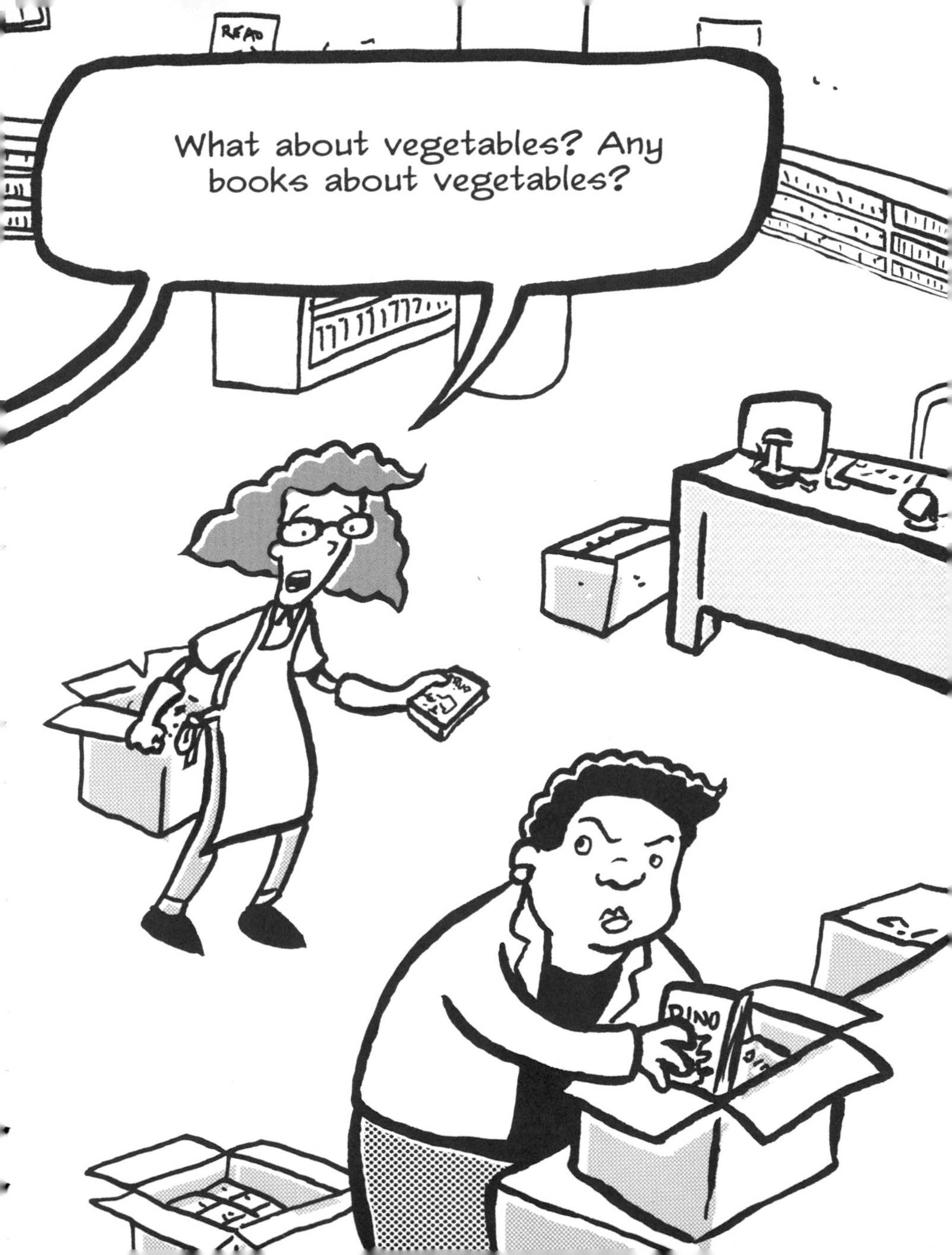
What about vegetables? Any books about vegetables?
READ
DINO

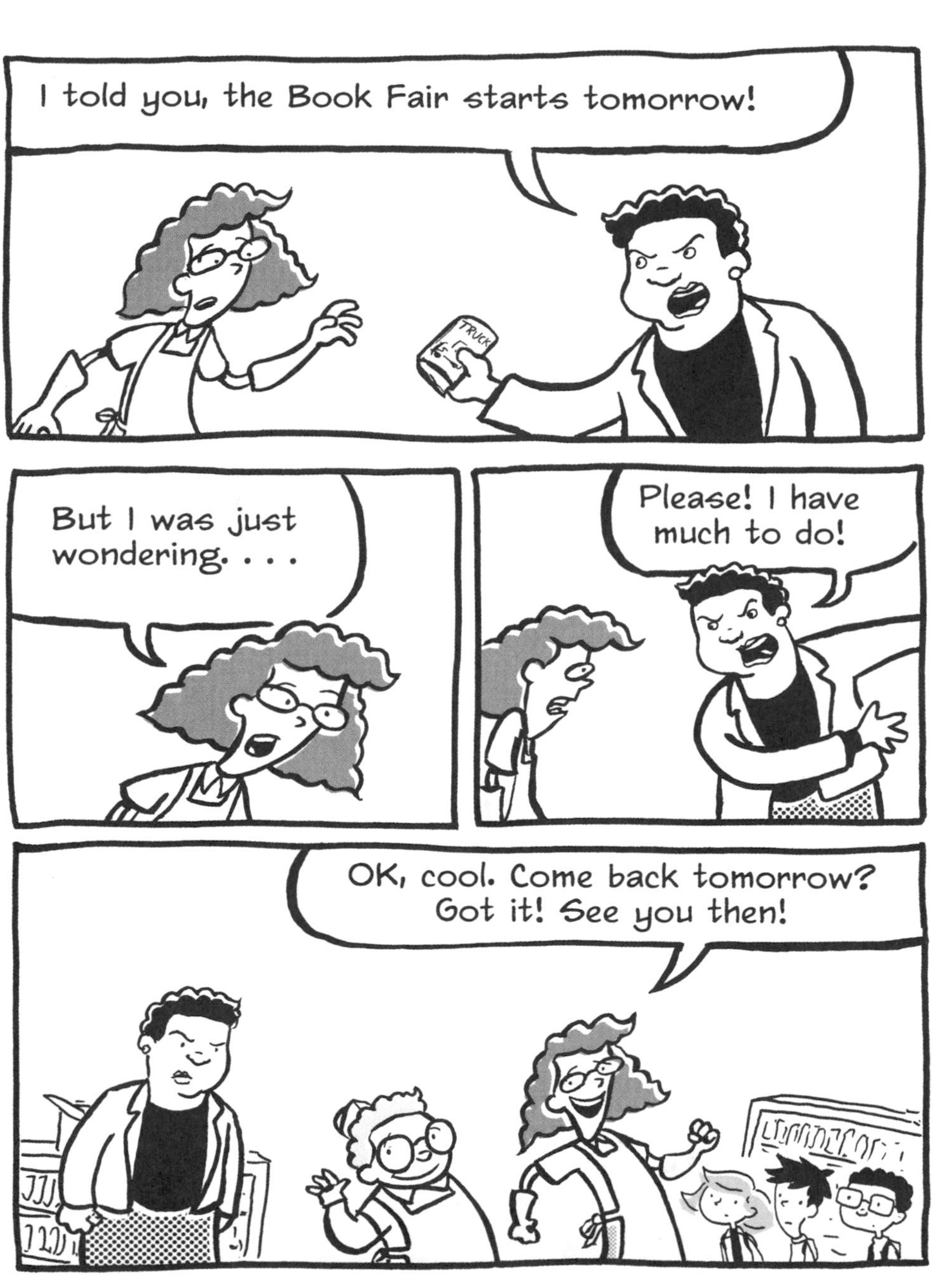
I told you, the Book Fair starts tomorrow!
TRUCK
But I was just wondering. . . .
Please! I have much to do!
OK, cool. Come back tomorrow? Got it! See you then!

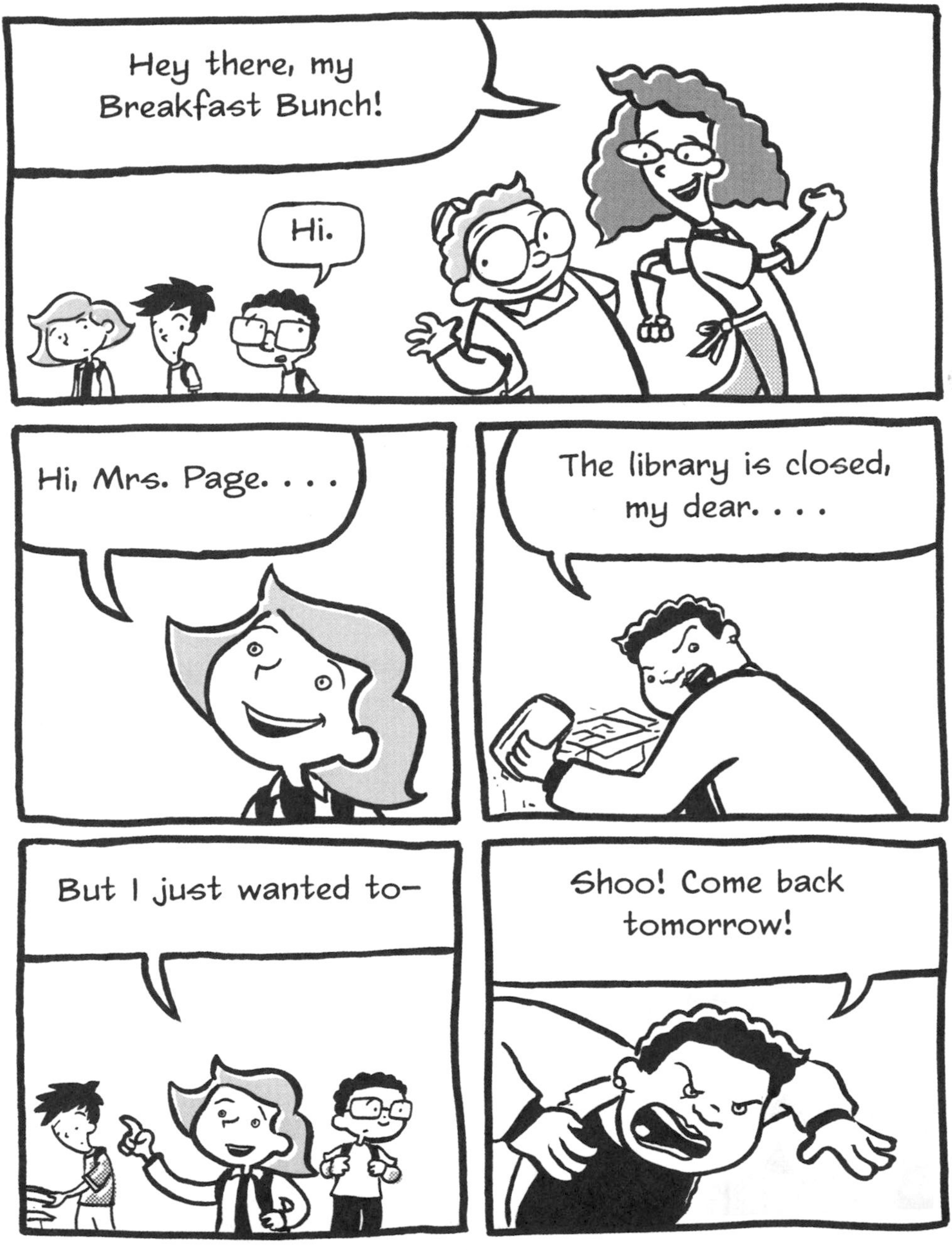
Hey there, my Breakfast Bunch!
Hi.
Hi, Mrs. Page. . . .
The library is closed, my dear. . . .
But I just wanted to–
Shoo! Come back tomorrow!

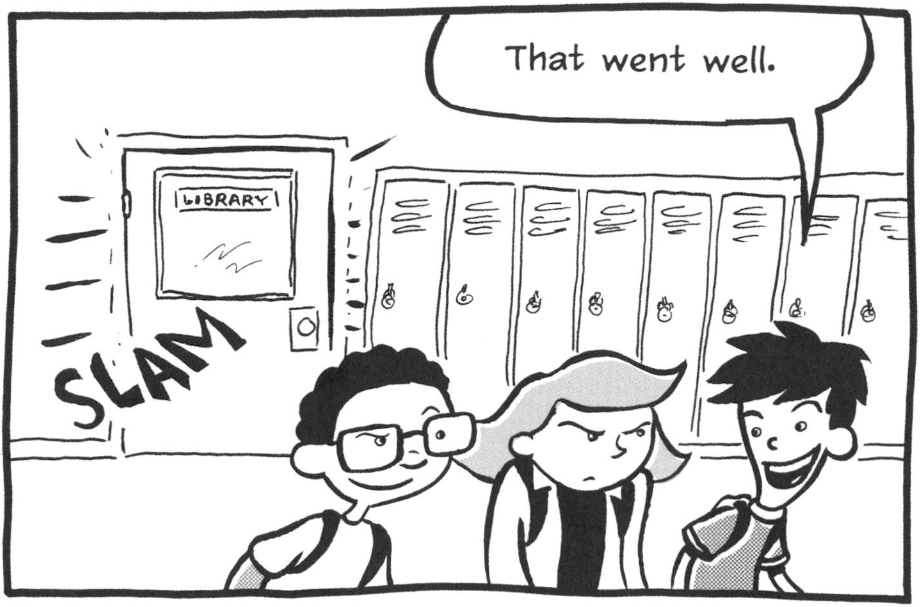
That went well.
LIBRARY
SLAM
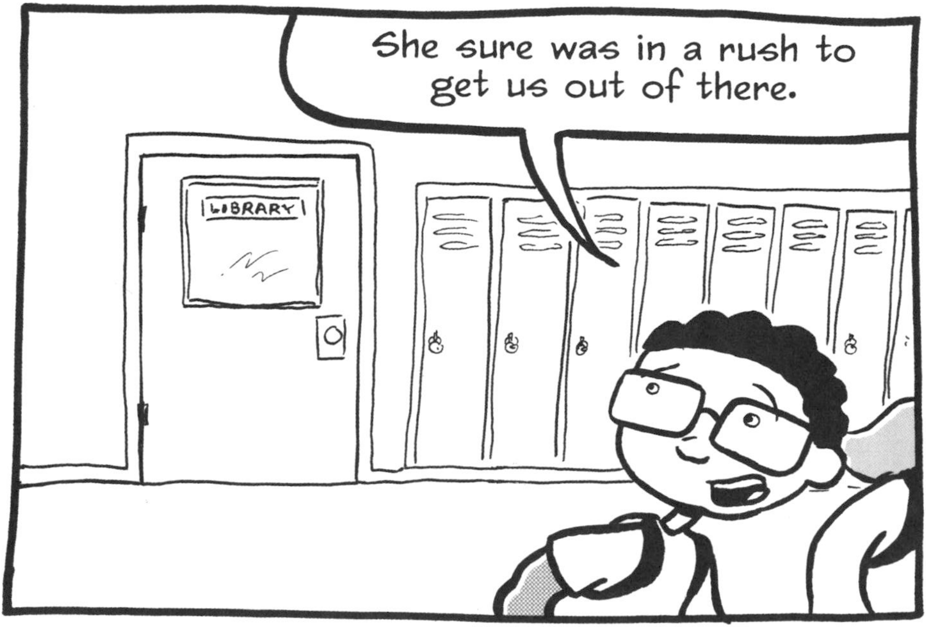
She sure was in a rush to get us out of there.
LIBRARY

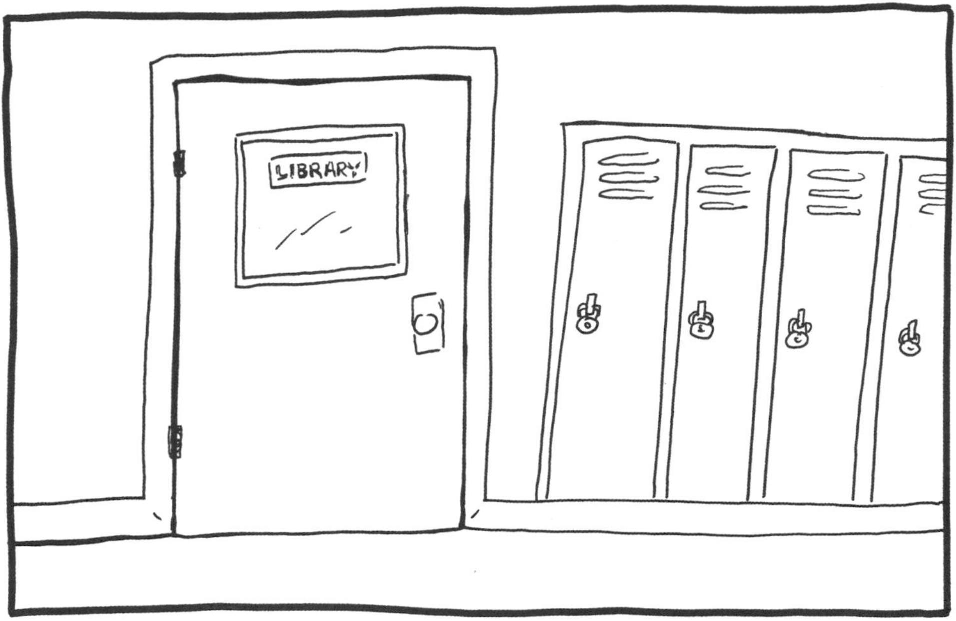
LIBRARY

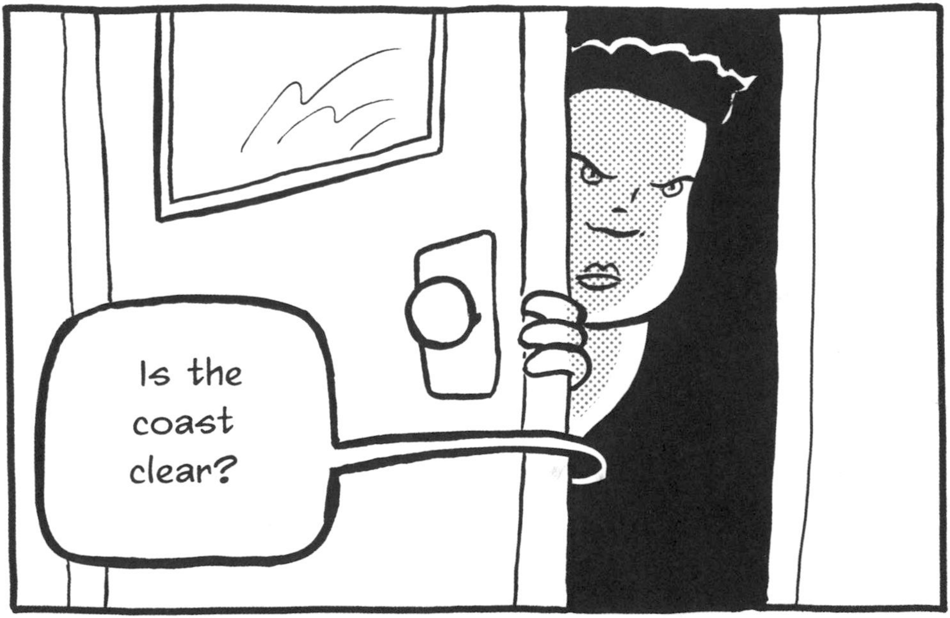
Is the coast clear?

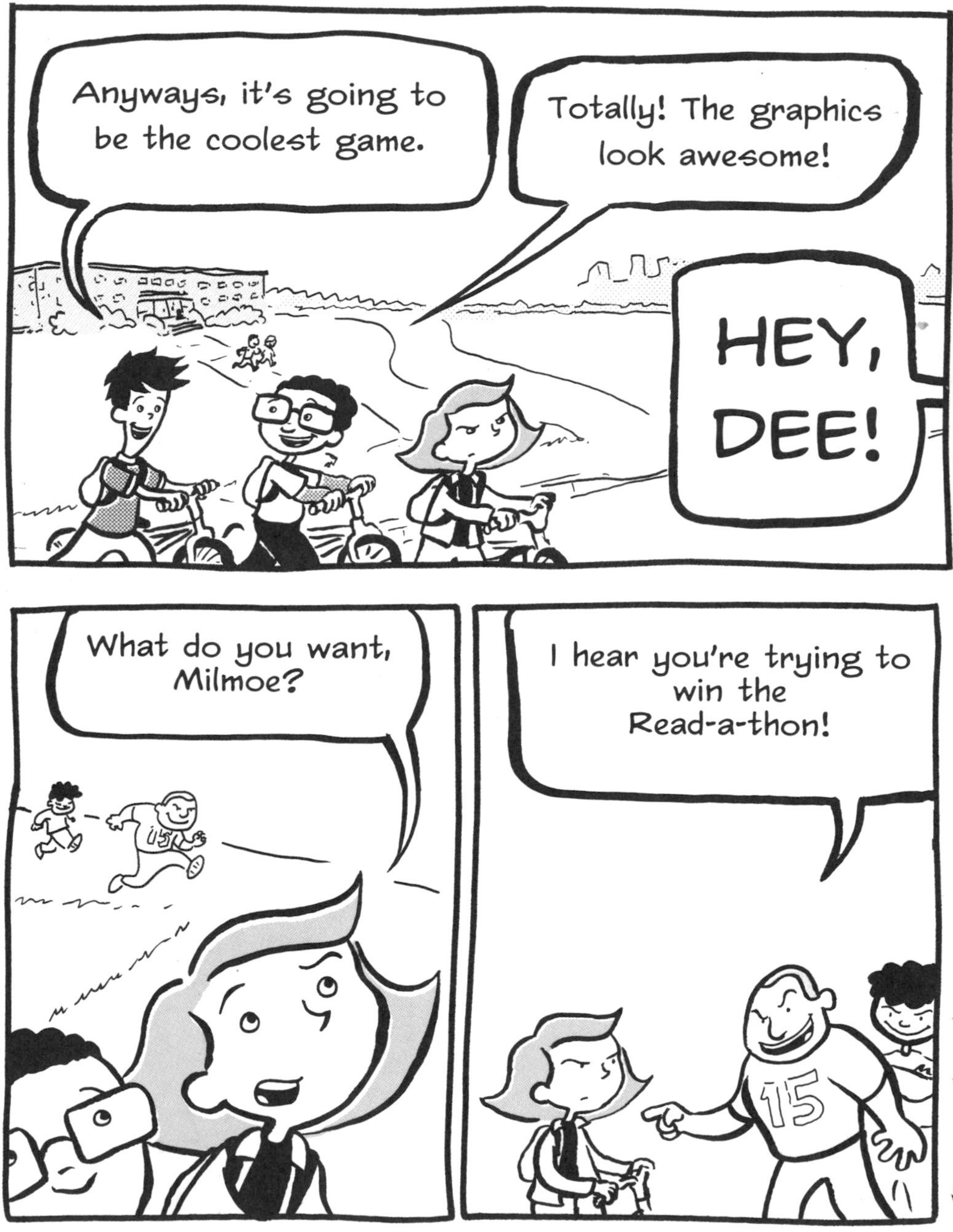
Anyways, it's going to be the coolest game.
Totally! The graphics look awesome!
HEY, DEE!
What do you want, Milmoe?
I hear you're trying to win the Read-a-thon!
15
15

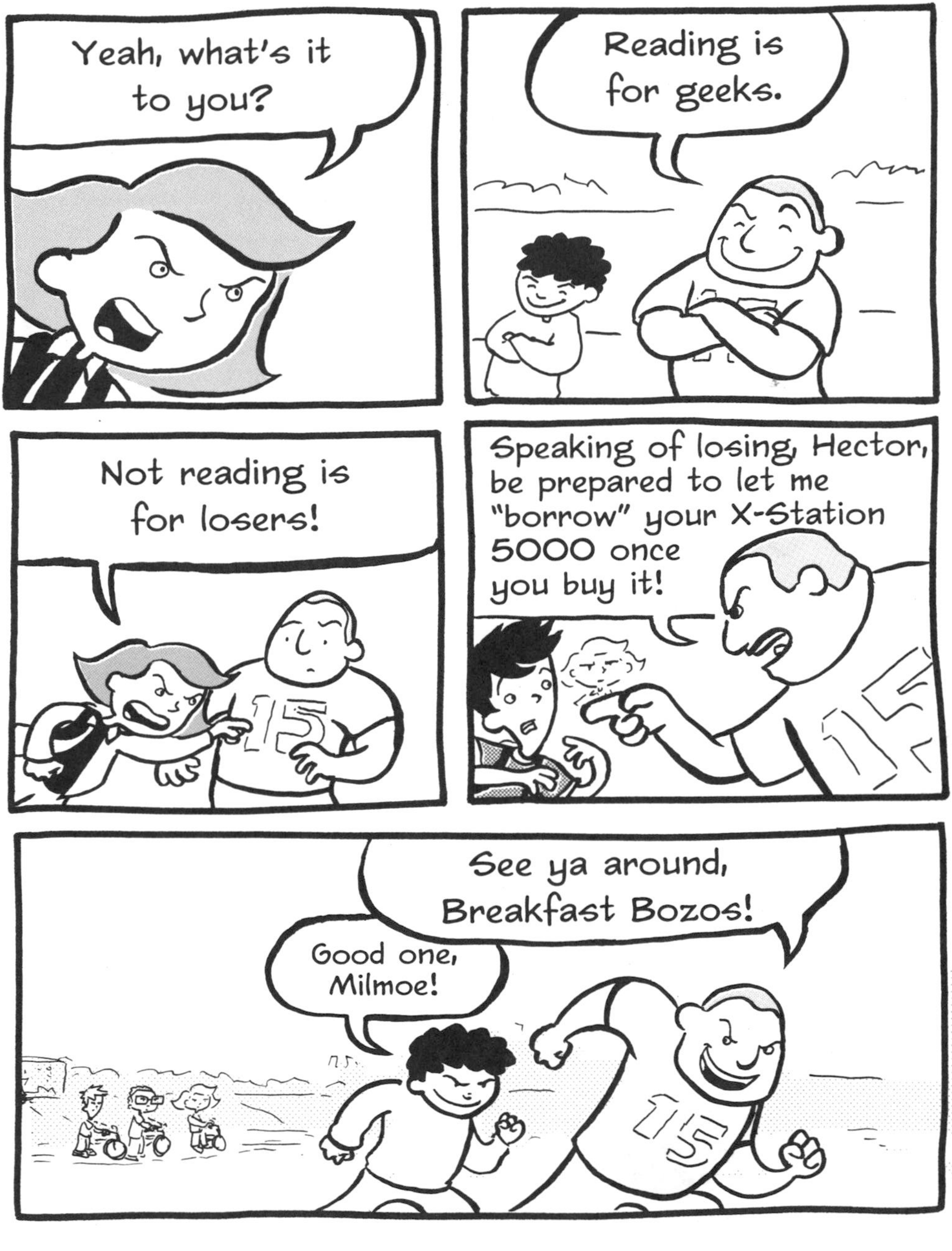

Yeah, what's it to you?
Reading is for geeks.
Not reading is for losers!
Speaking of losing, Hector, be prepared to let me "borrow" your X-Station 5000 once you buy it!
See ya around, Breakfast Bozos!
Good one, Milmoe!

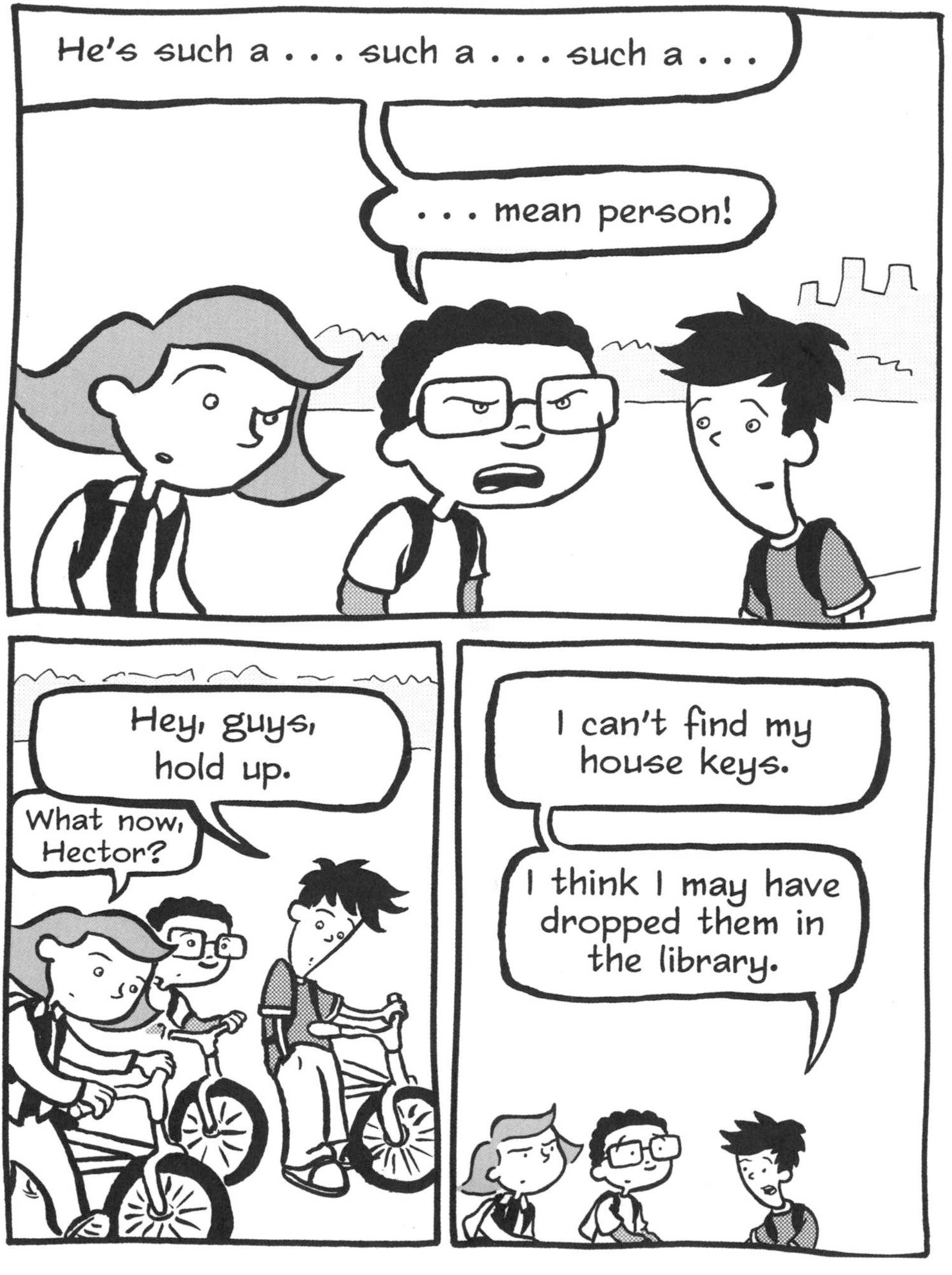
He's such a . . . such a . . . such a . . .
. . . mean person!
Hey, guys, hold up.
What now, Hector?
I can't find my house keys.
I think I may have dropped them in the library.

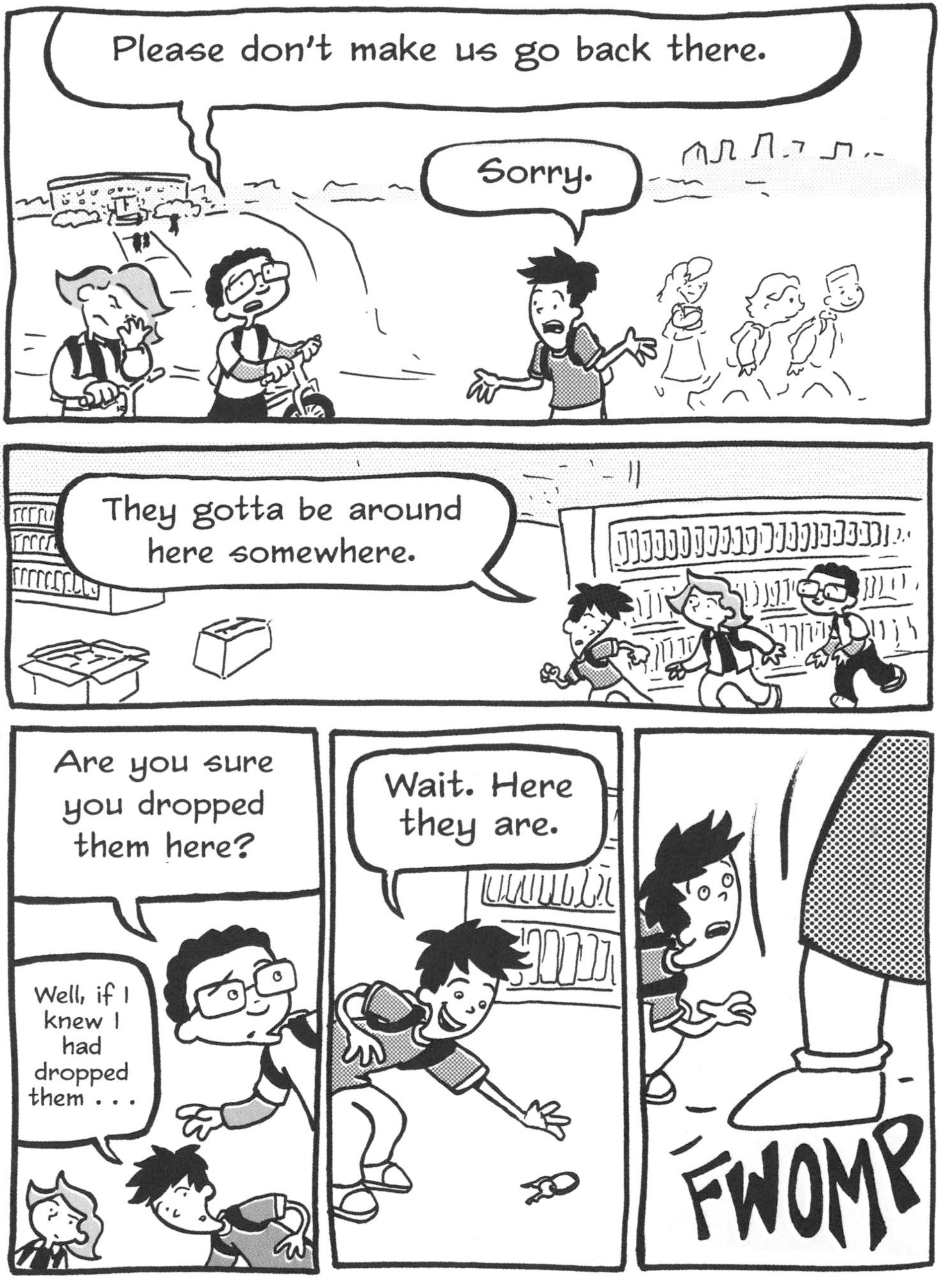
Please don't make us go back there.
Sorry.
They gotta be around here somewhere.
Are you sure you dropped them here?
Well, if I knew I had dropped them . . .
Wait. Here they are.
FWOMP

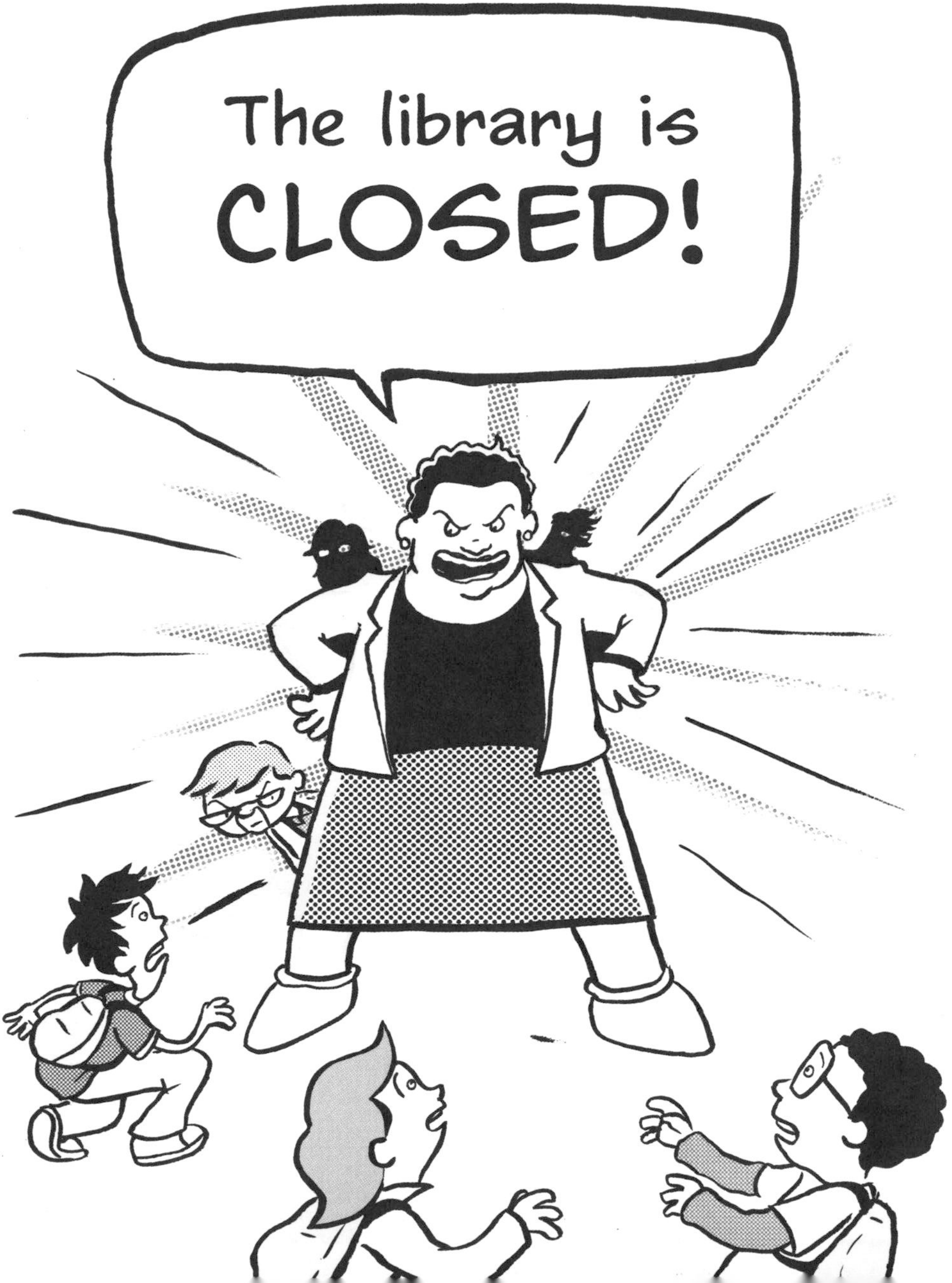
The library is CLOSED!

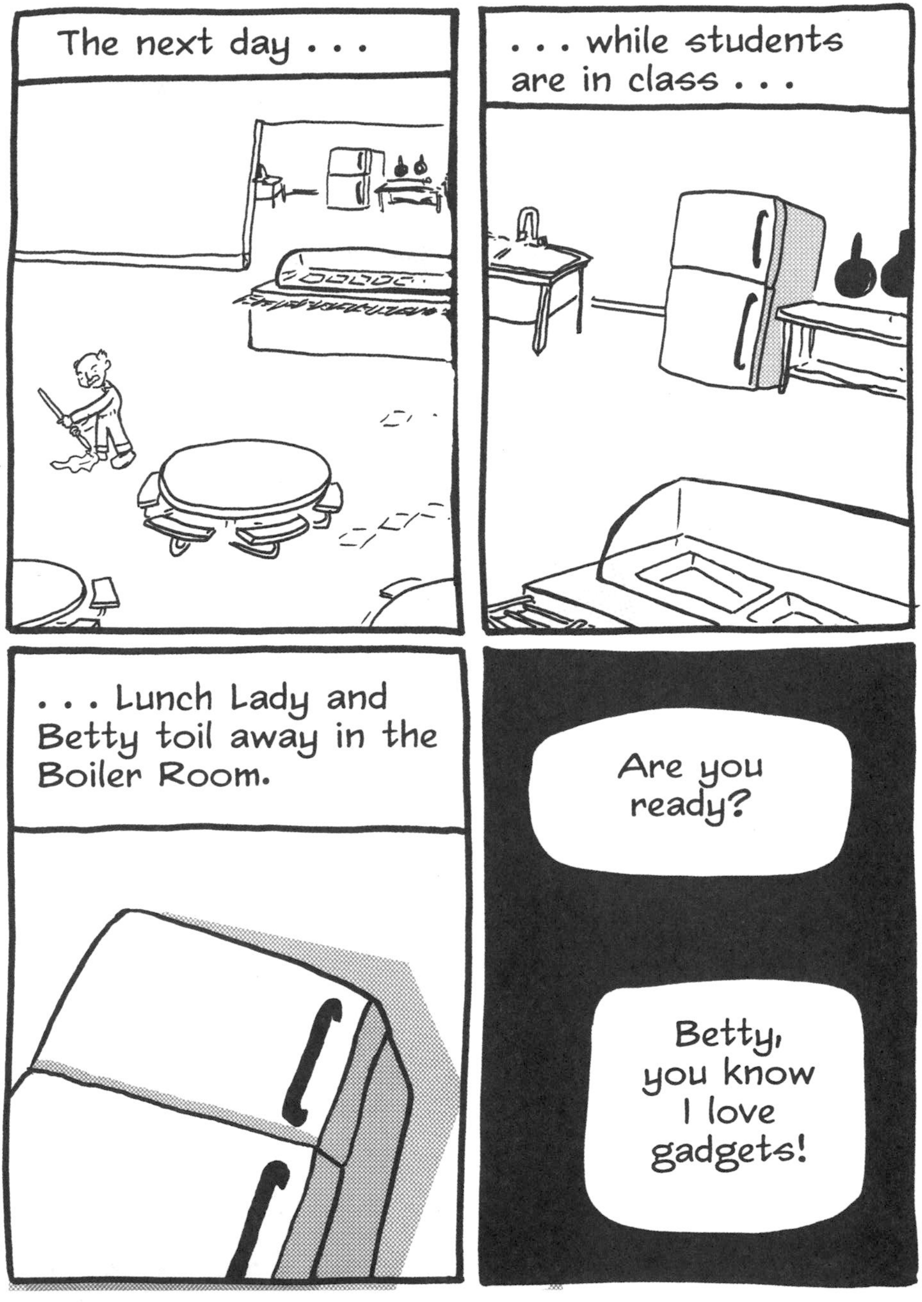
The next day . . .
. . . while students are in class . . .
. . . Lunch Lady and Betty toil away in the Boiler Room.
Are you ready?
Betty, you know I love gadgets!

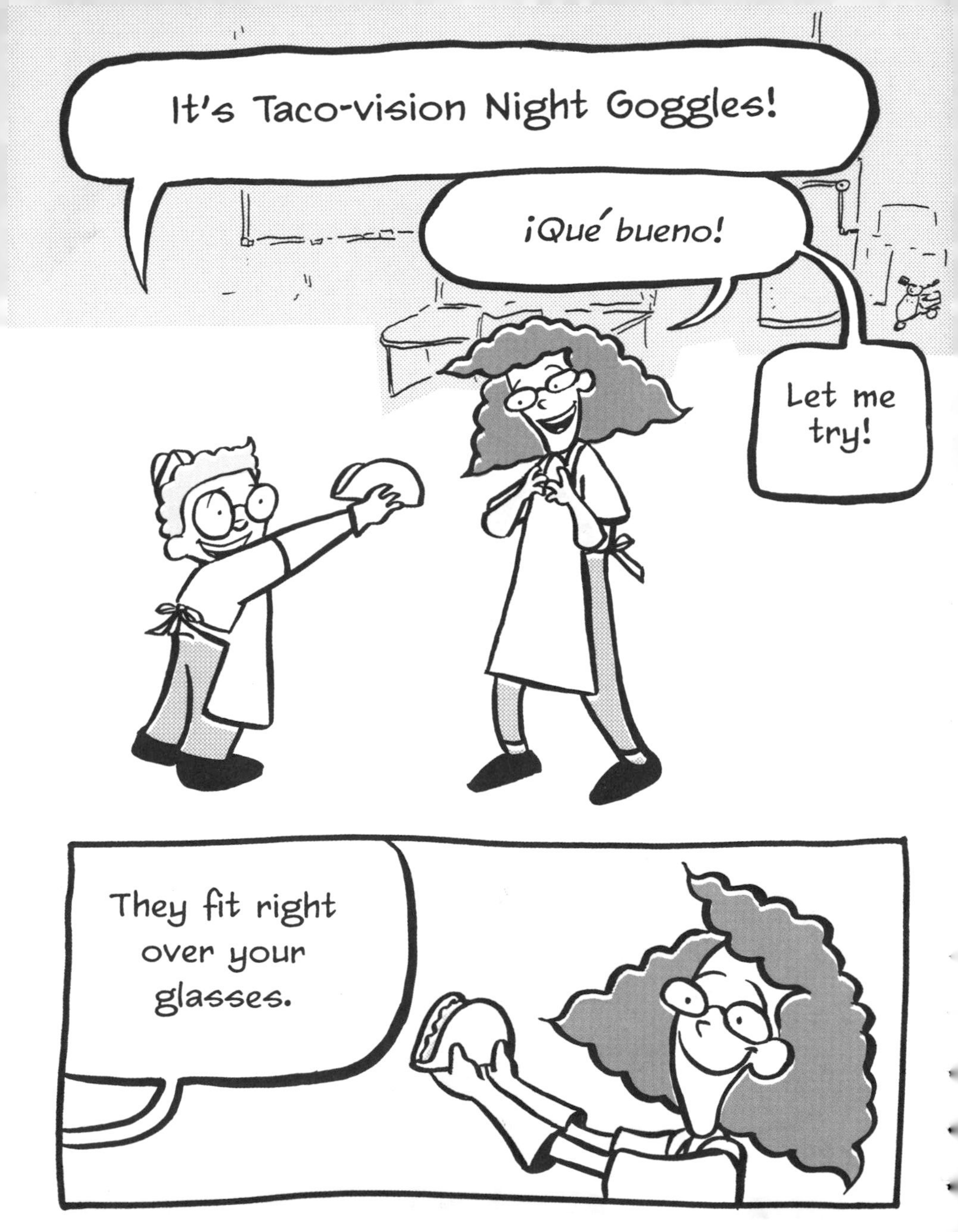
It's Taco-vision Night Goggles!
¡Qué bueno!
Let me try!
They fit right over your glasses.

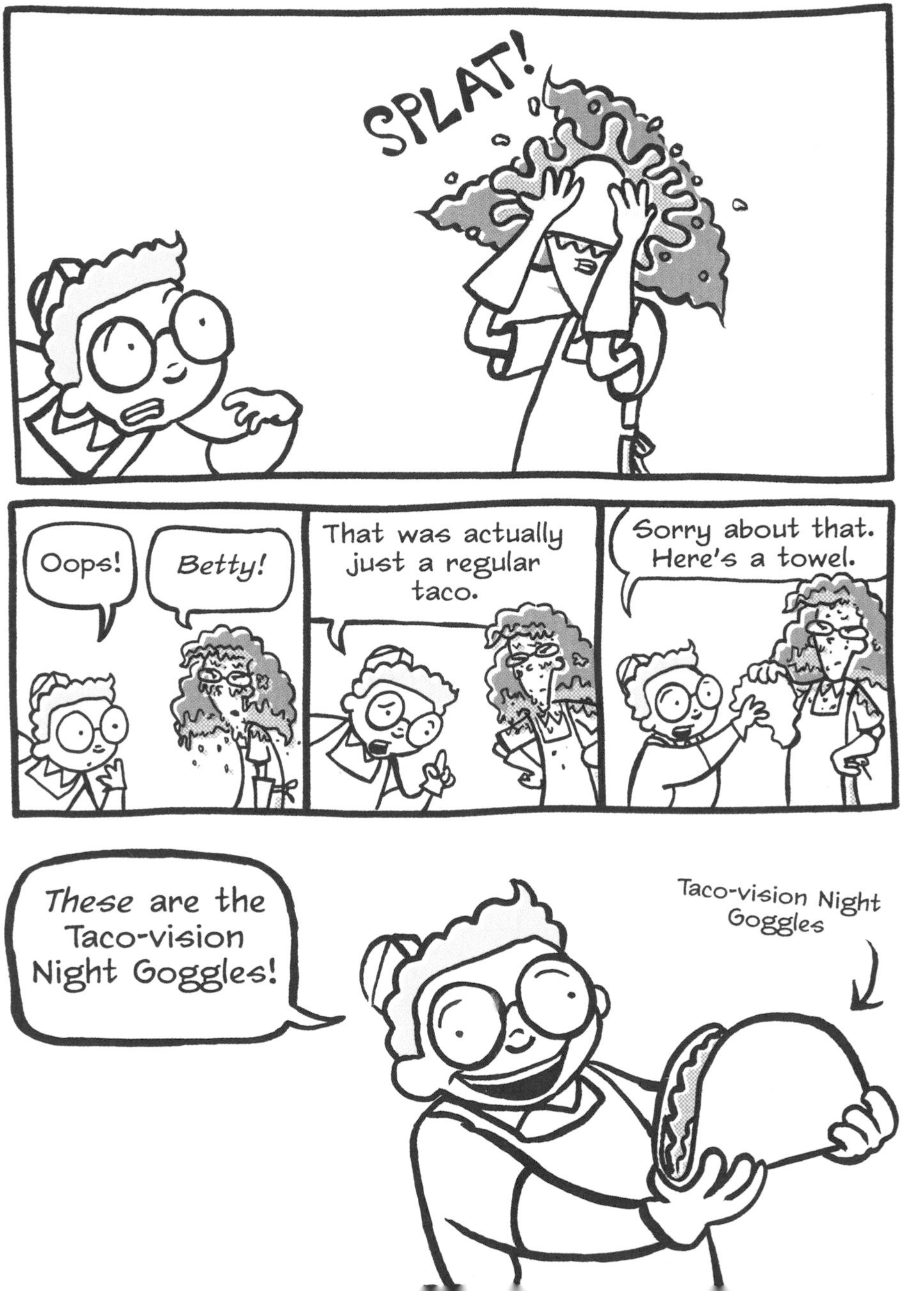
SPLAT!
Oops!
Betty!
That was actually just a regular taco.
Sorry about that. Here's a towel.
These are the Taco-vision Night Goggles!
Taco-vision Night Goggles

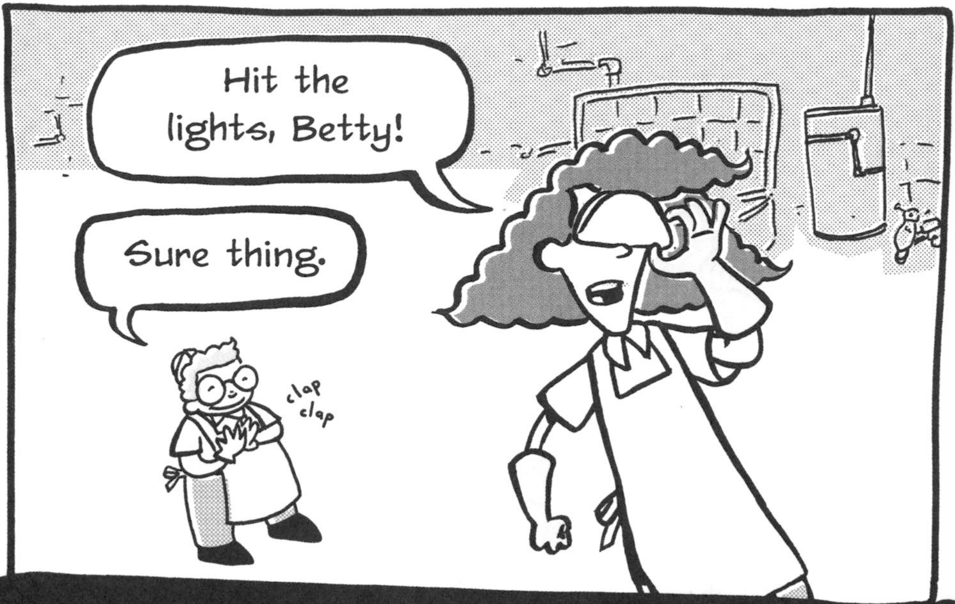

Hit the lights, Betty!
Sure thing.
clap clap

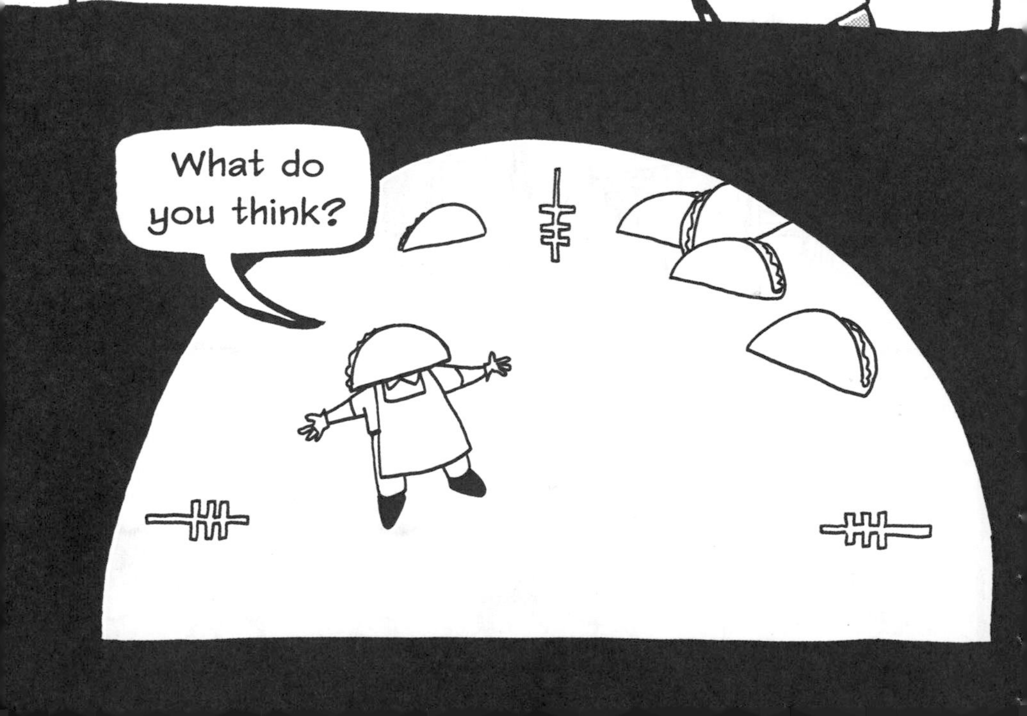

What do you think?

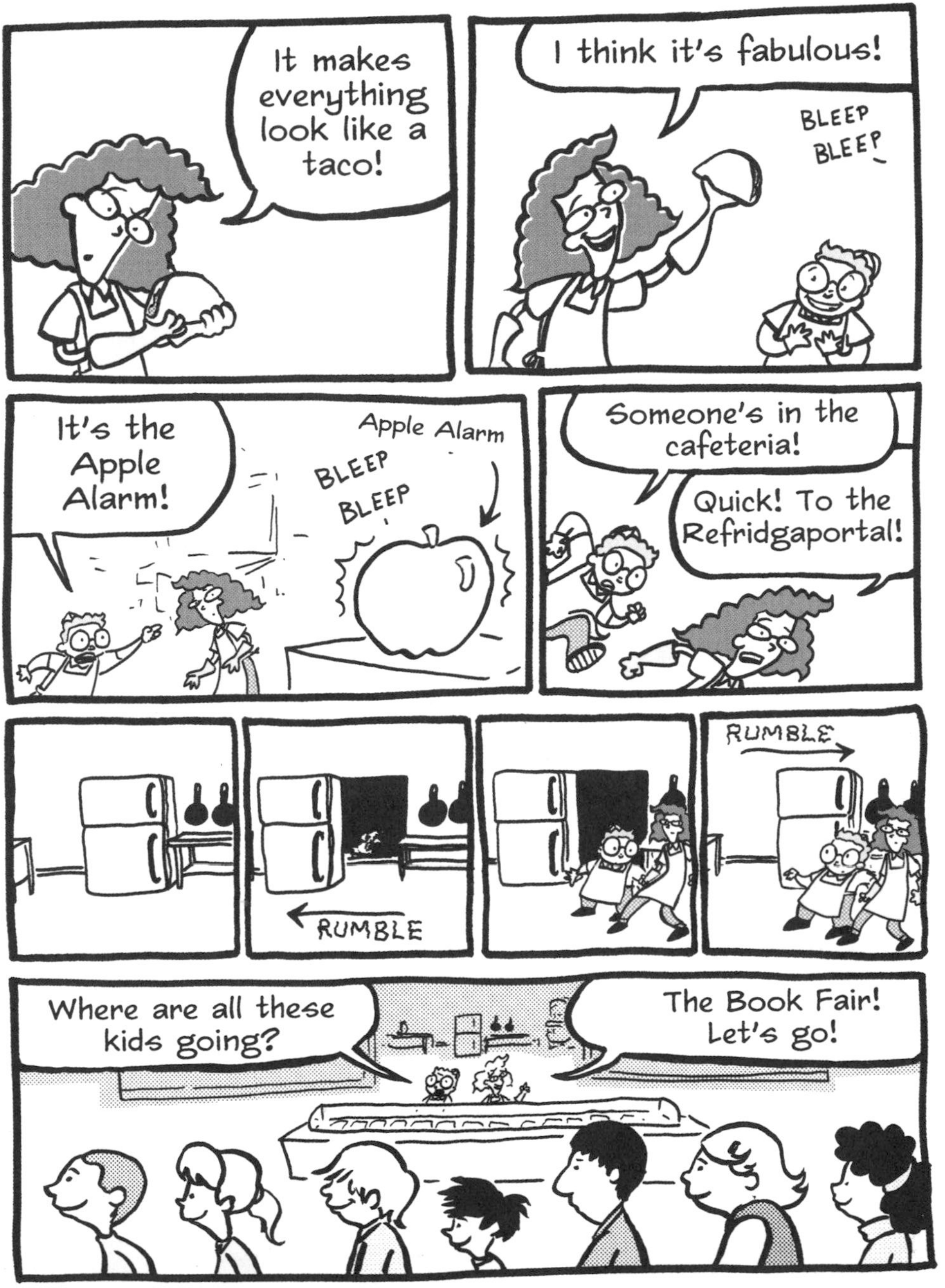
It makes everything look like a taco!
I think it's fabulous!
BLEEP BLEEP
It's the Apple Alarm!
Apple Alarm
BLEEP BLEEP
Someone's in the cafeteria!
Quick! To the Refridgaportal!
RUMBLE
RUMBLE
Where are all these kids going?
The Book Fair! Let's go!

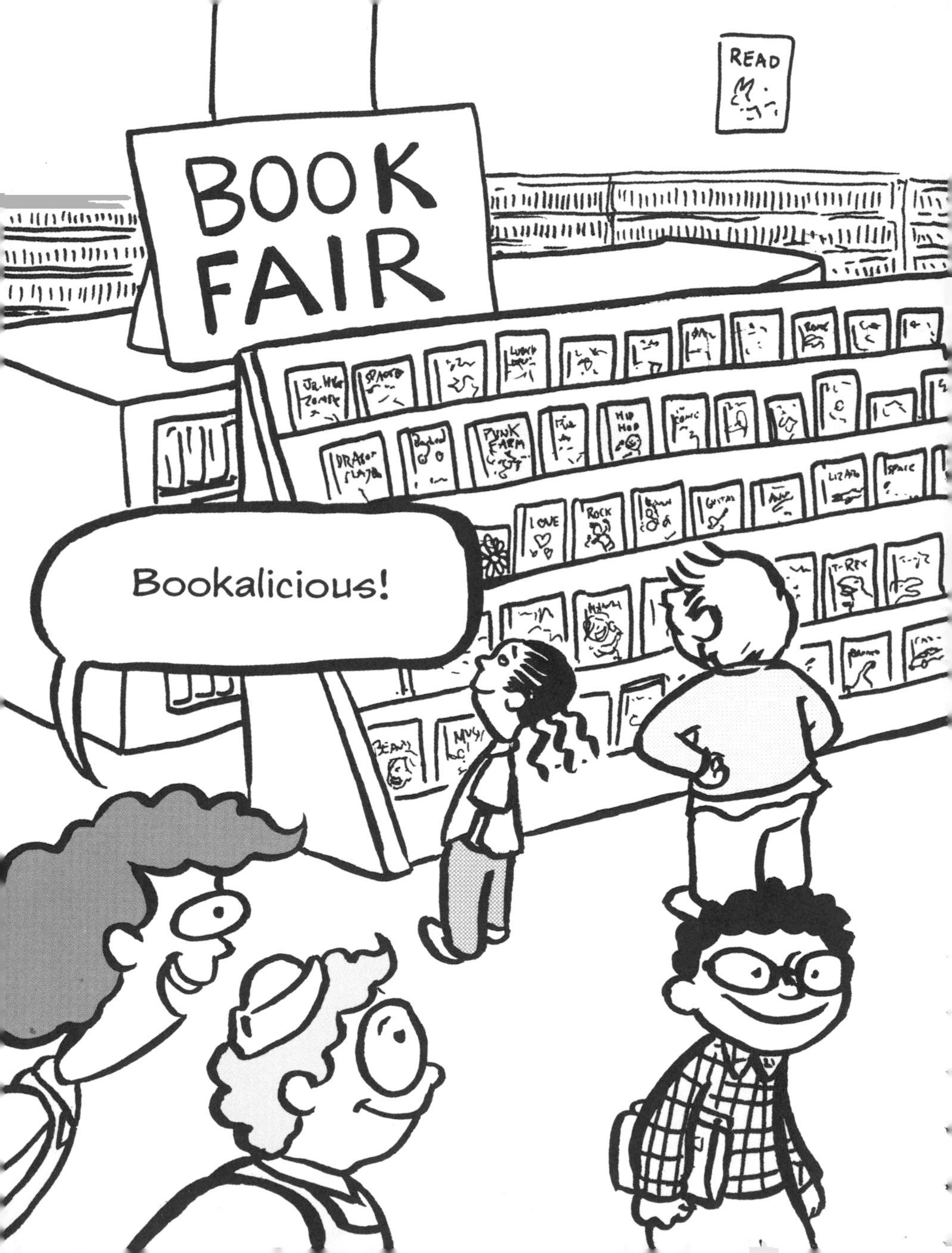
BOOK FAIR
READ
PUNK FARM
HIP HOP
LOVE
ROCK
T-REX
Bookalicious!

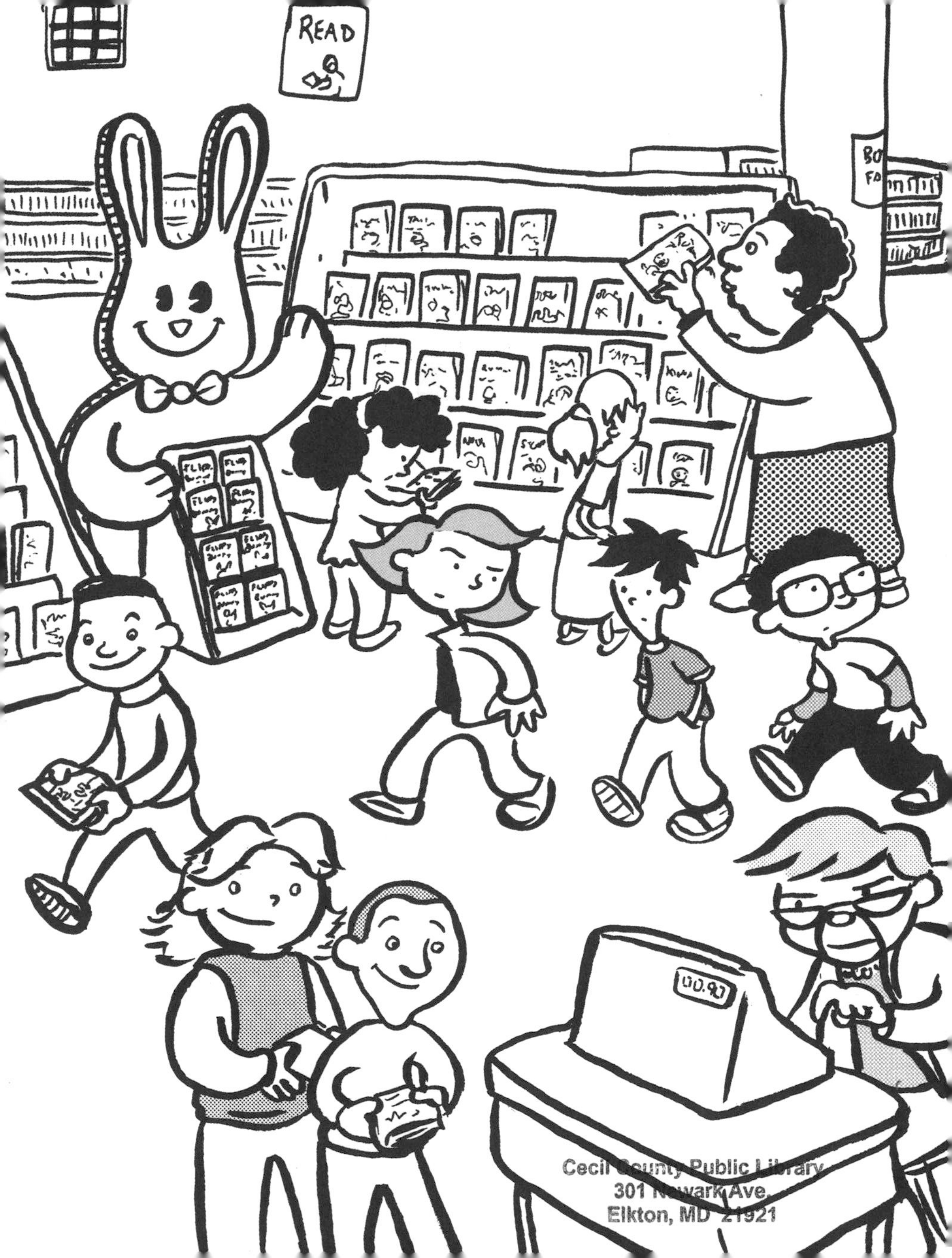
READ

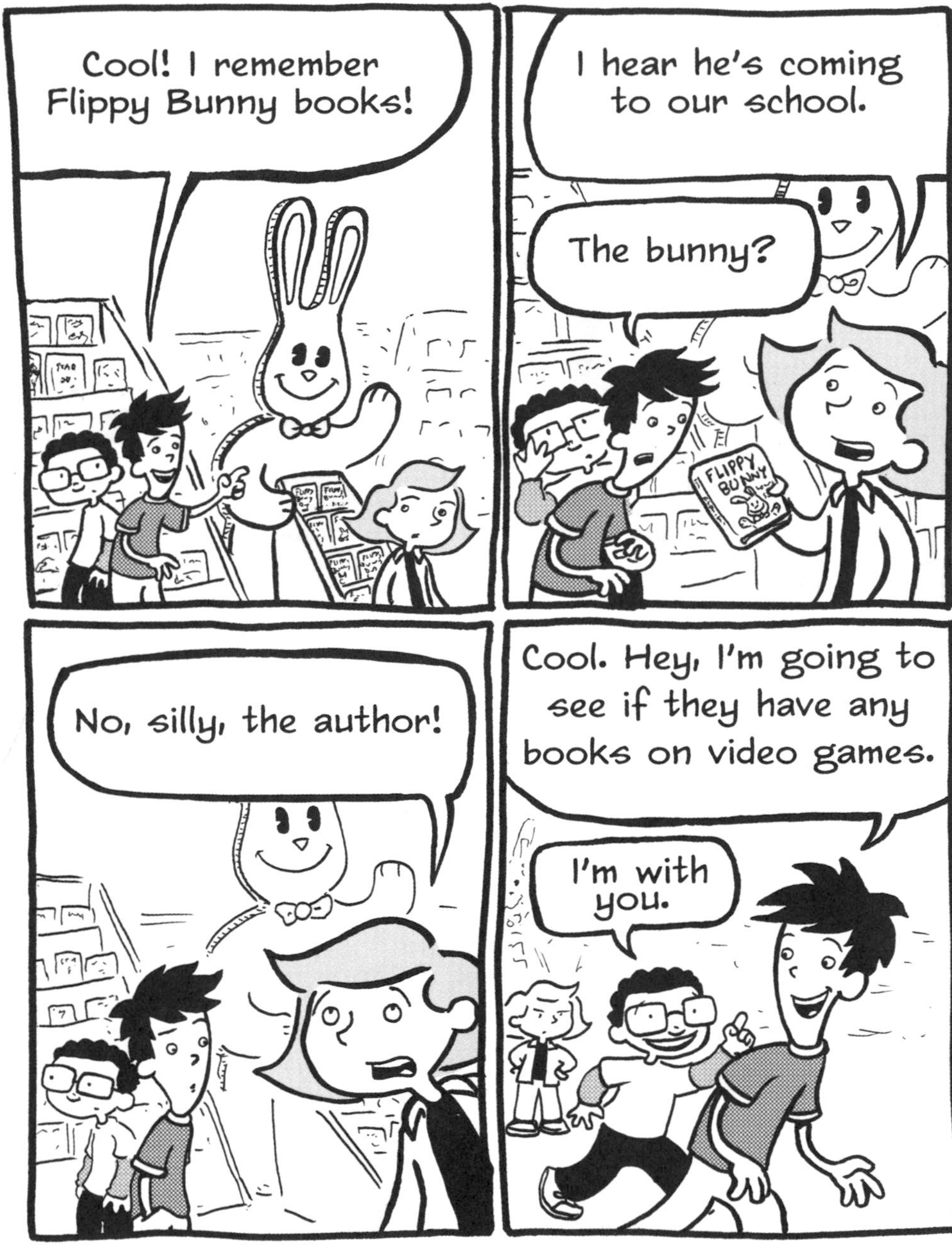
Cool! I remember Flippy Bunny books!
I hear he's coming to our school.
The bunny?
FLIPPY BUNNY
No, silly, the author!
Cool. Hey, I'm going to see if they have any books on video games.
I'm with you.

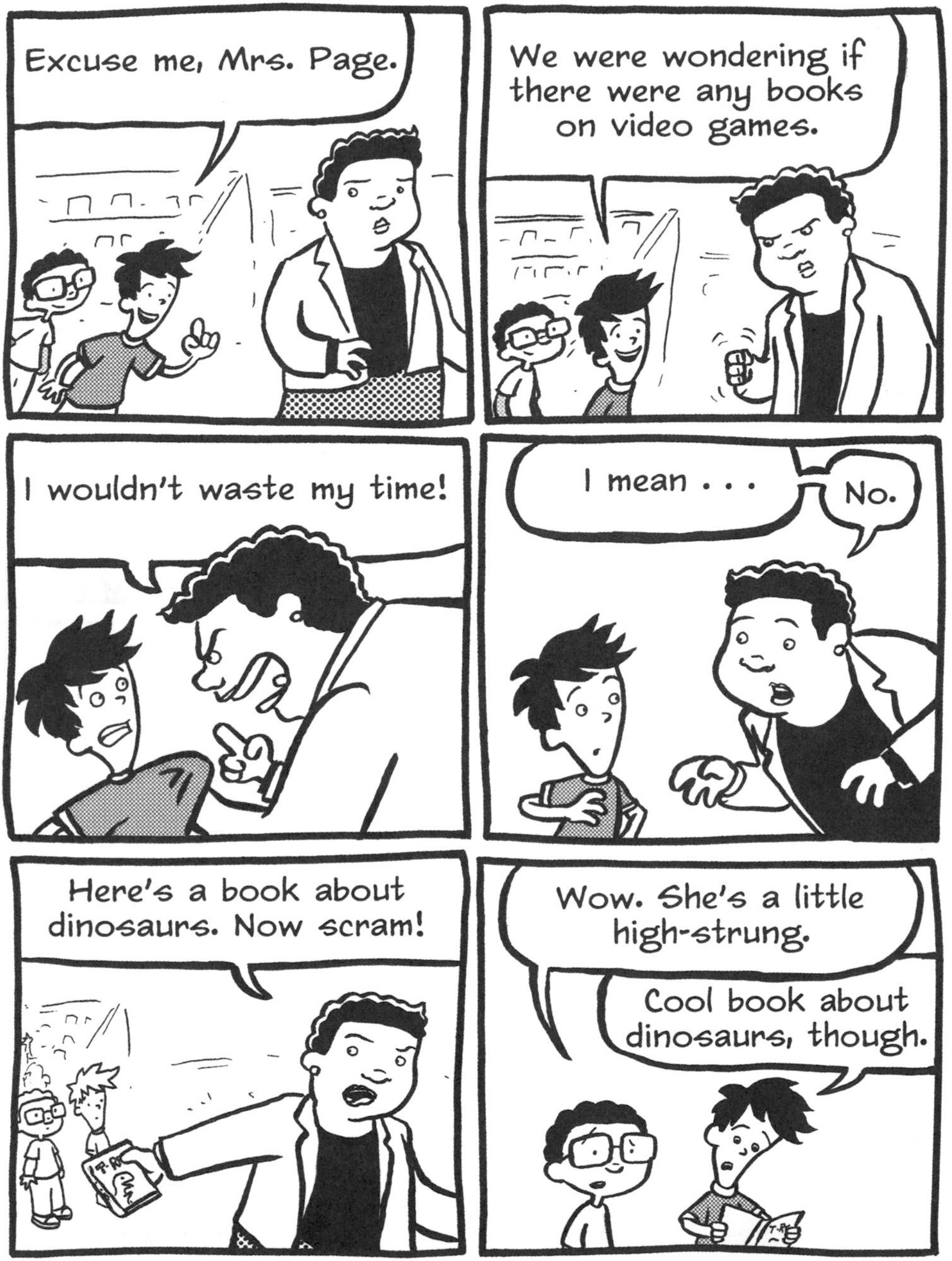
Excuse me, Mrs. Page.
We were wondering if there were any books on video games.
I wouldn't waste my time!
I mean . . .
No.
Here's a book about dinosaurs. Now scram!
T-REX
Wow. She's a little high-strung.
Cool book about dinosaurs, though.

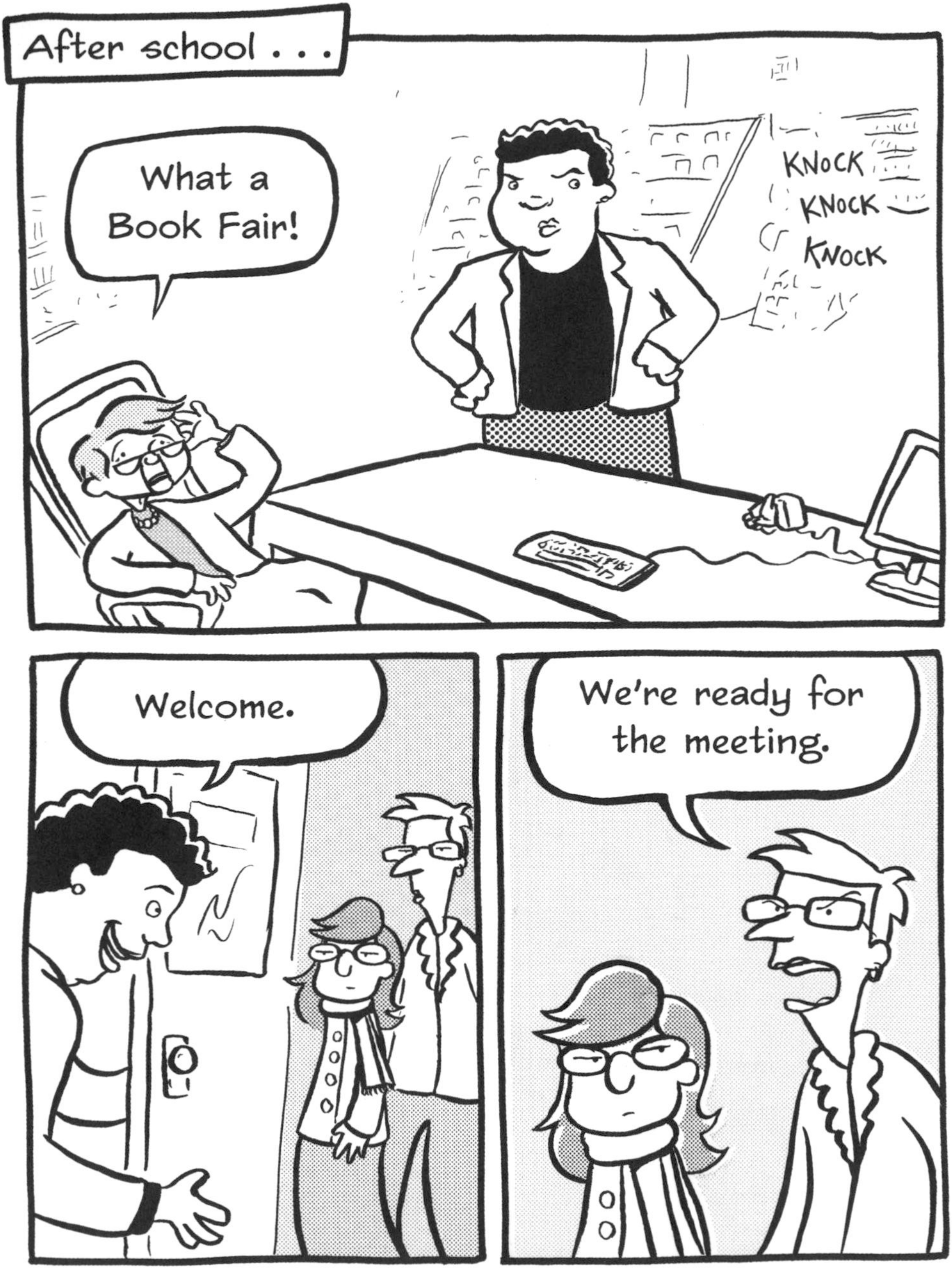
After school . . .
What a Book Fair!
KNOCK
KNOCK
KNOCK
Welcome.
We're ready for the meeting.

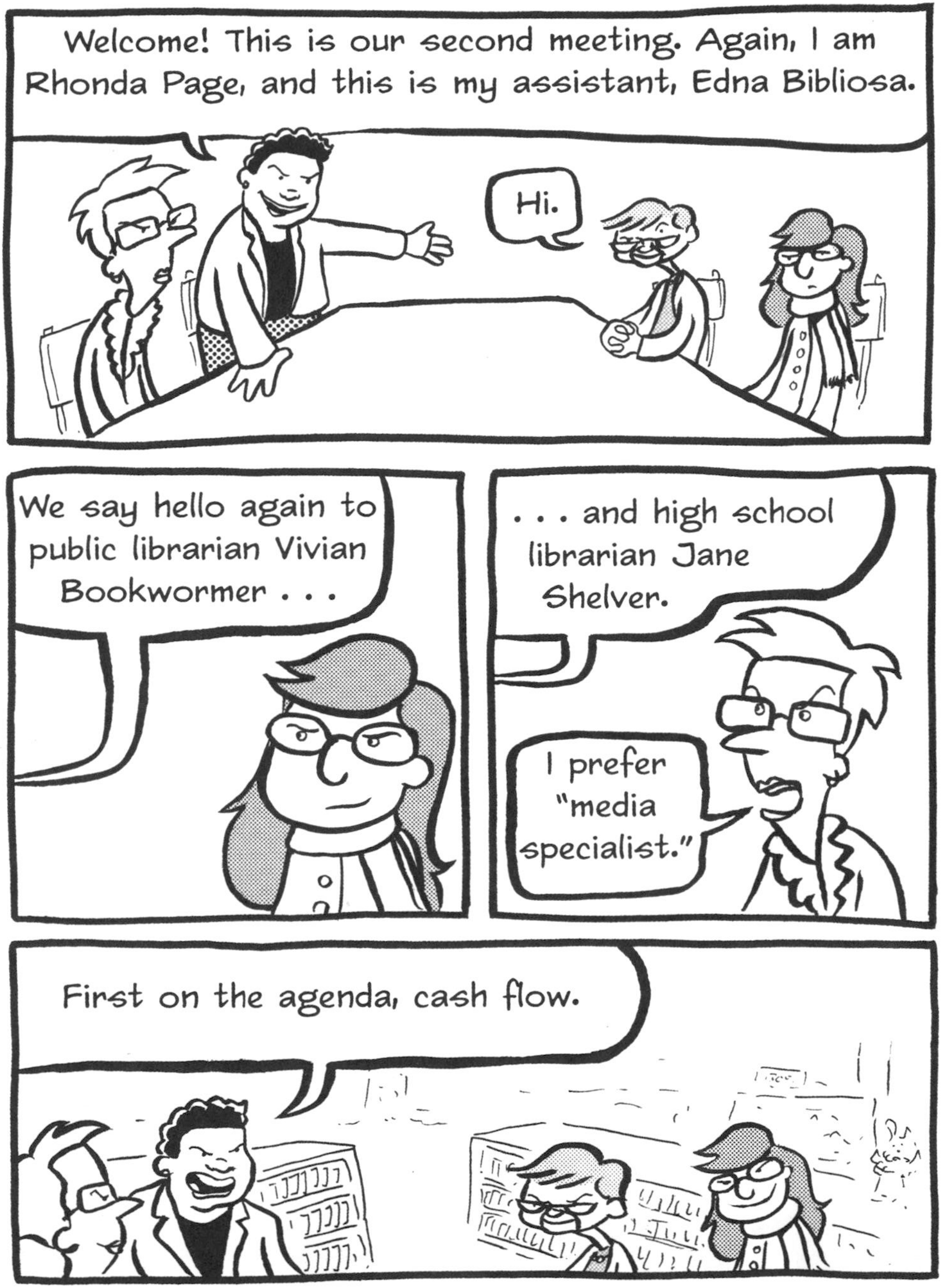
Welcome! This is our second meeting. Again, I am Rhonda Page, and this is my assistant, Edna Bibliosa.
Hi.
We say hello again to public librarian Vivian Bookwormer . . .
. . . and high school librarian Jane Shelver.
I prefer "media specialist."
First on the agenda, cash flow.

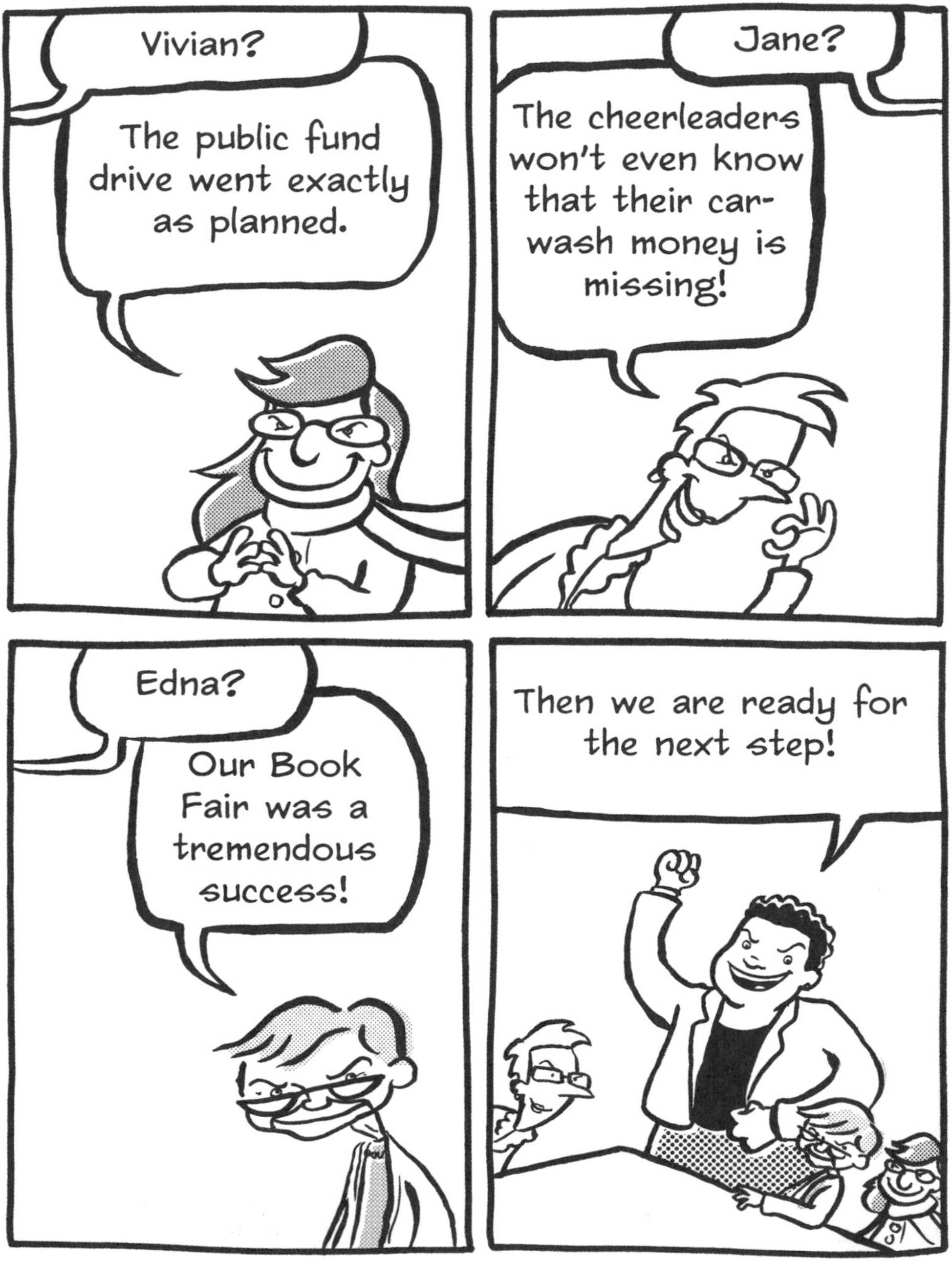
Vivian?
The public fund drive went exactly as planned.
Jane?
The cheerleaders won't even know that their car-wash money is missing!
Edna?
Our Book Fair was a tremendous success!
Then we are ready for the next step!

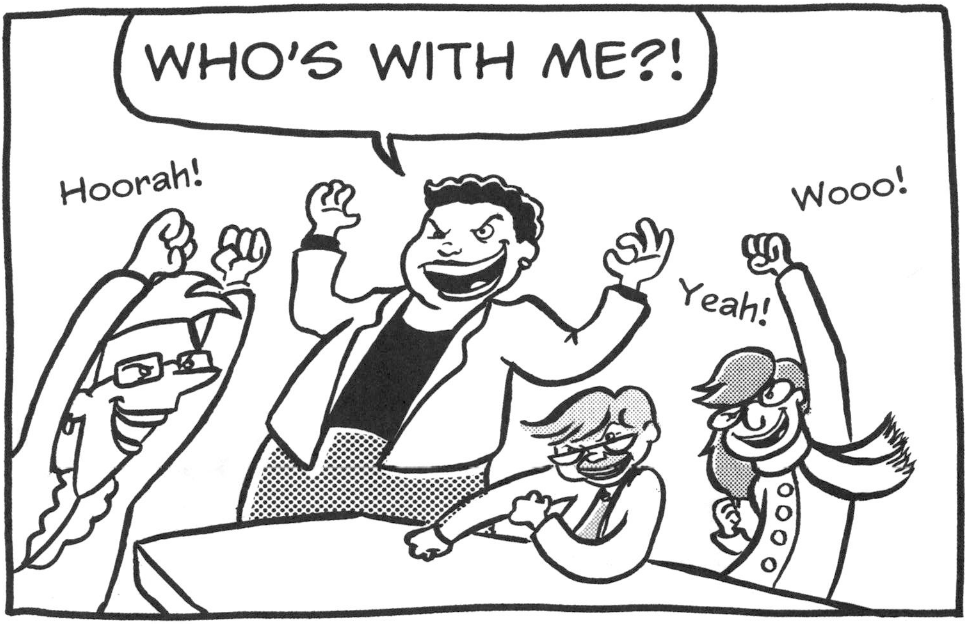
WHO'S WITH ME?!
Hoorah!
Yeah!
Wooo!

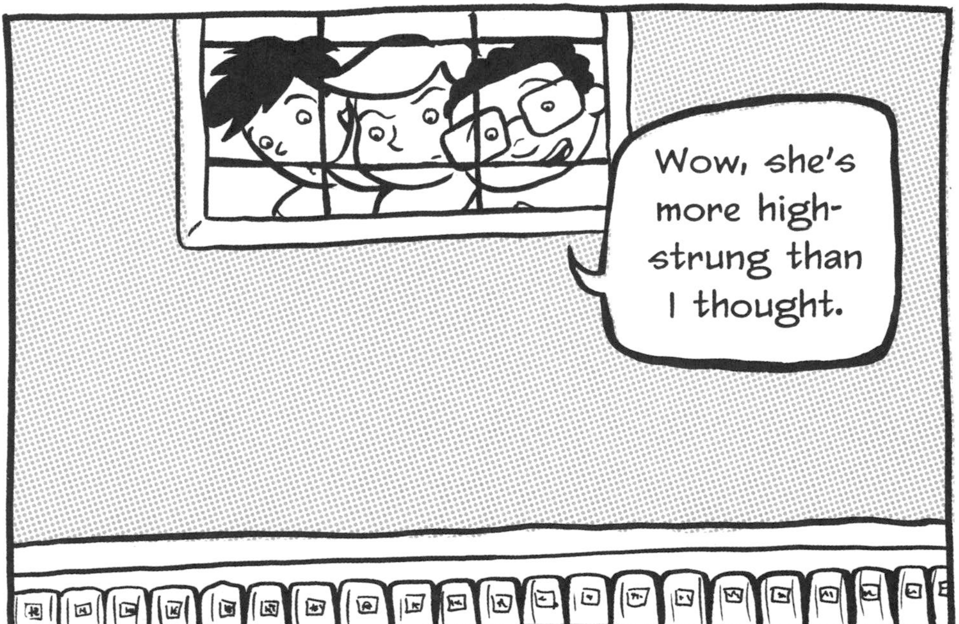
Wow, she's more high-strung than I thought.

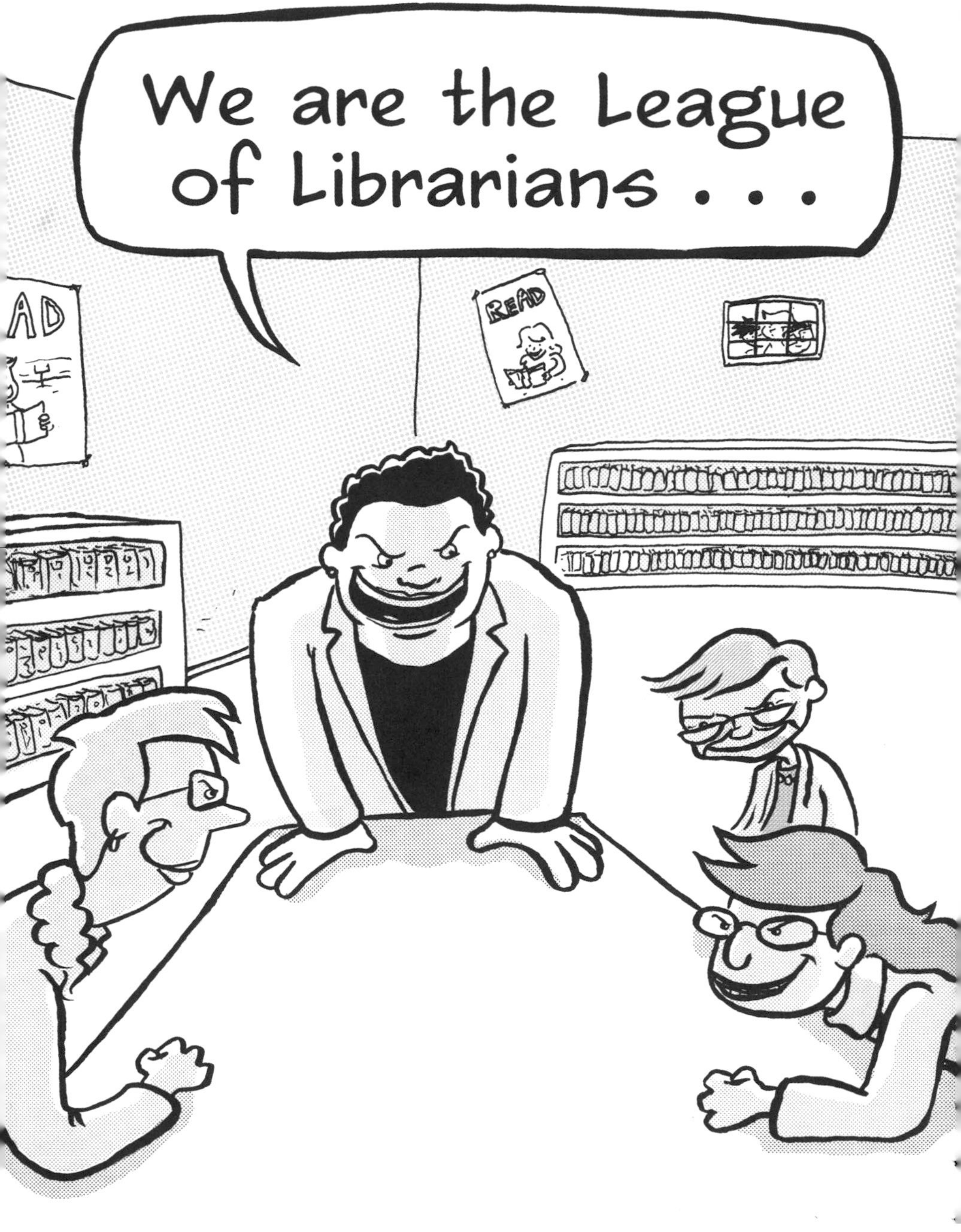
We are the League of Librarians . . .
READ

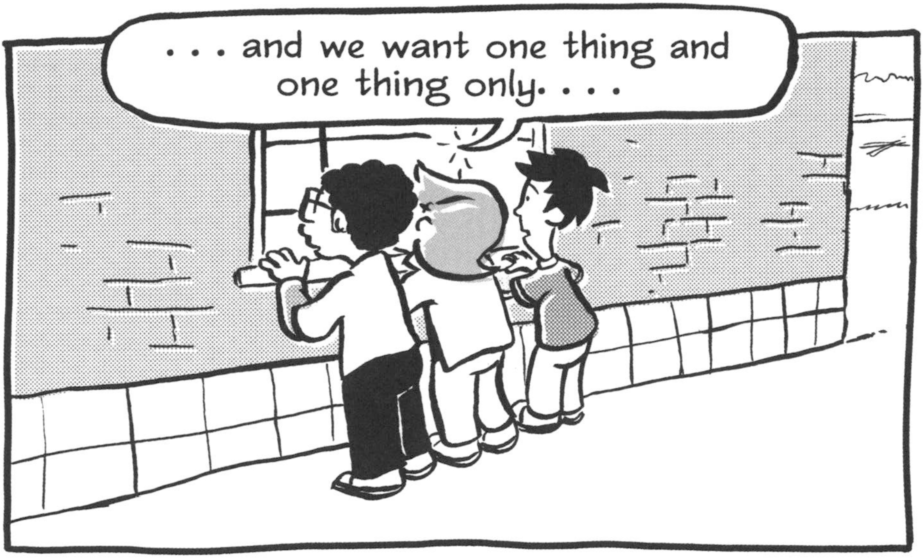
. . . and we want one thing and one thing only. . . .

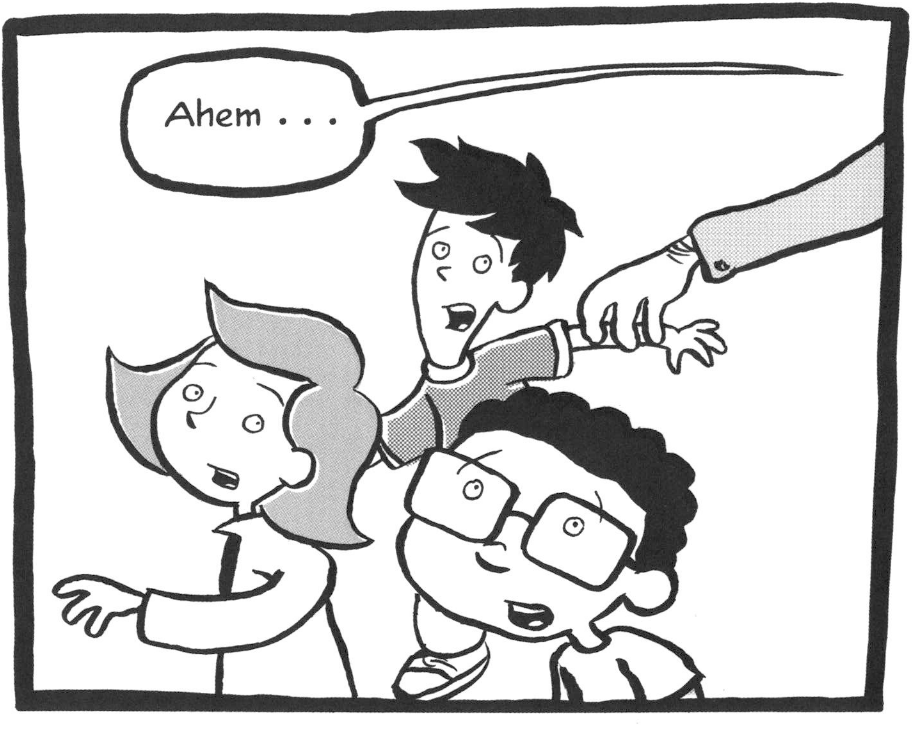
Ahem . . .

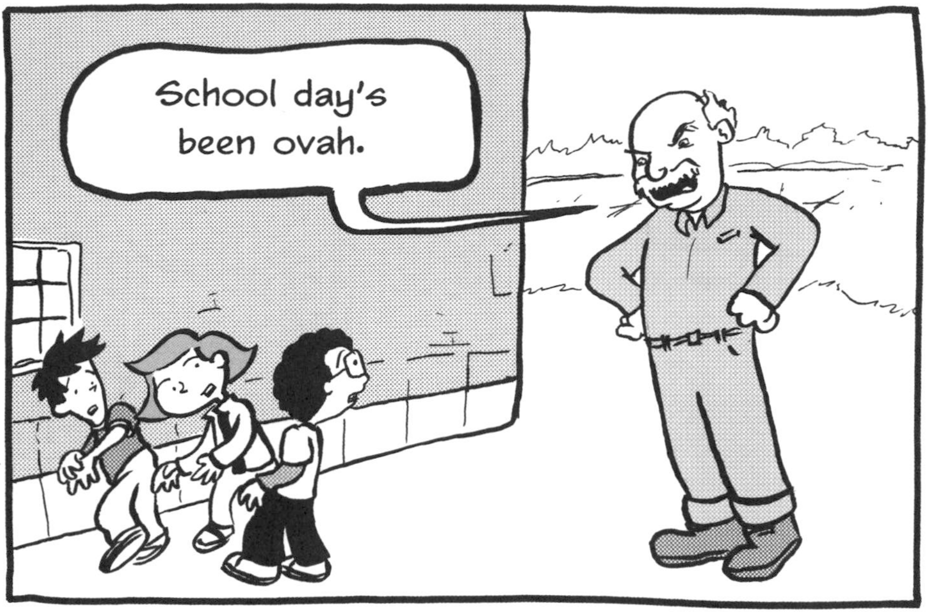
School day's been ovah.

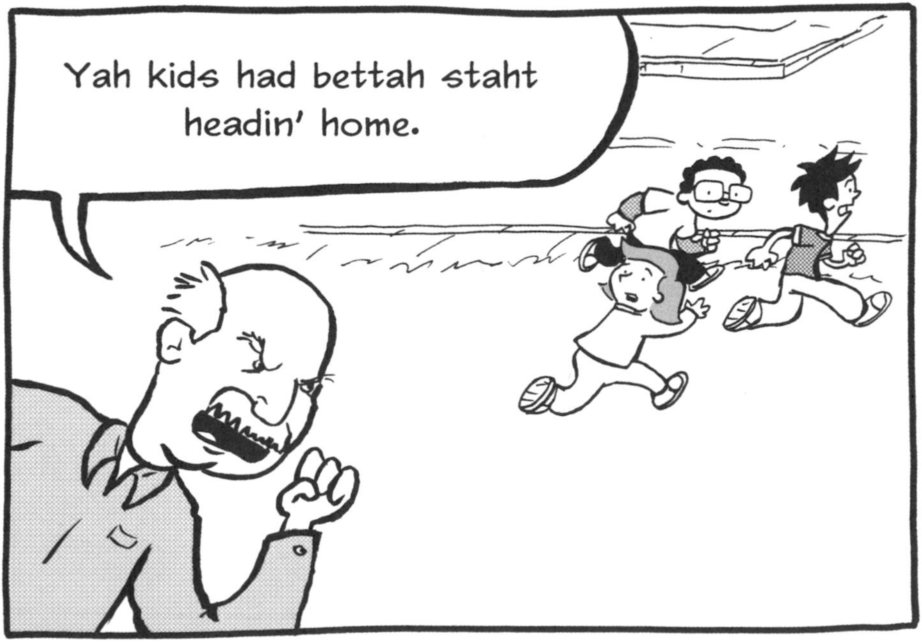
Yah kids had bettah staht headin' home.

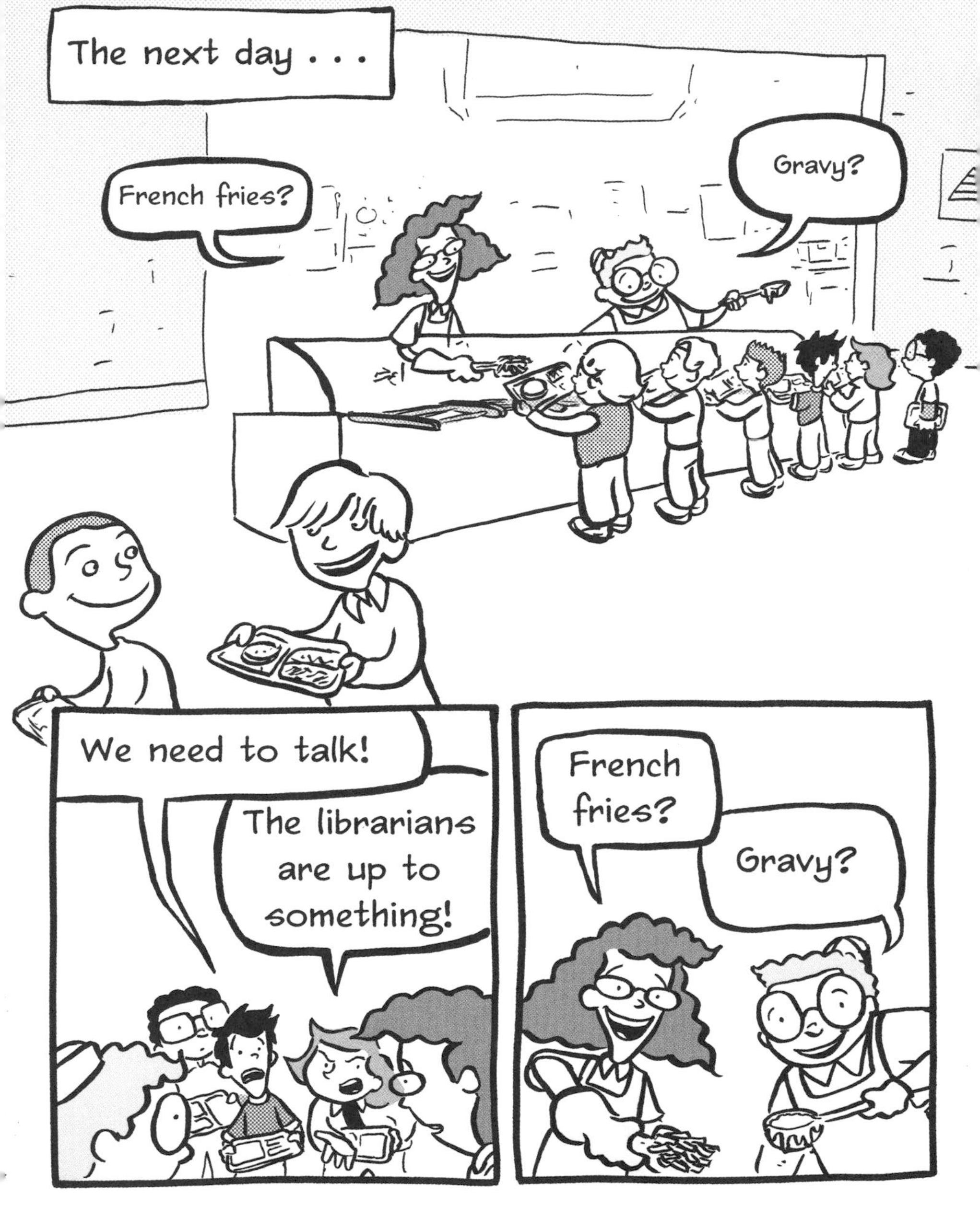
The next day . . .
French fries?
Gravy?
We need to talk!
The librarians are up to something!
French fries?
Gravy?

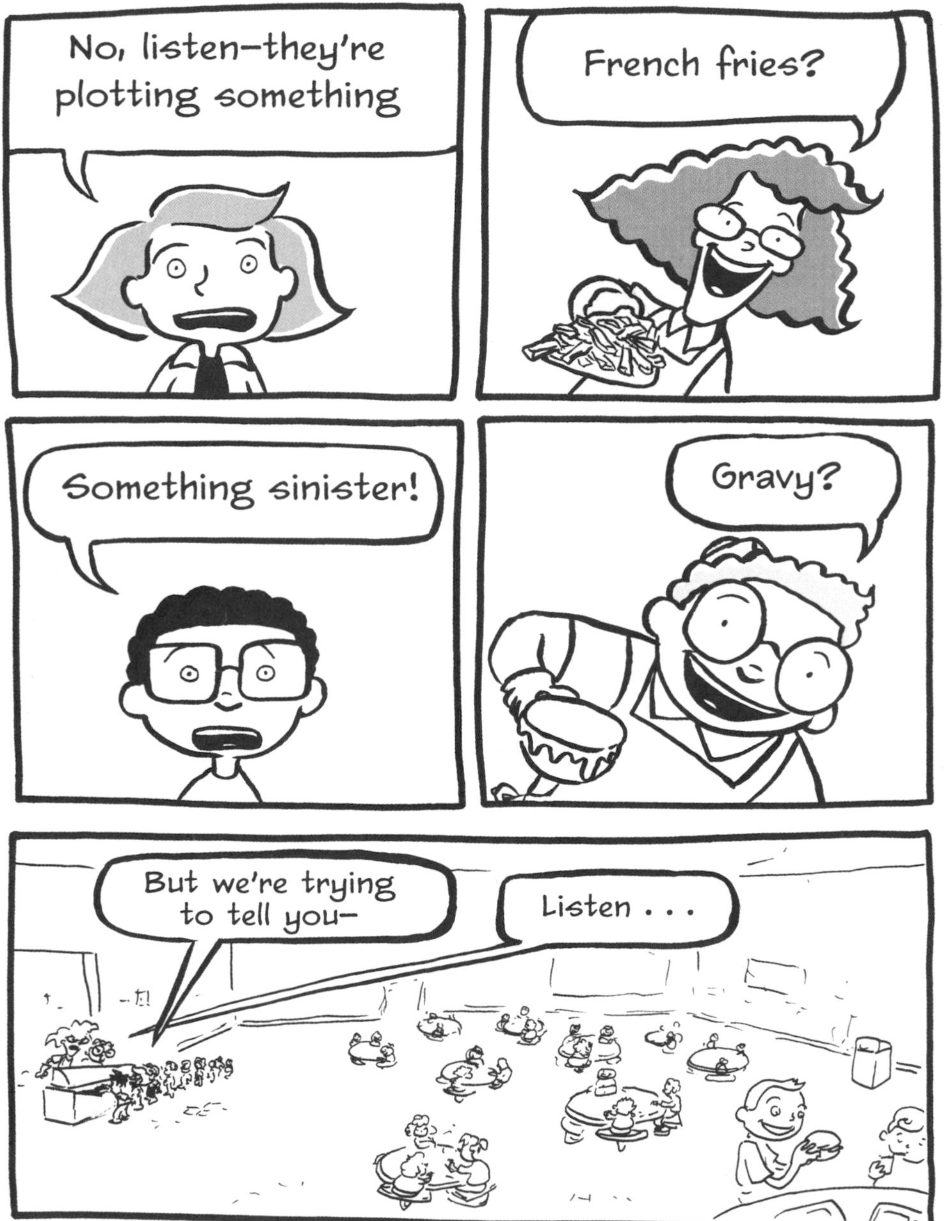
No, listen—they're plotting something
French fries?
Something sinister!
Gravy?
But we're trying to tell you—
Listen . . .

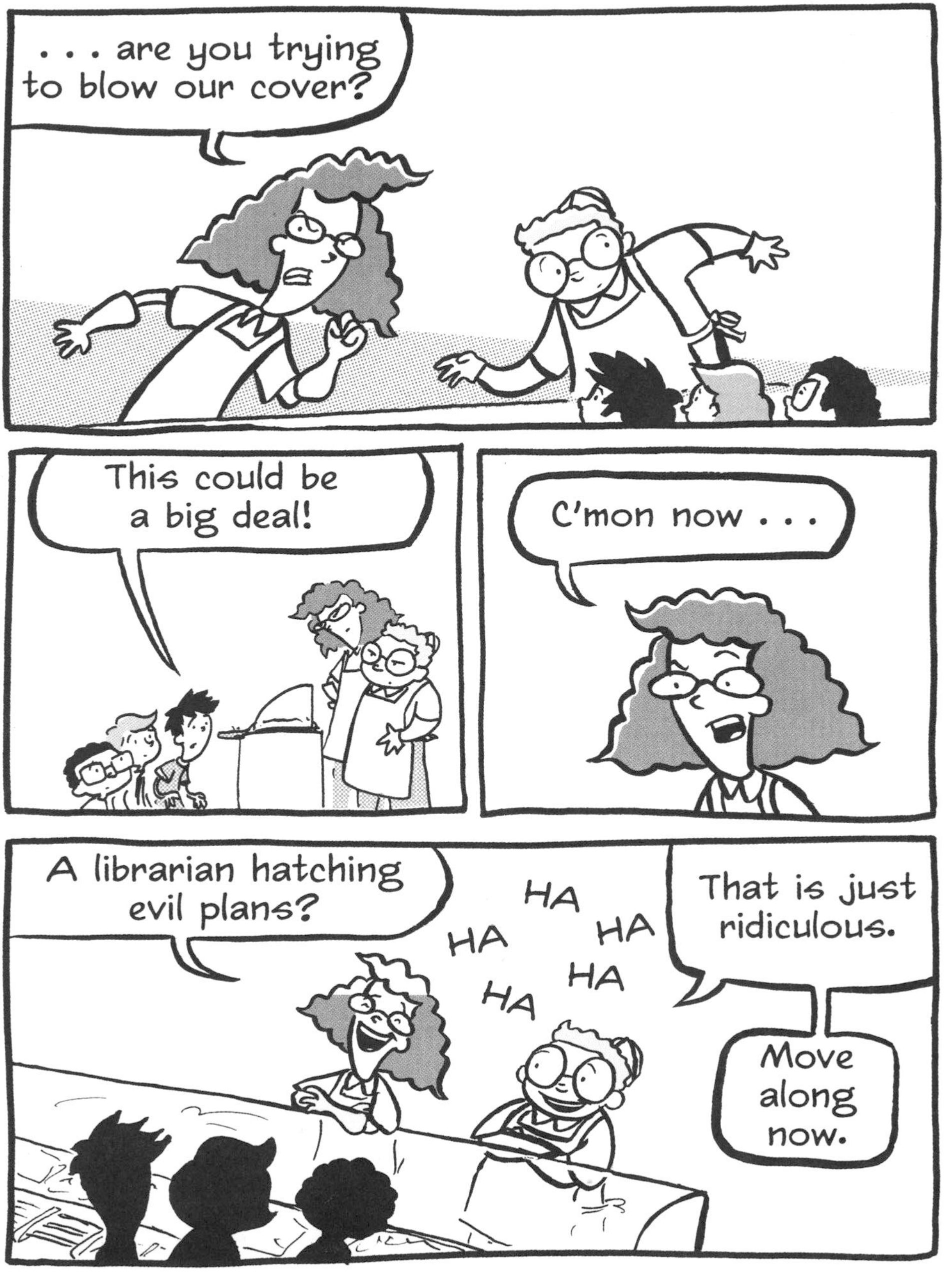
. . . are you trying to blow our cover?
This could be a big deal!
C'mon now . . .
A librarian hatching evil plans?
HA HA HA HA HA
That is just ridiculous.
Move along now.

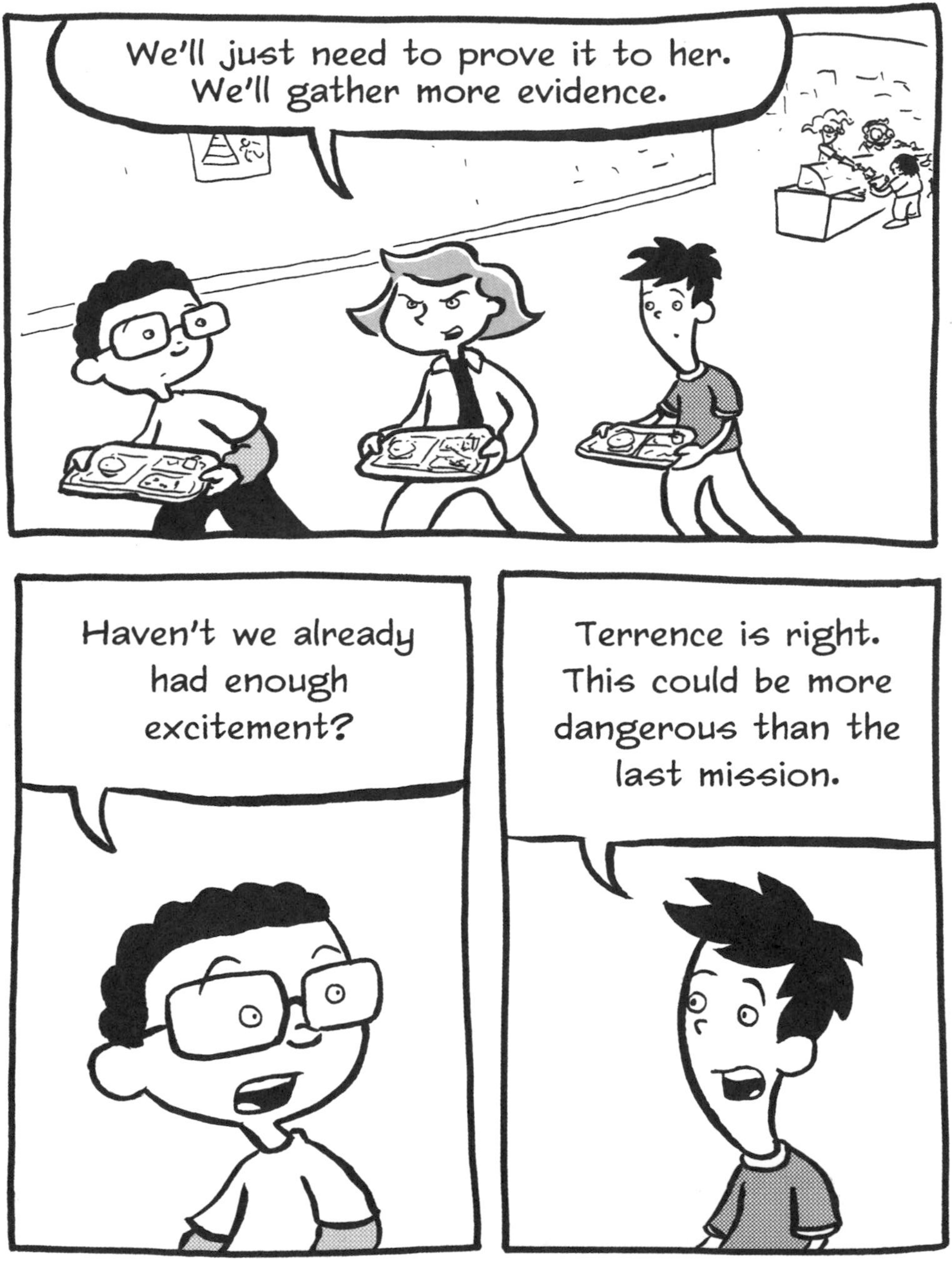
We'll just need to prove it to her. We'll gather more evidence.
Haven't we already had enough excitement?
Terrence is right. This could be more dangerous than the last mission.

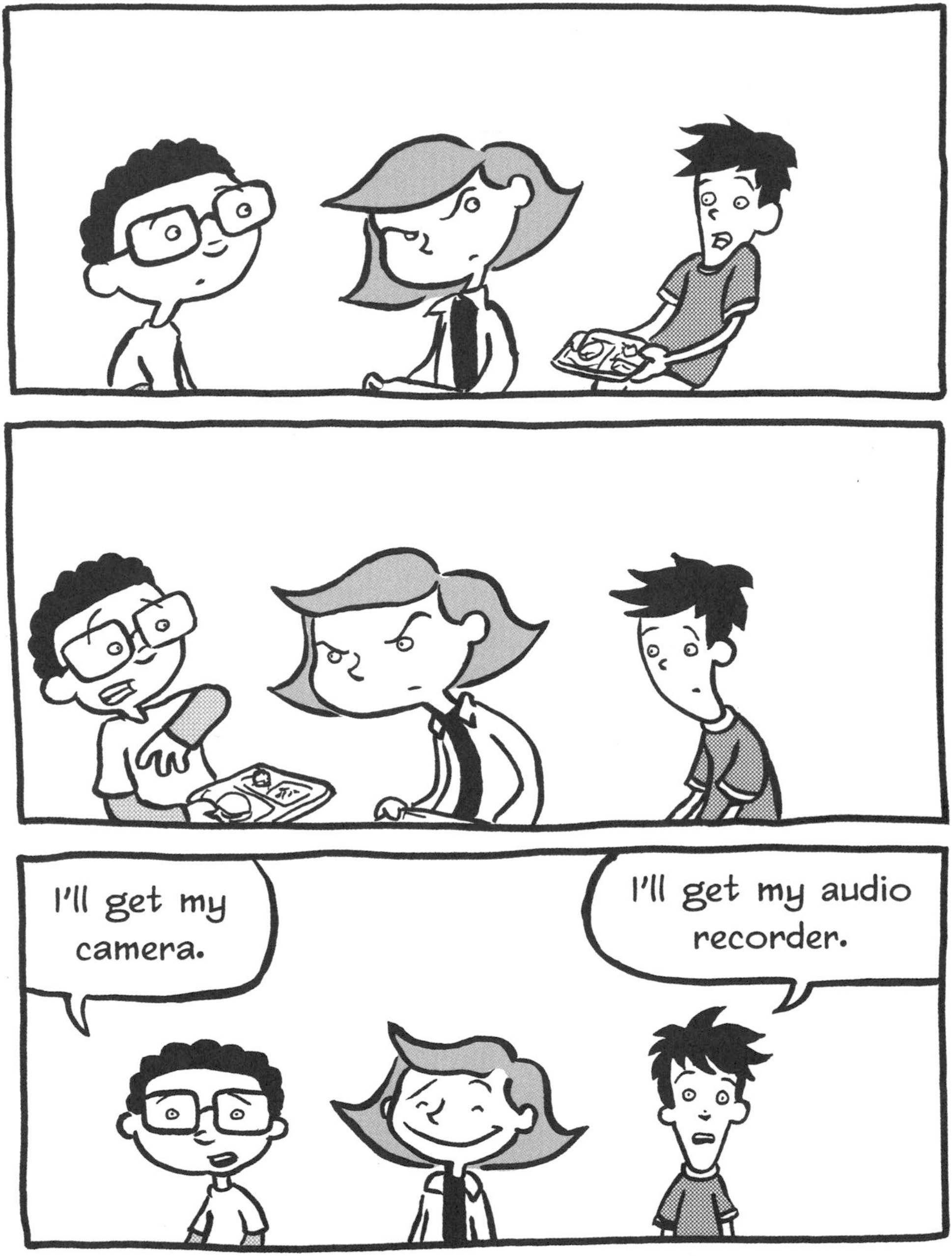
I'll get my camera.
I'll get my audio recorder.

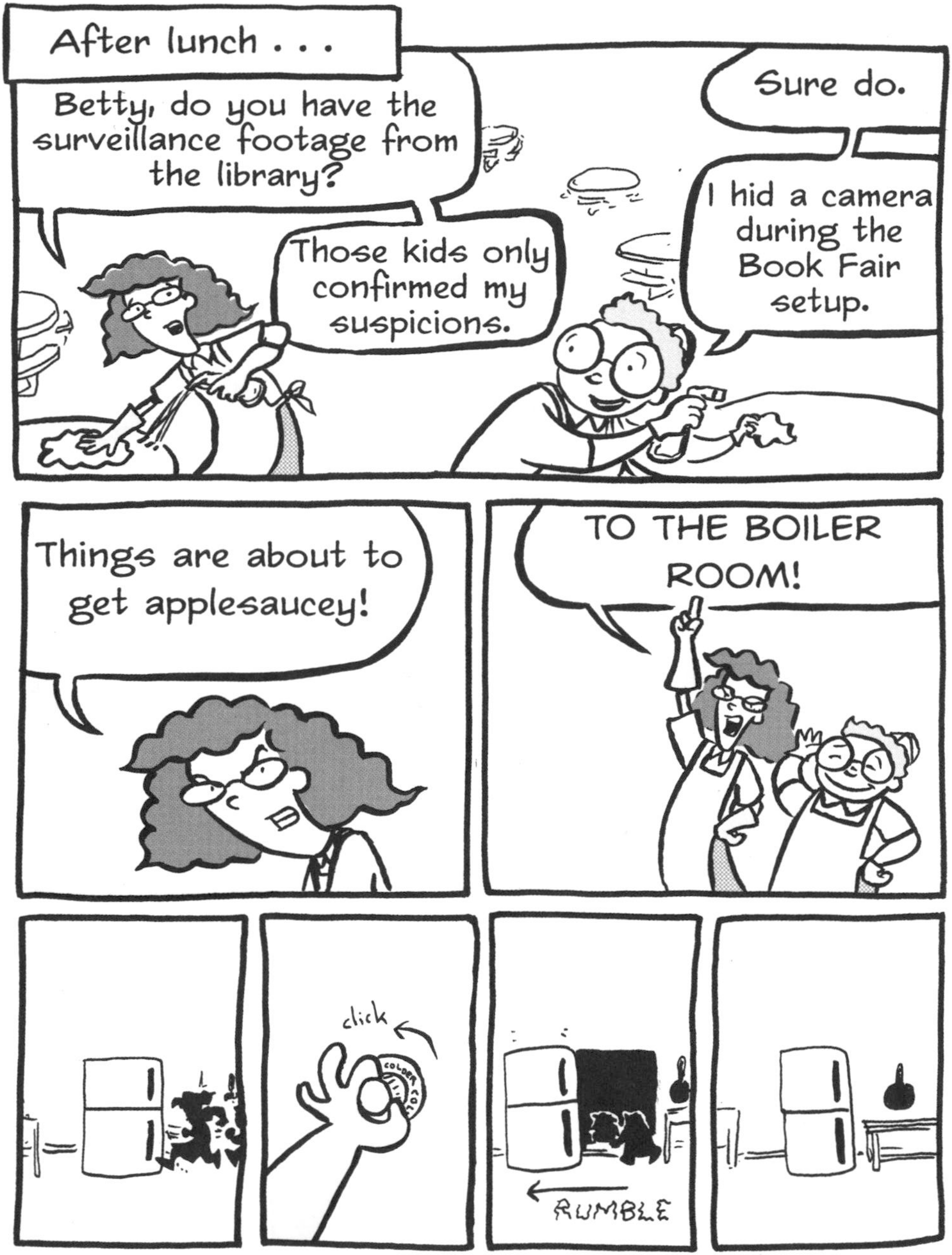
After lunch . . .
Betty, do you have the surveillance footage from the library?
Those kids only confirmed my suspicions.
Sure do.
I hid a camera during the Book Fair setup.
Things are about to get applesaucey!
TO THE BOILER ROOM!
click
RUMBLE

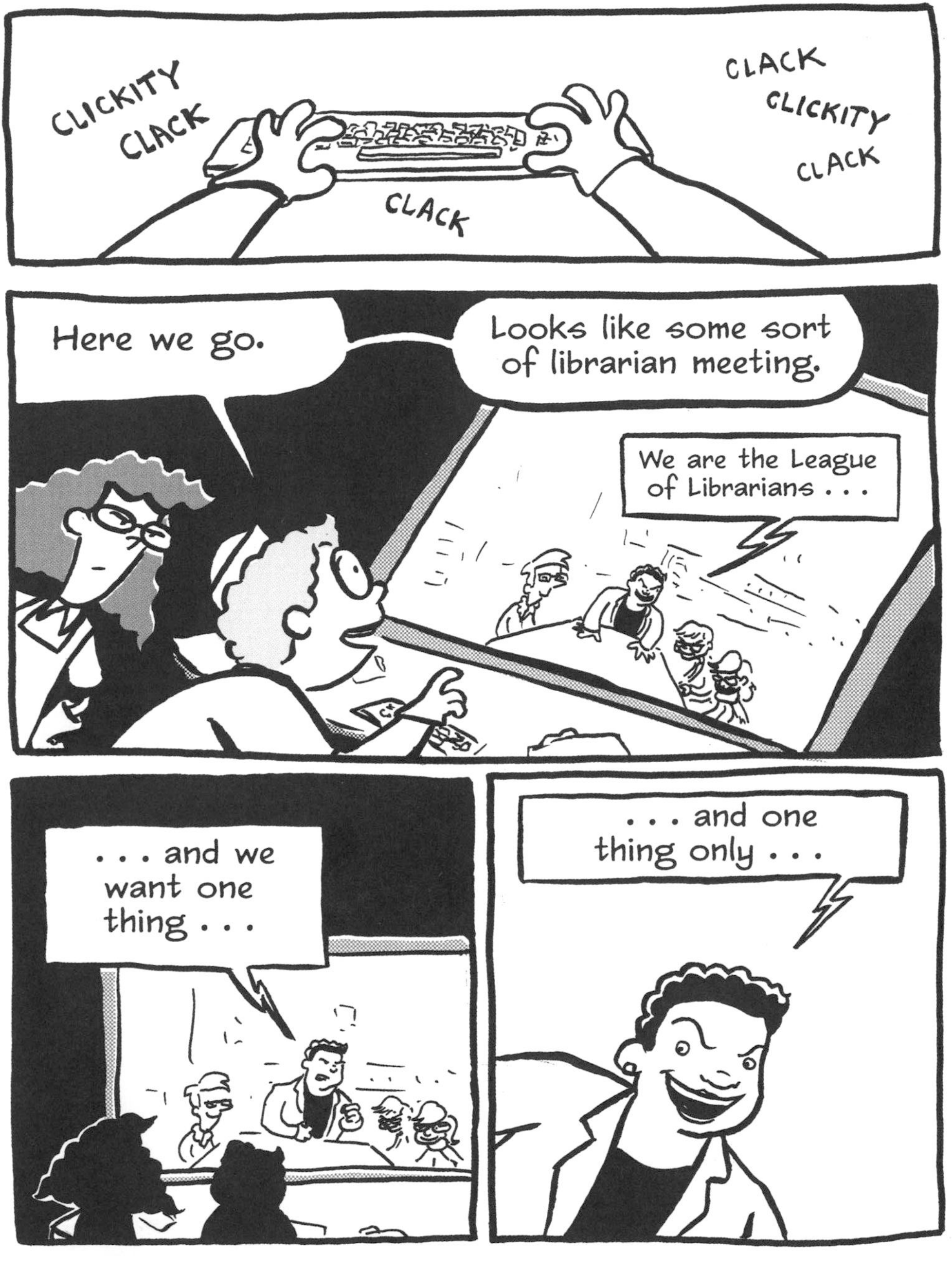
CLICKITY CLACK
CLACK
CLACK CLICKITY CLACK
Here we go.
Looks like some sort of librarian meeting.
We are the League of Librarians . . .
. . . and we want one thing . . .
. . . and one thing only . . .

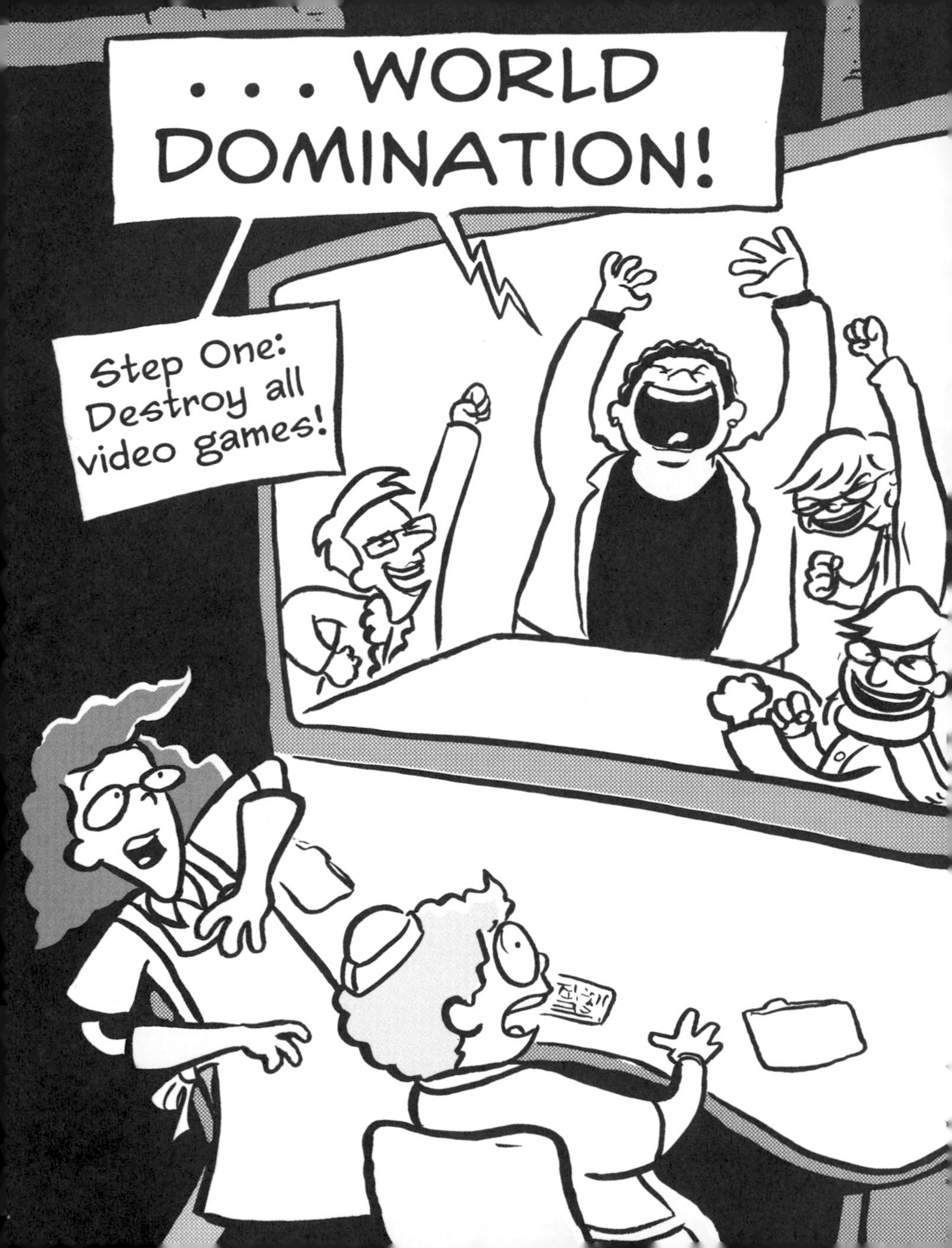
. . . WORLD DOMINATION!
Step One: Destroy all video games!

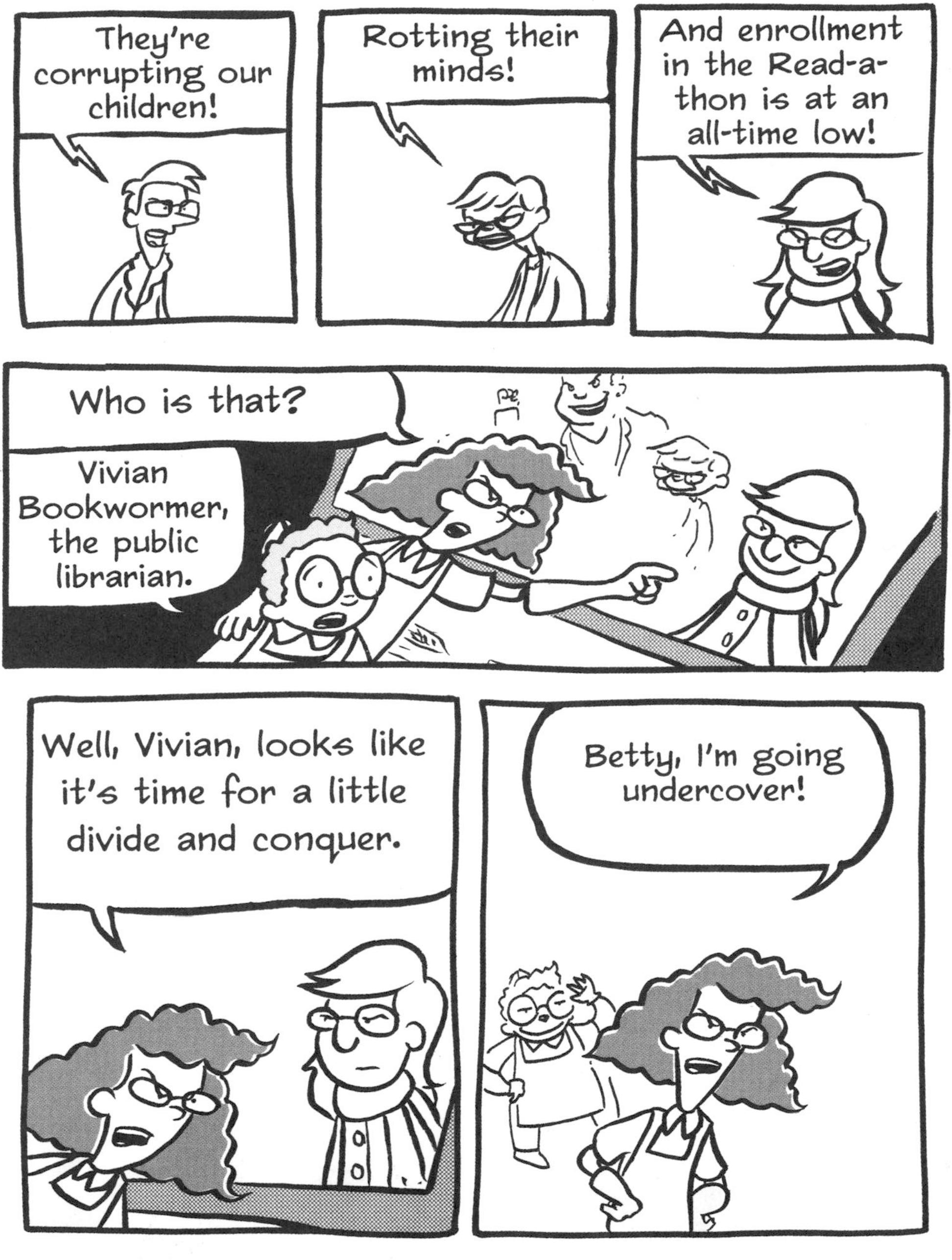
They're corrupting our children!
Rotting their minds!
And enrollment in the Read-a-thon is at an all-time low!
Who is that?
Vivian Bookwormer, the public librarian.
Well, Vivian, looks like it's time for a little divide and conquer.
Betty, I'm going undercover!

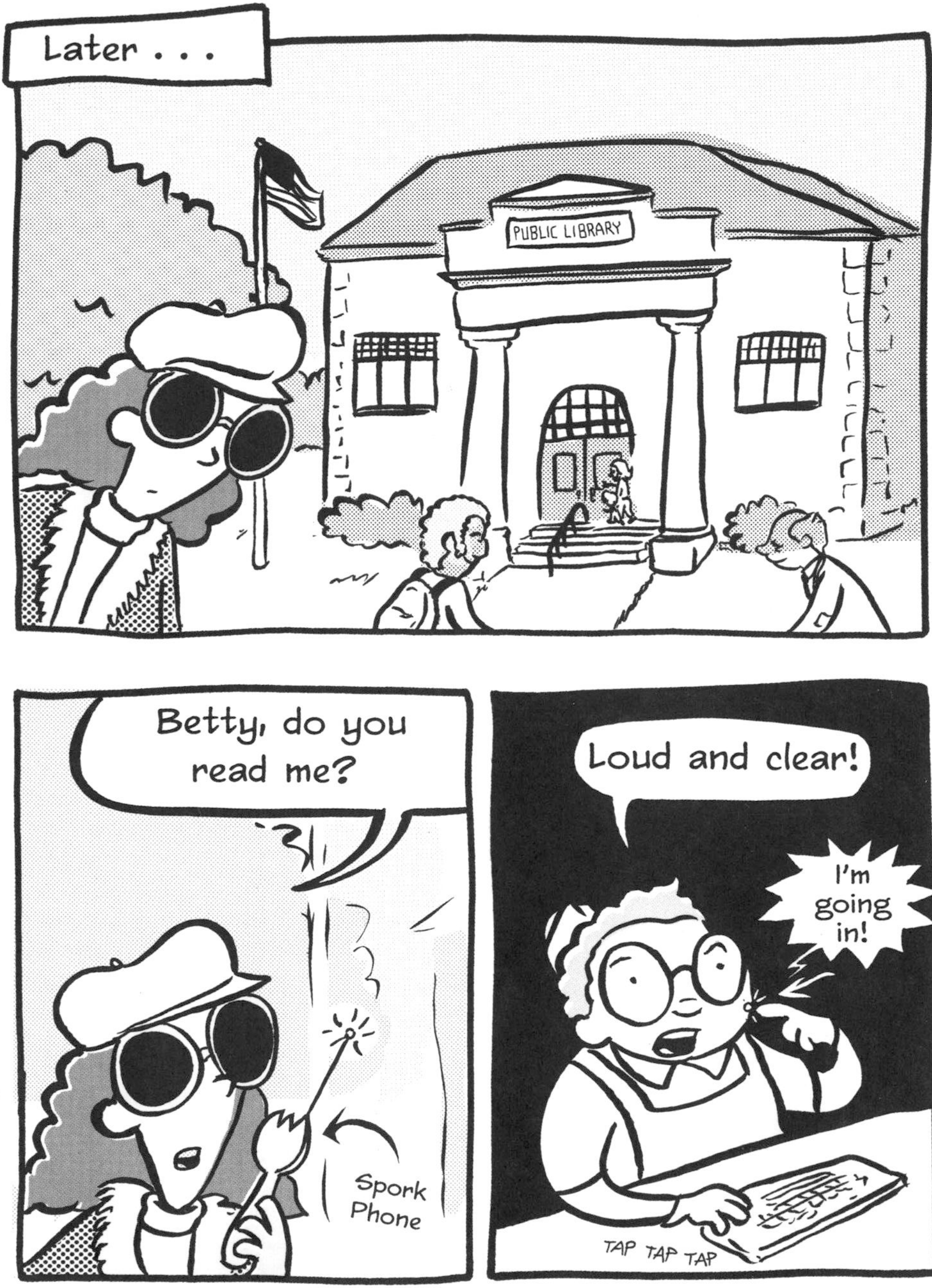
Later . . .
PUBLIC LIBRARY
Betty, do you read me?
Spork Phone
Loud and clear!
I'm going in!
TAP TAP TAP

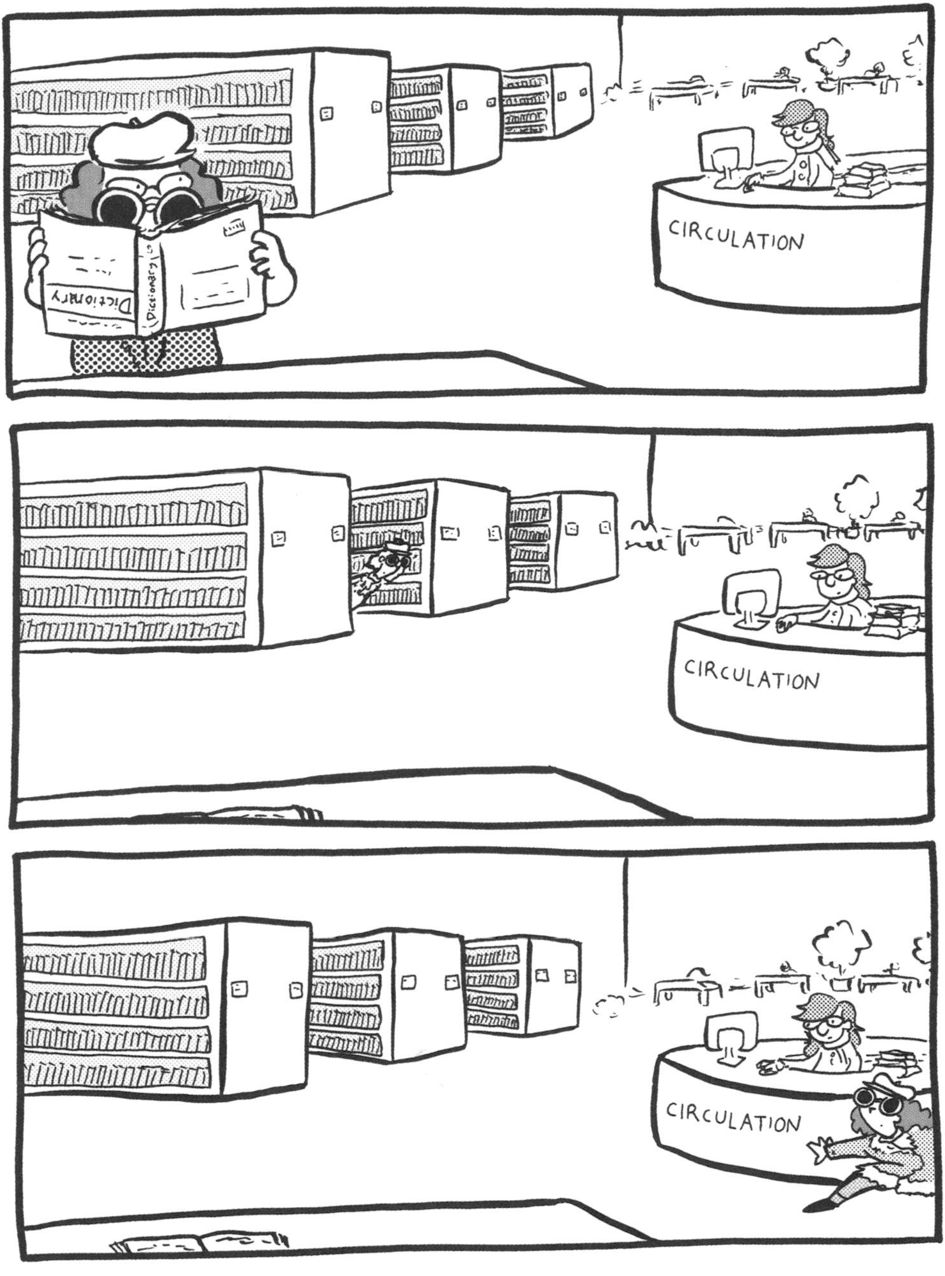
Dictionary
Dictionary
CIRCULATION
CIRCULATION
CIRCULATION

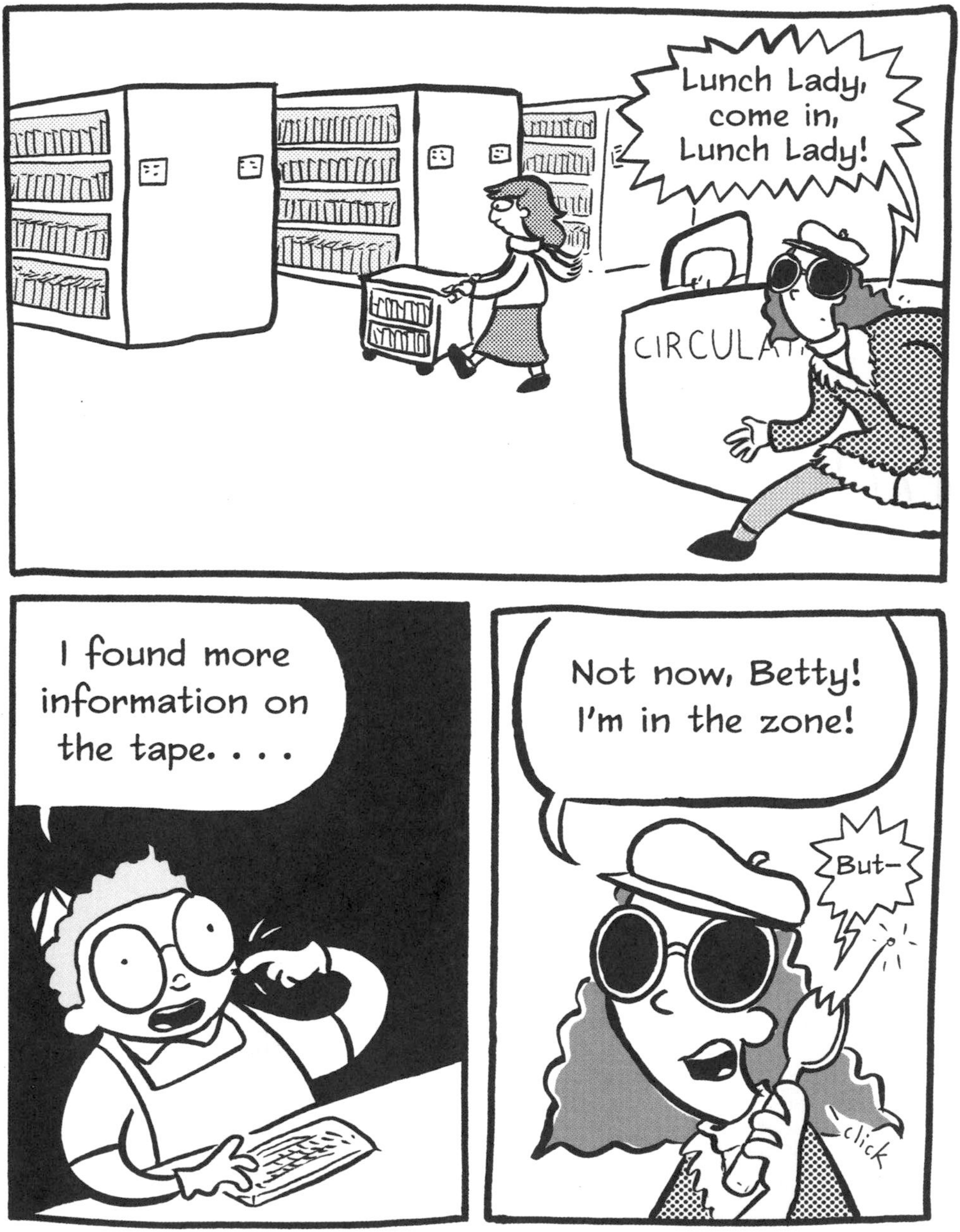

Lunch Lady, come in, Lunch Lady!
I found more information on the tape. . . .
Not now, Betty! I'm in the zone!
But–
click

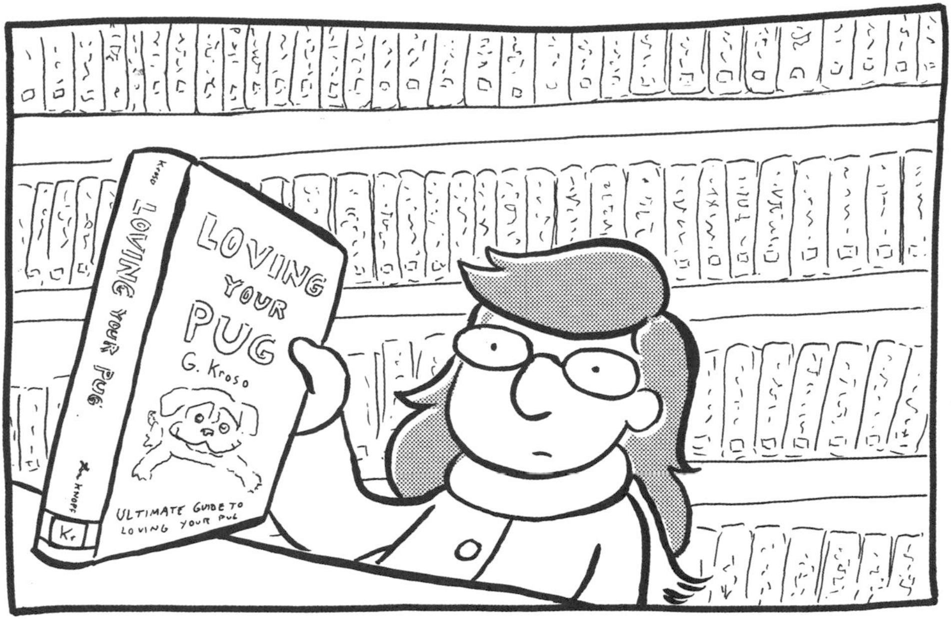
KROSO
LOVING YOUR PUG
KNOPF
Kr
LOVING YOUR PUG
G. Kroso
ULTIMATE GUIDE TO LOVING YOUR PUG

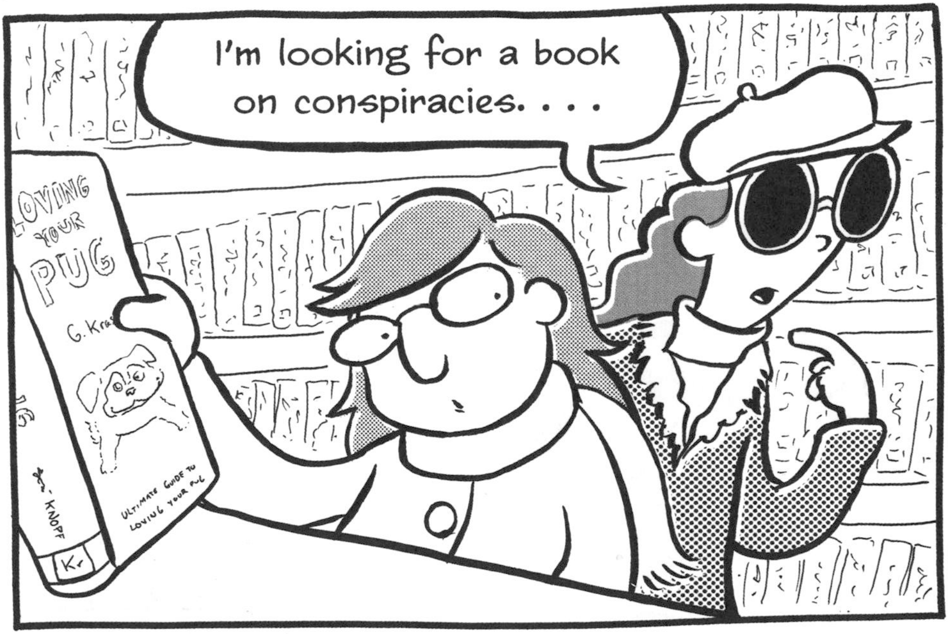
I'm looking for a book on conspiracies. . . .
LOVING YOUR PUG
KNOPF
Kr
ULTIMATE GUIDE TO LOVING YOUR PUG

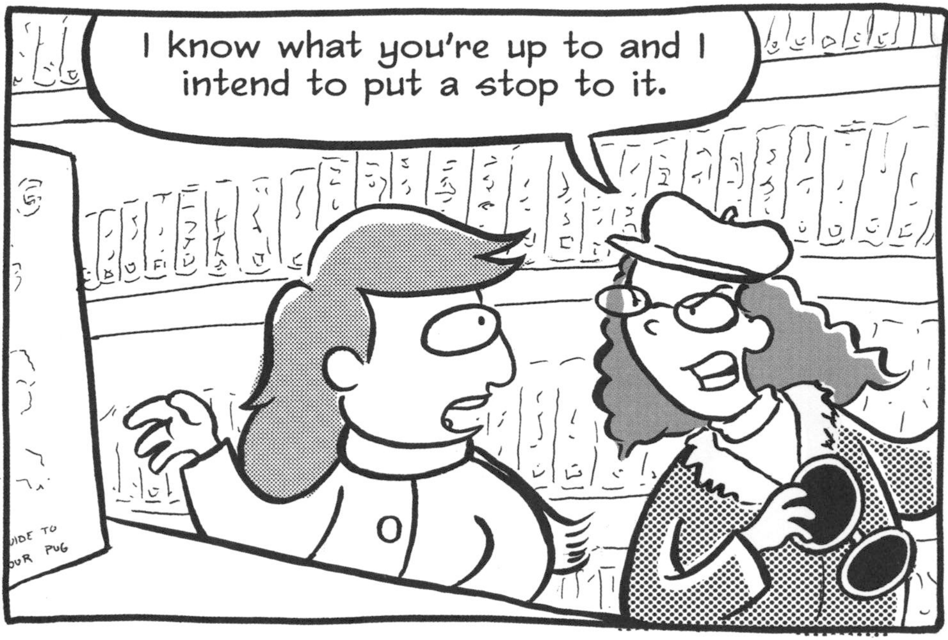
I know what you're up to and I intend to put a stop to it.

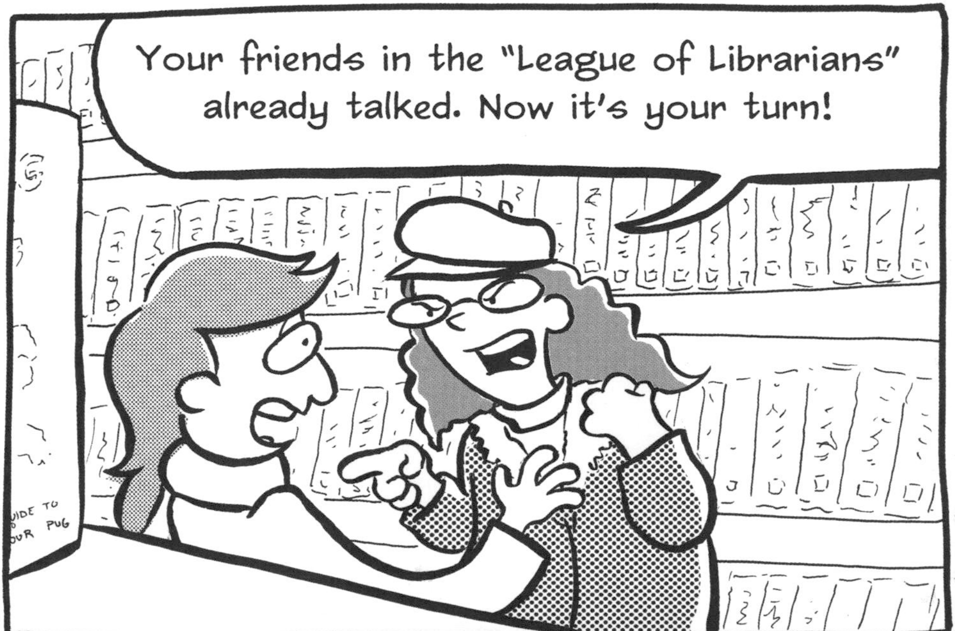
Your friends in the "League of Librarians" already talked. Now it's your turn!

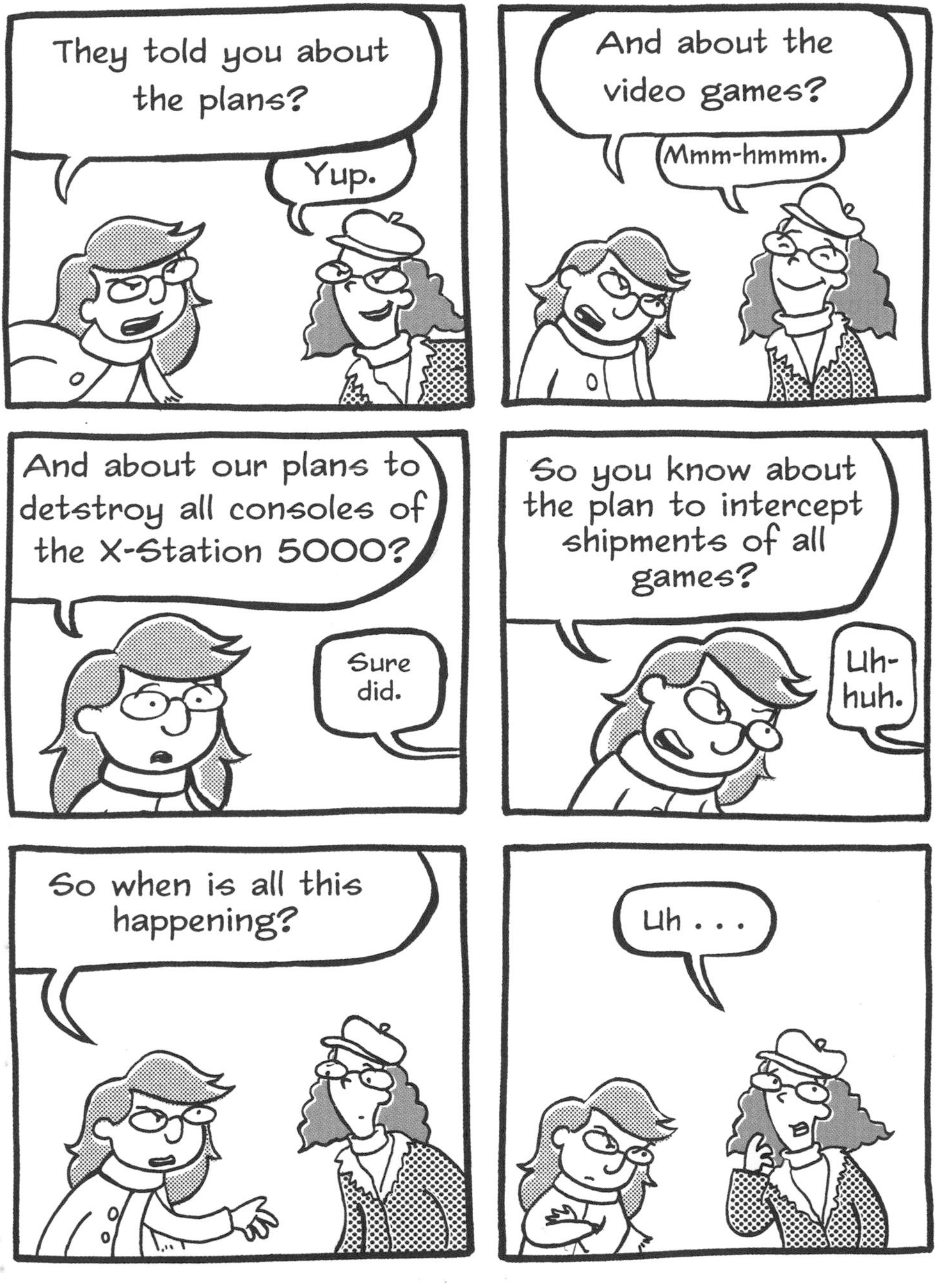
They told you about the plans?
Yup.
And about the video games?
Mmm-hmmm.
And about our plans to detstroy all consoles of the X-Station 5000?
Sure did.
So you know about the plan to intercept shipments of all games?
Uh-huh.
So when is all this happening?
Uh . . .

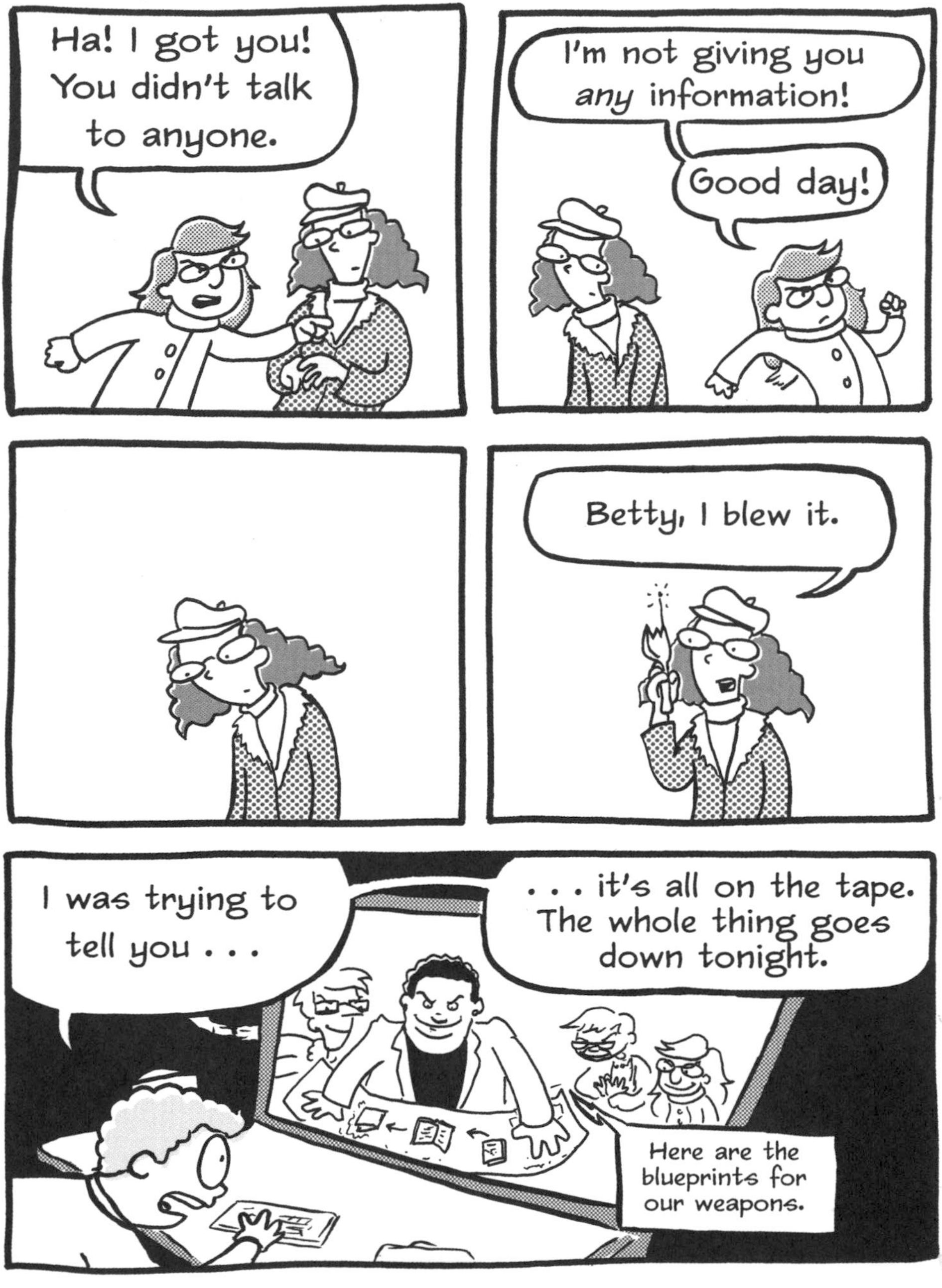
Ha! I got you! You didn't talk to anyone.
I'm not giving you *any* information!
Good day!
Betty, I blew it.
I was trying to tell you . . .
. . . it's all on the tape. The whole thing goes down tonight.
Here are the blueprints for our weapons.

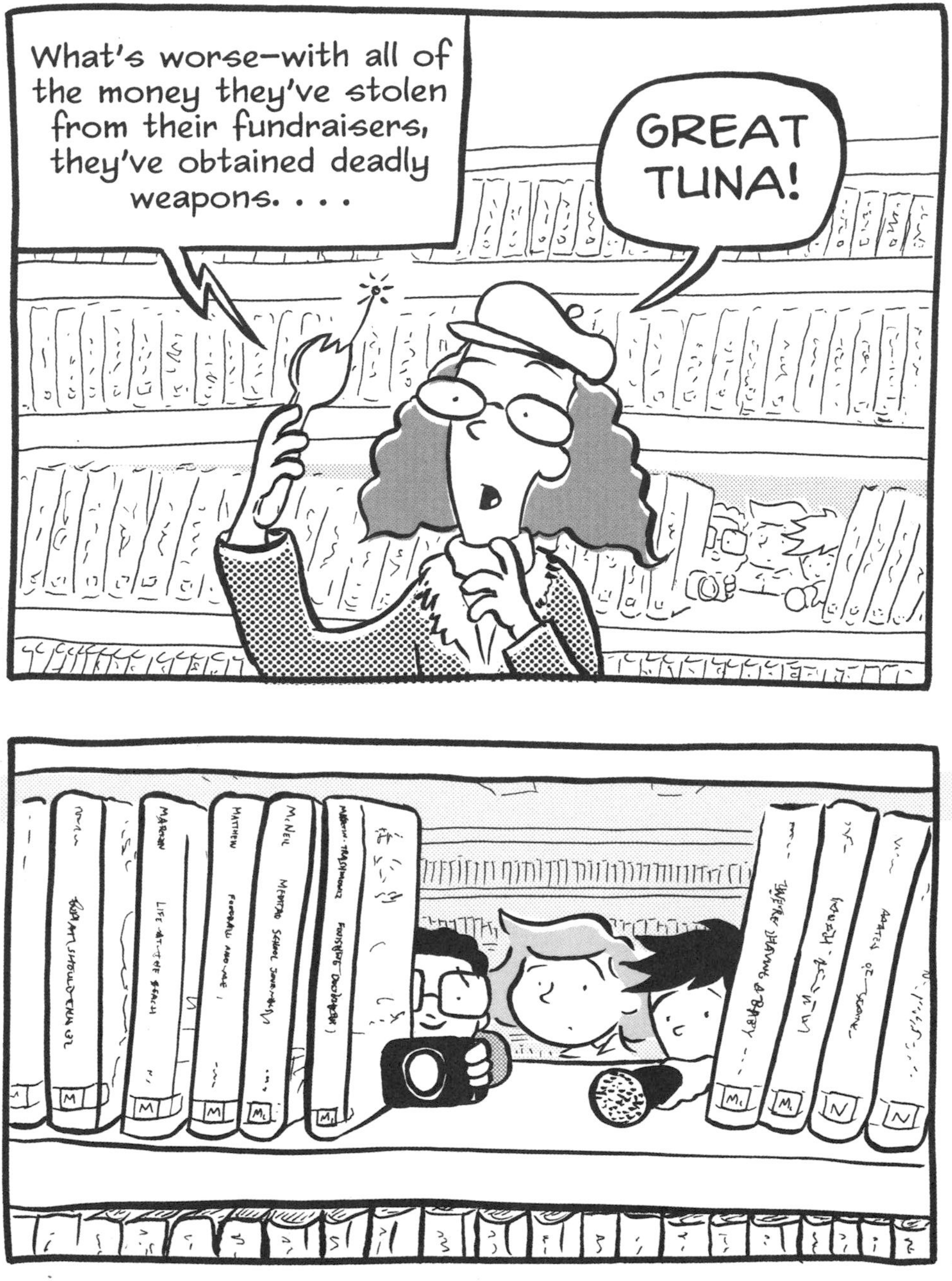
What's worse—with all of the money they've stolen from their fundraisers, they've obtained deadly weapons. . . .
GREAT TUNA!

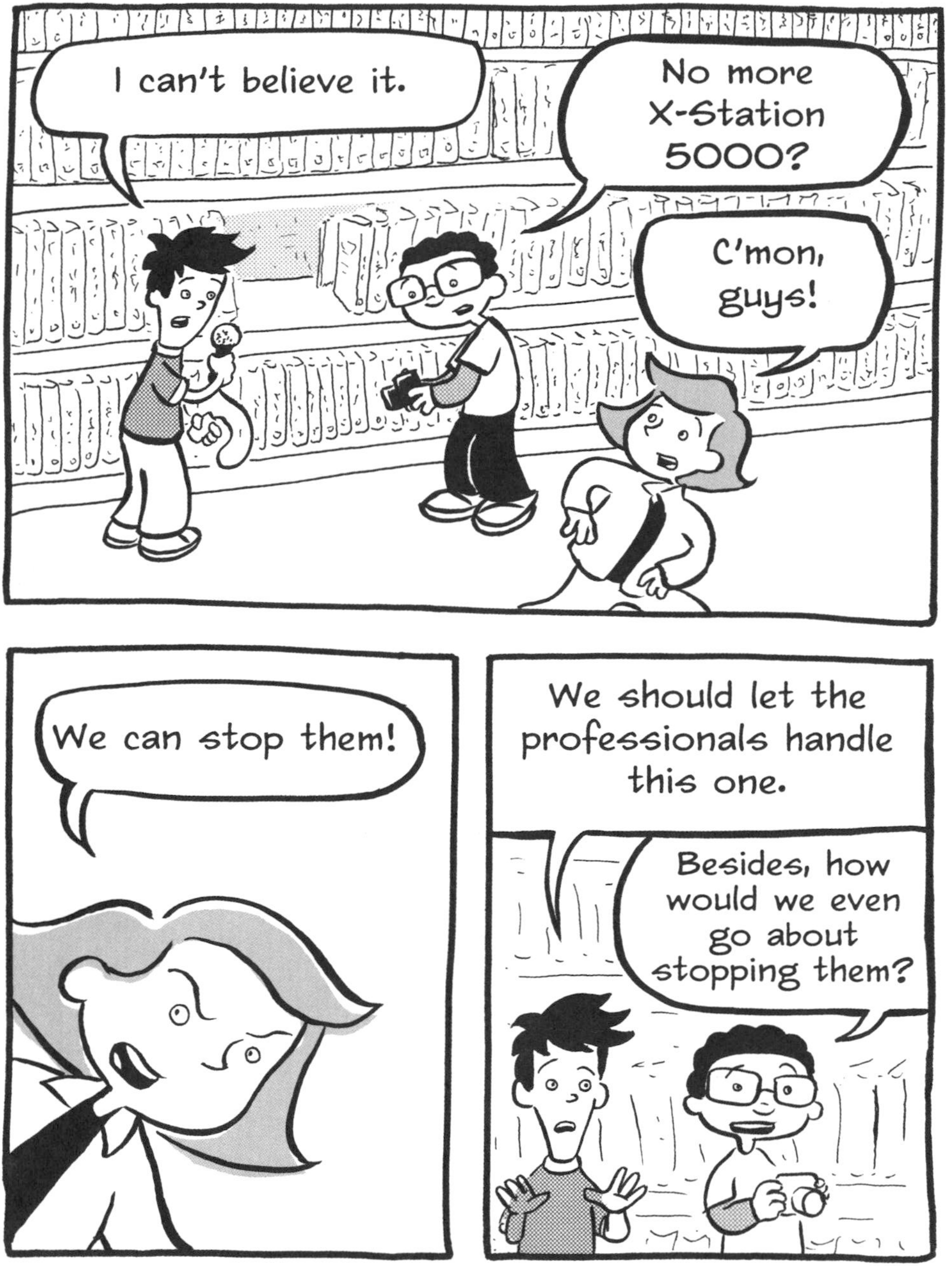
I can't believe it.
No more X-Station 5000?
C'mon, guys!
We can stop them!
We should let the professionals handle this one.
Besides, how would we even go about stopping them?

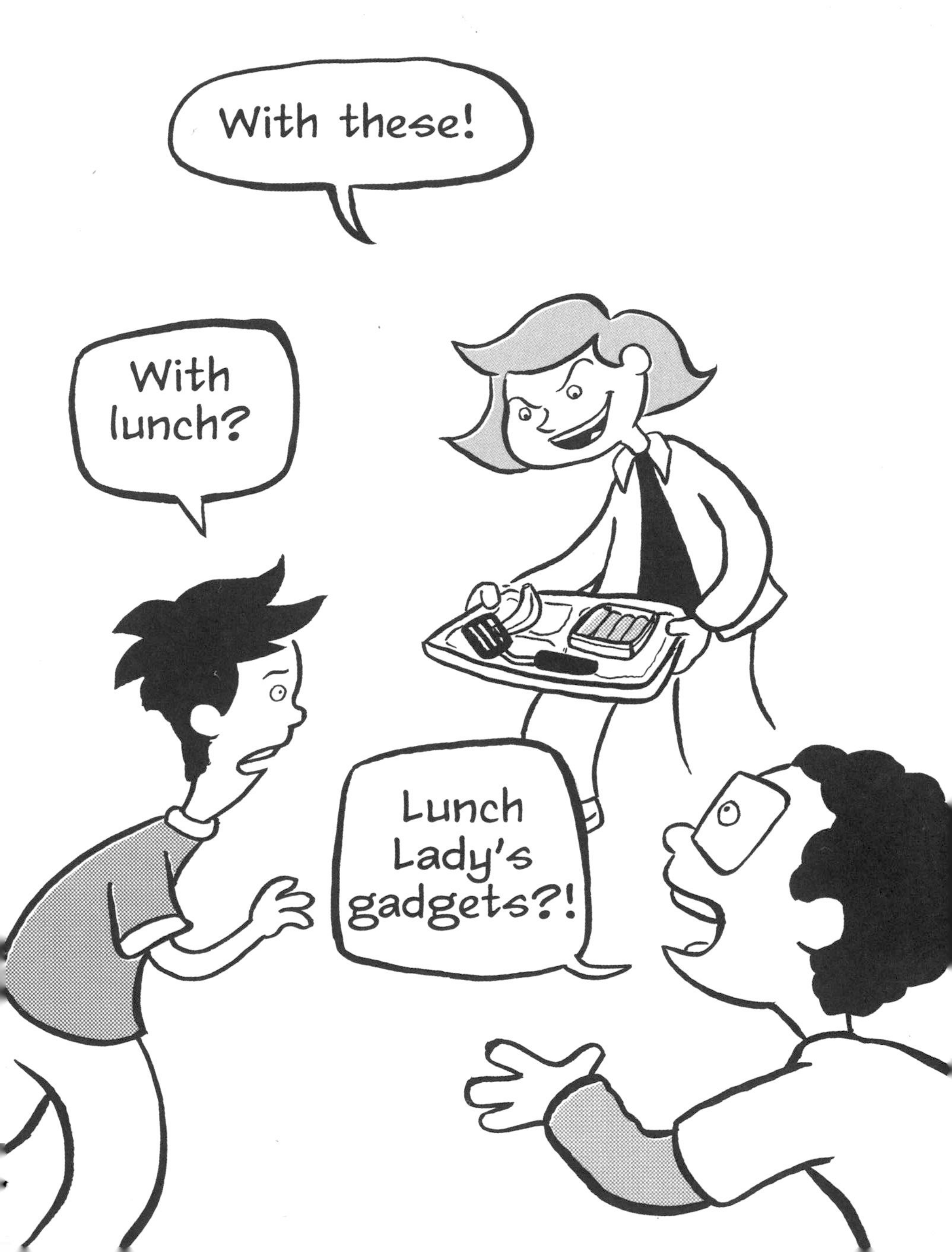
With these!
With lunch?
Lunch Lady's gadgets?!

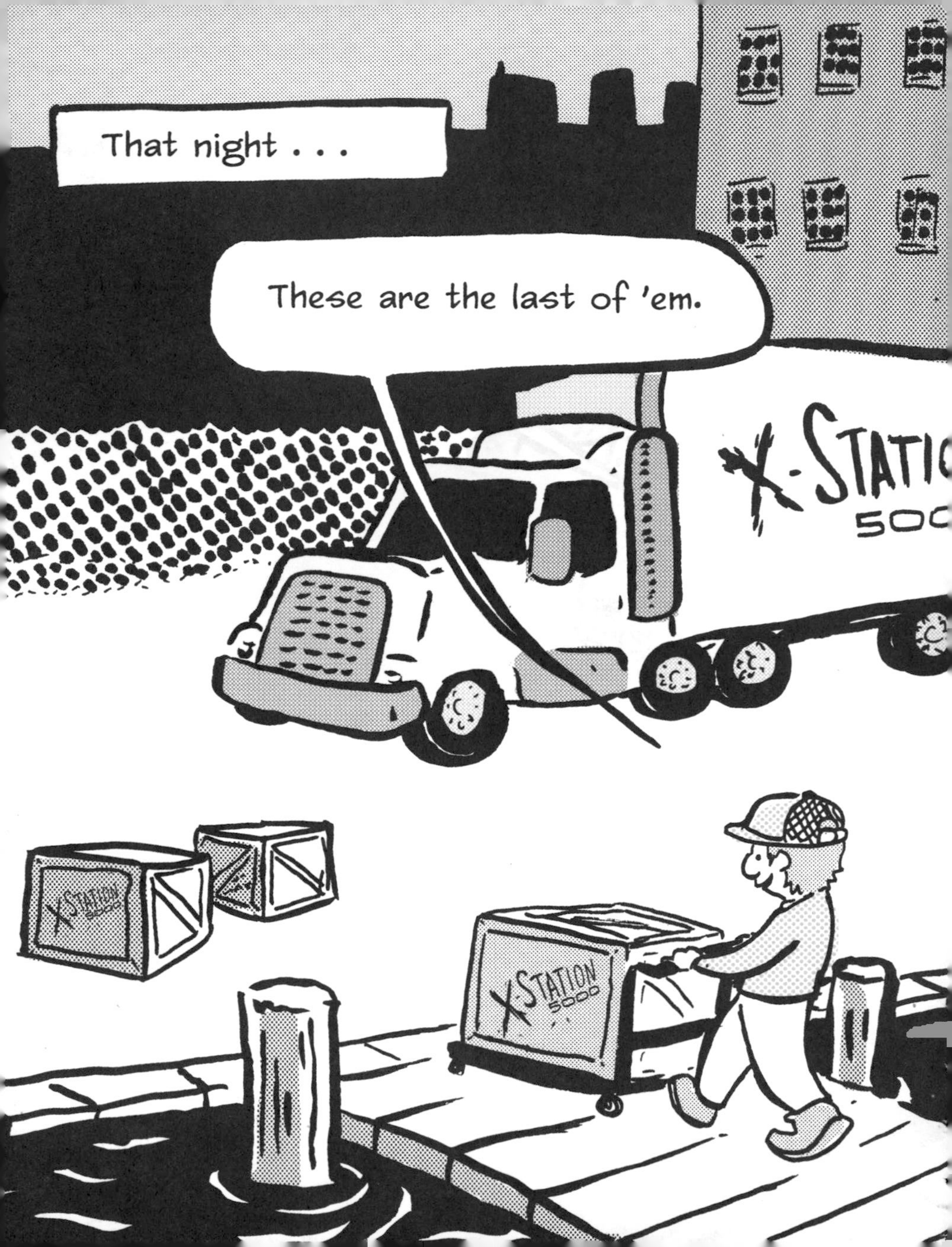
That night . . .
These are the last of 'em.
X-STATI
500
X-STATION 5000
X-STATION 5000

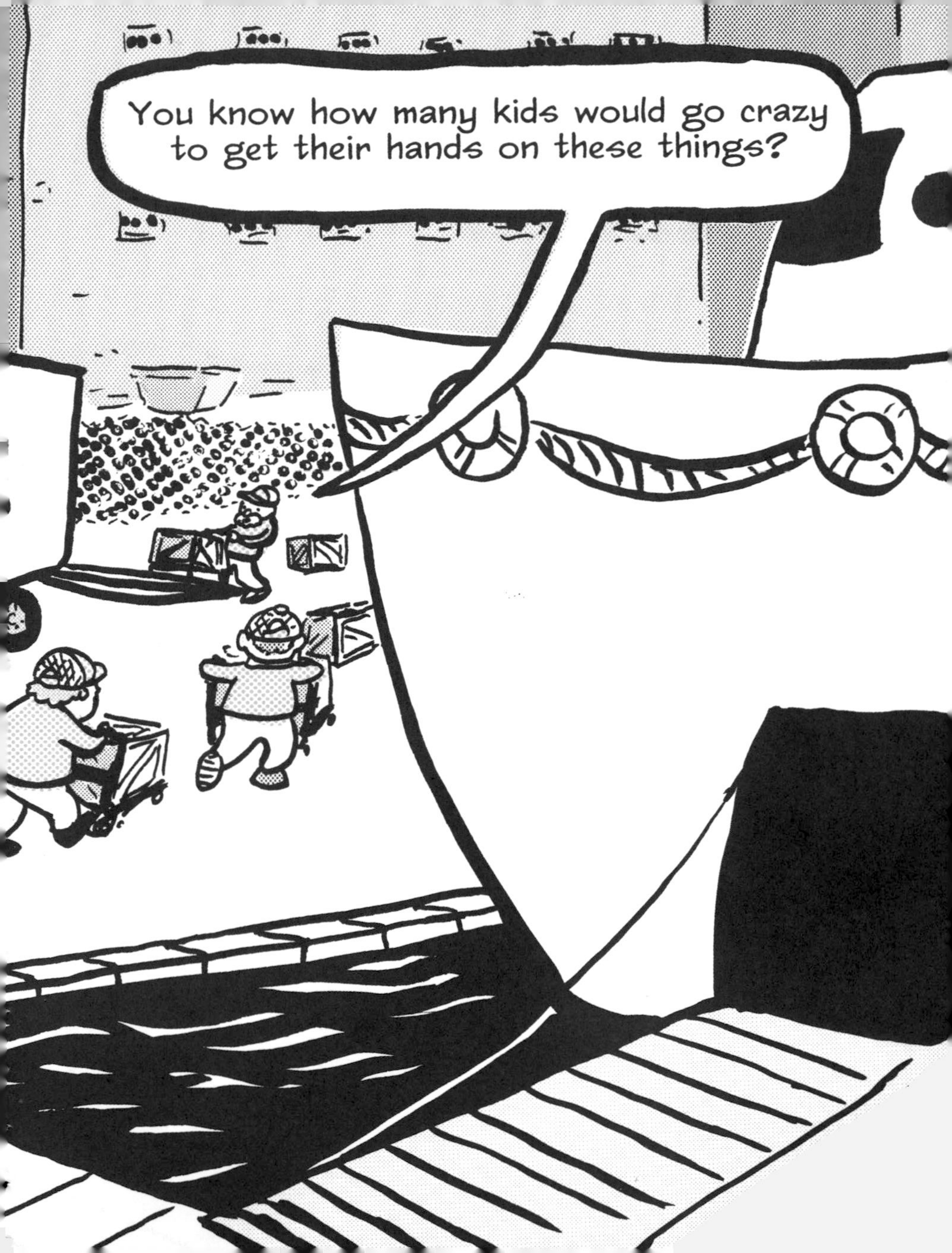
You know how many kids would go crazy to get their hands on these things?

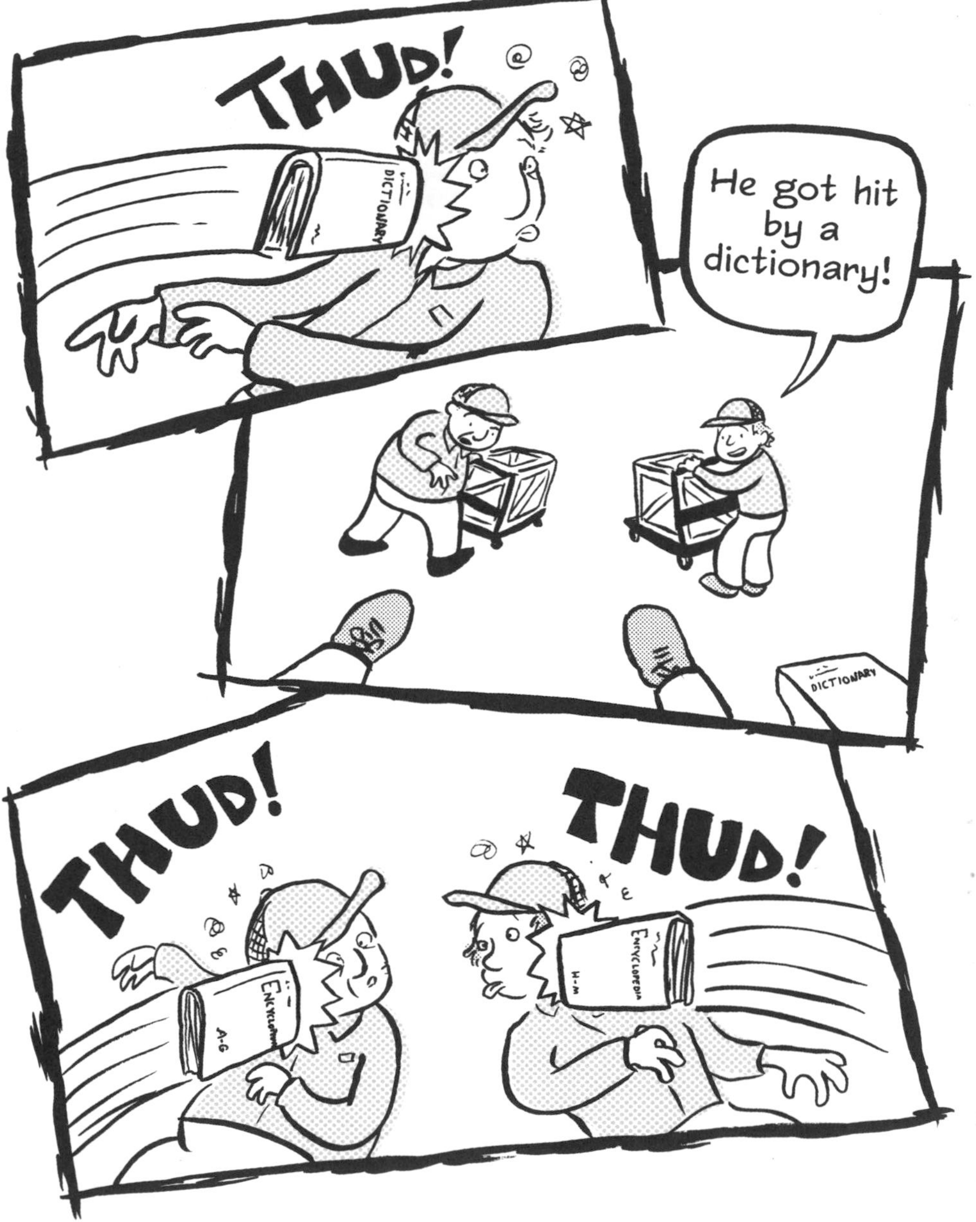
THUD!
DICTIONARY
He got hit by a dictionary!
DICTIONARY
THUD!
A-G
THUD!
ENCYCLOPEDIA
H-M

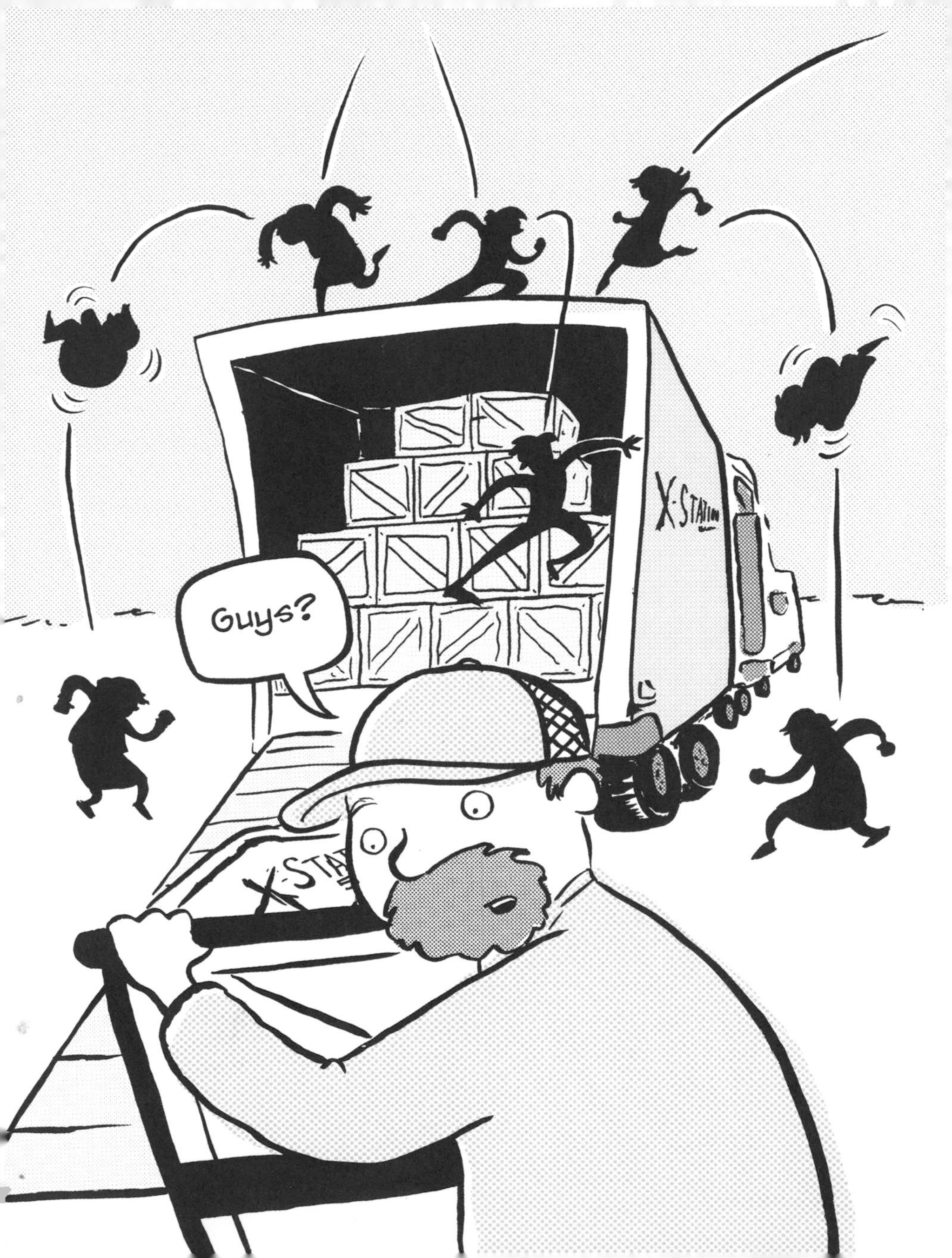
X-STATION
Guys?

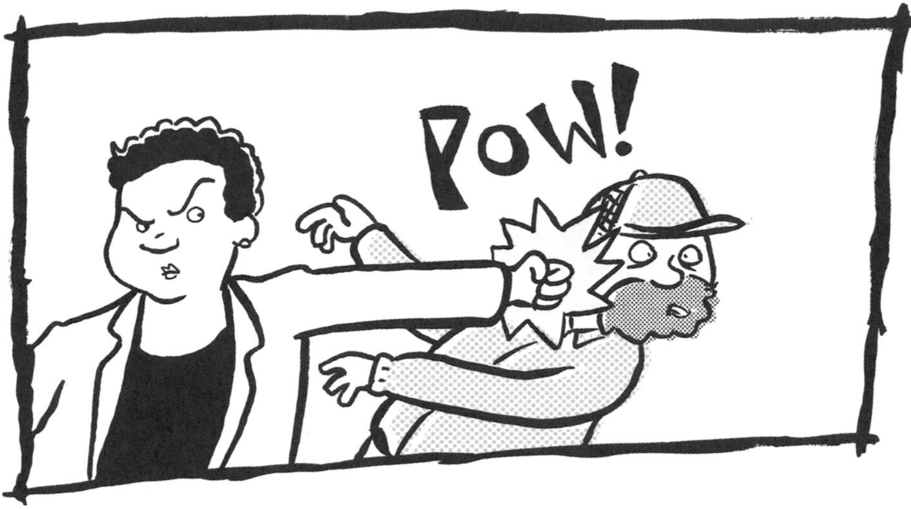
POW!

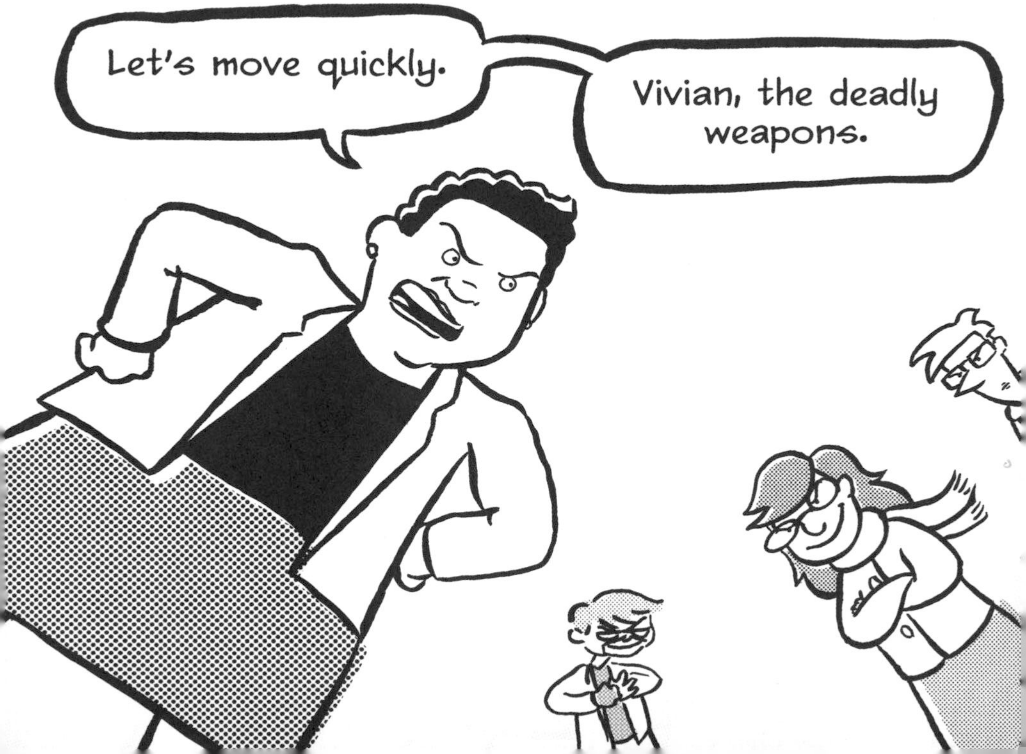
Let's move quickly.
Vivian, the deadly weapons.

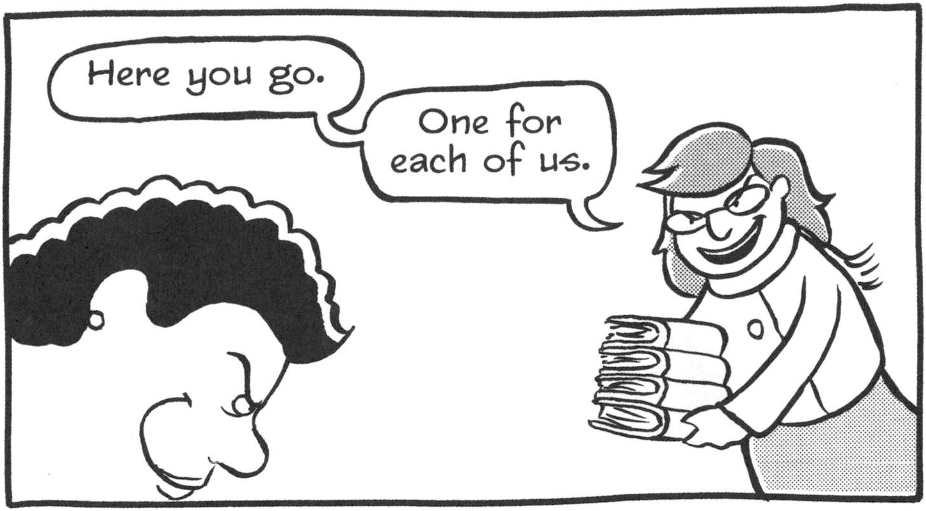
Here you go.
One for each of us.

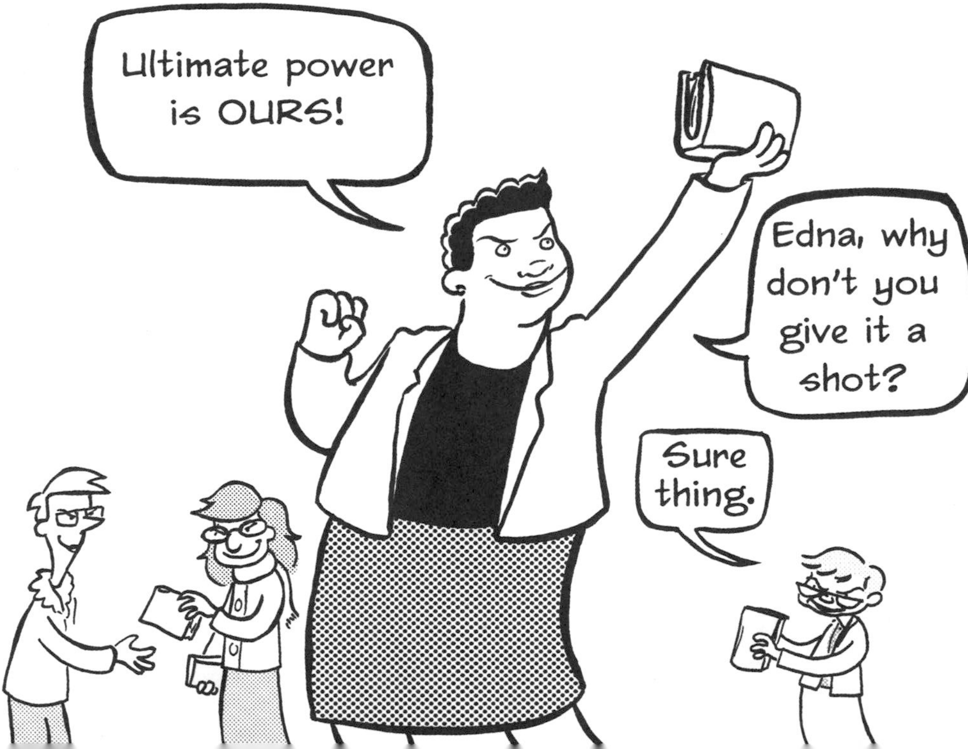
Ultimate power is OURS!
Edna, why don't you give it a shot?
Sure thing.

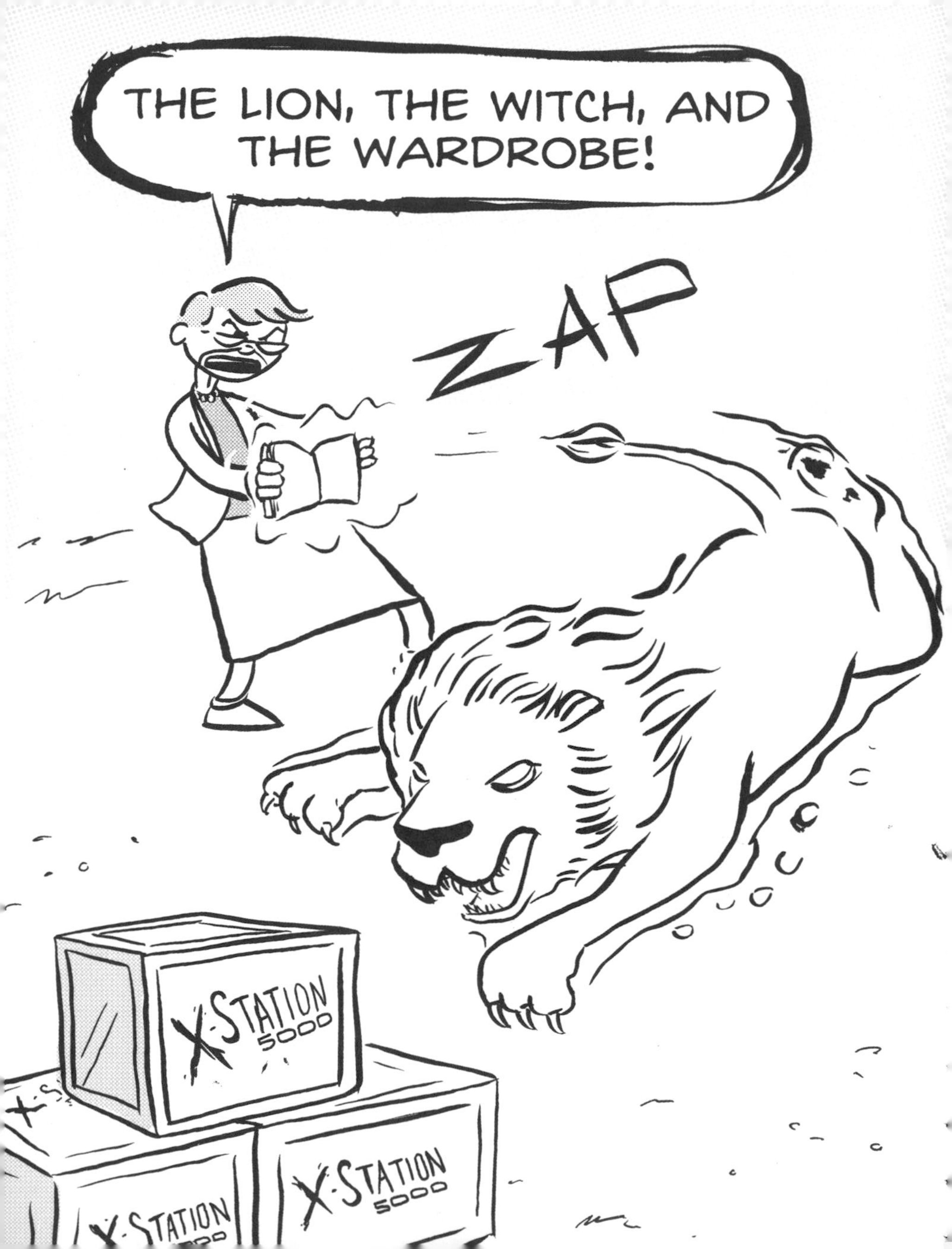
THE LION, THE WITCH, AND THE WARDROBE!
ZAP
X-STATION 5000
X-STATION 5000
X-STATION

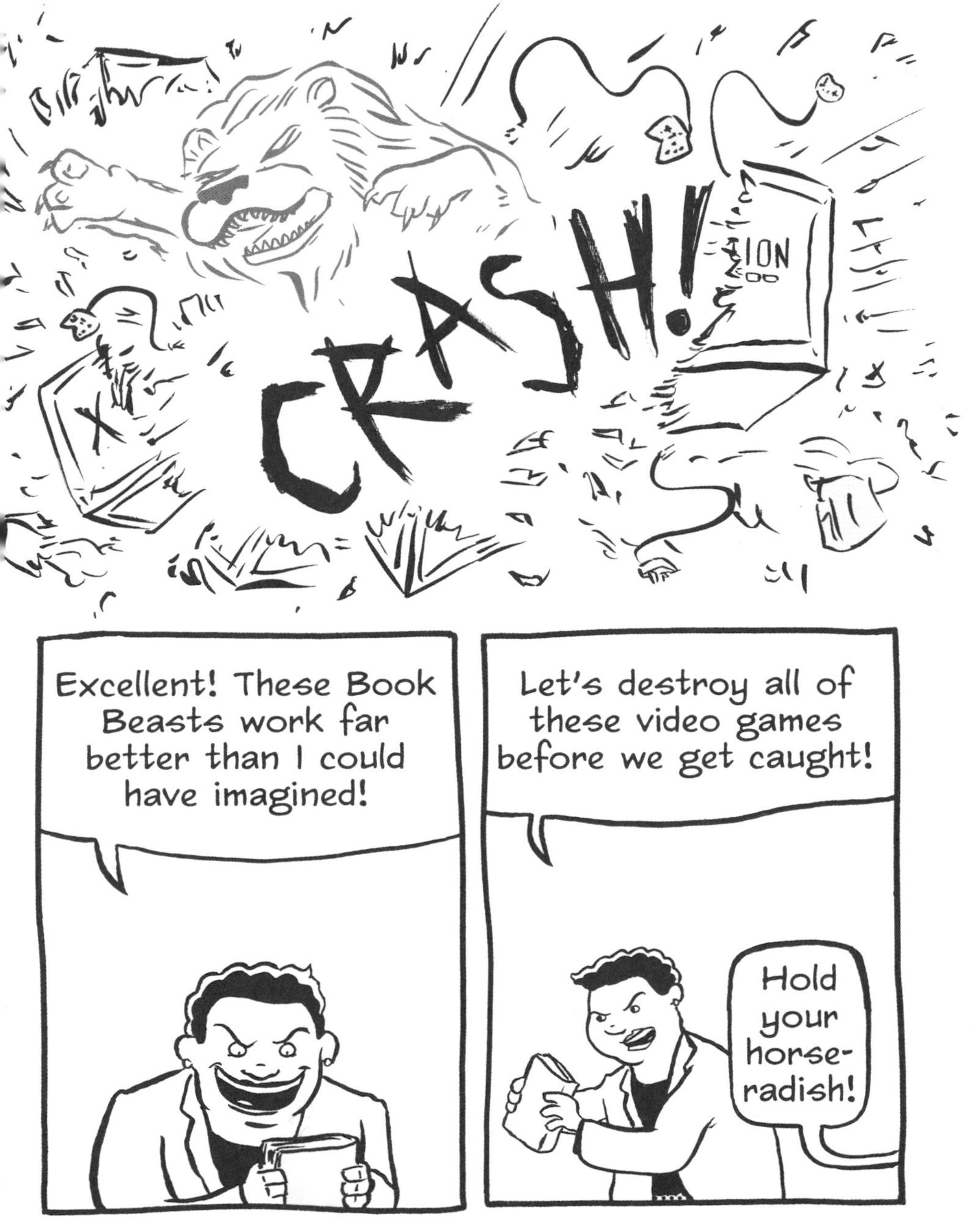
CRASH!
ION
Excellent! These Book Beasts work far better than I could have imagined!
Let's destroy all of these video games before we get caught!
Hold your horse-radish!

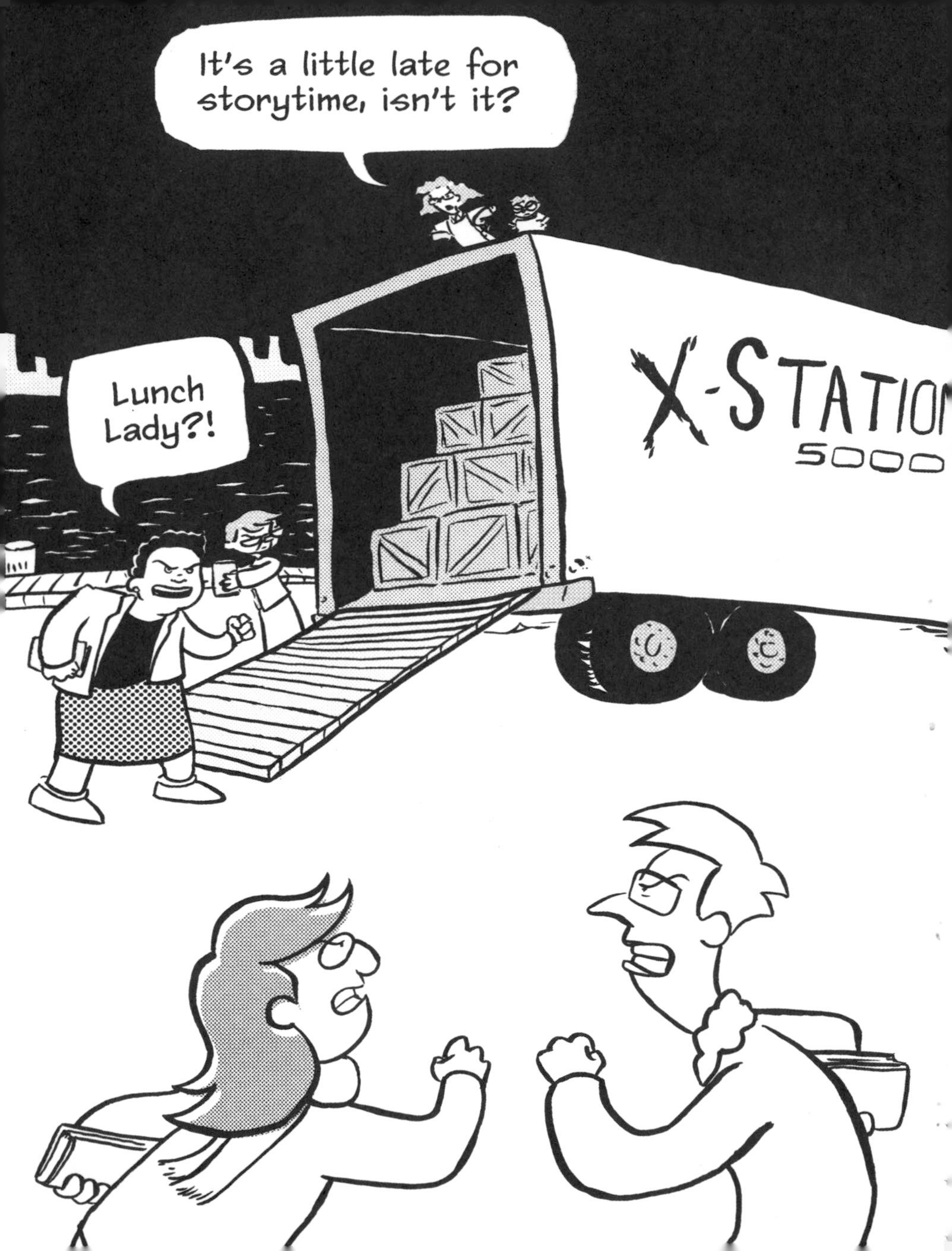
It's a little late for storytime, isn't it?
Lunch Lady?!
X-STATION
5000

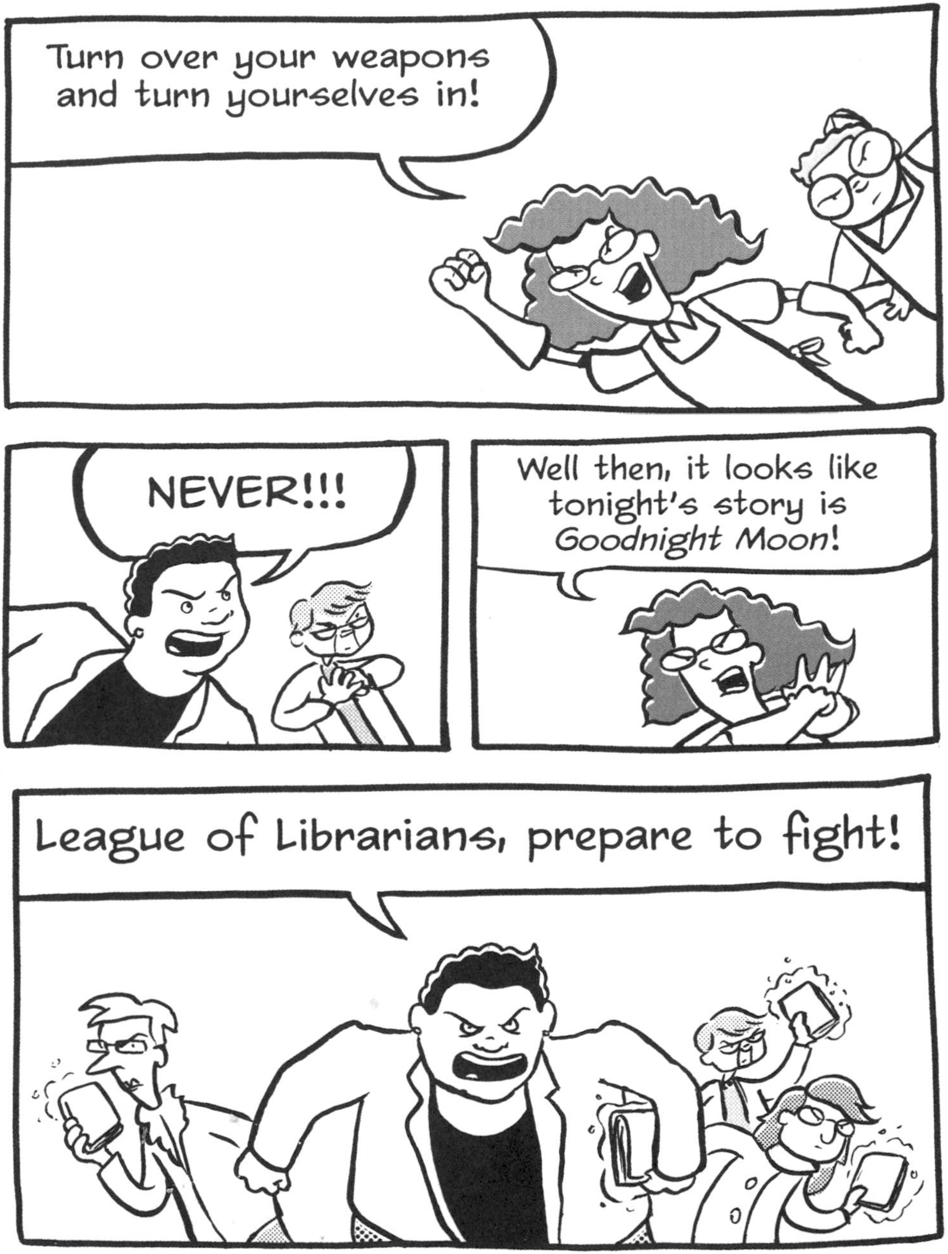
Turn over your weapons and turn yourselves in!
NEVER!!!
Well then, it looks like tonight's story is *Goodnight Moon*!
League of Librarians, prepare to fight!

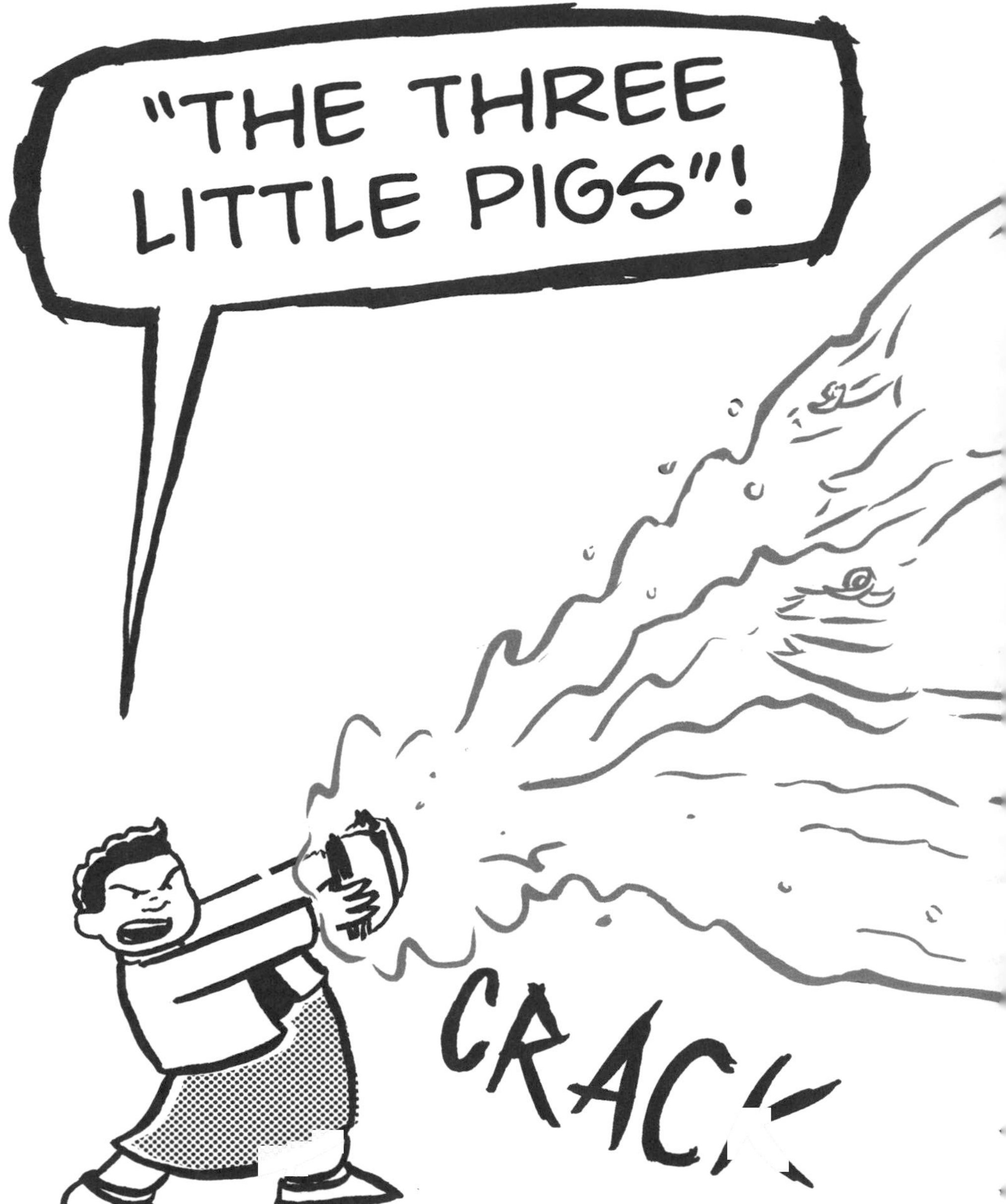
"THE THREE LITTLE PIGS"!
CRACK

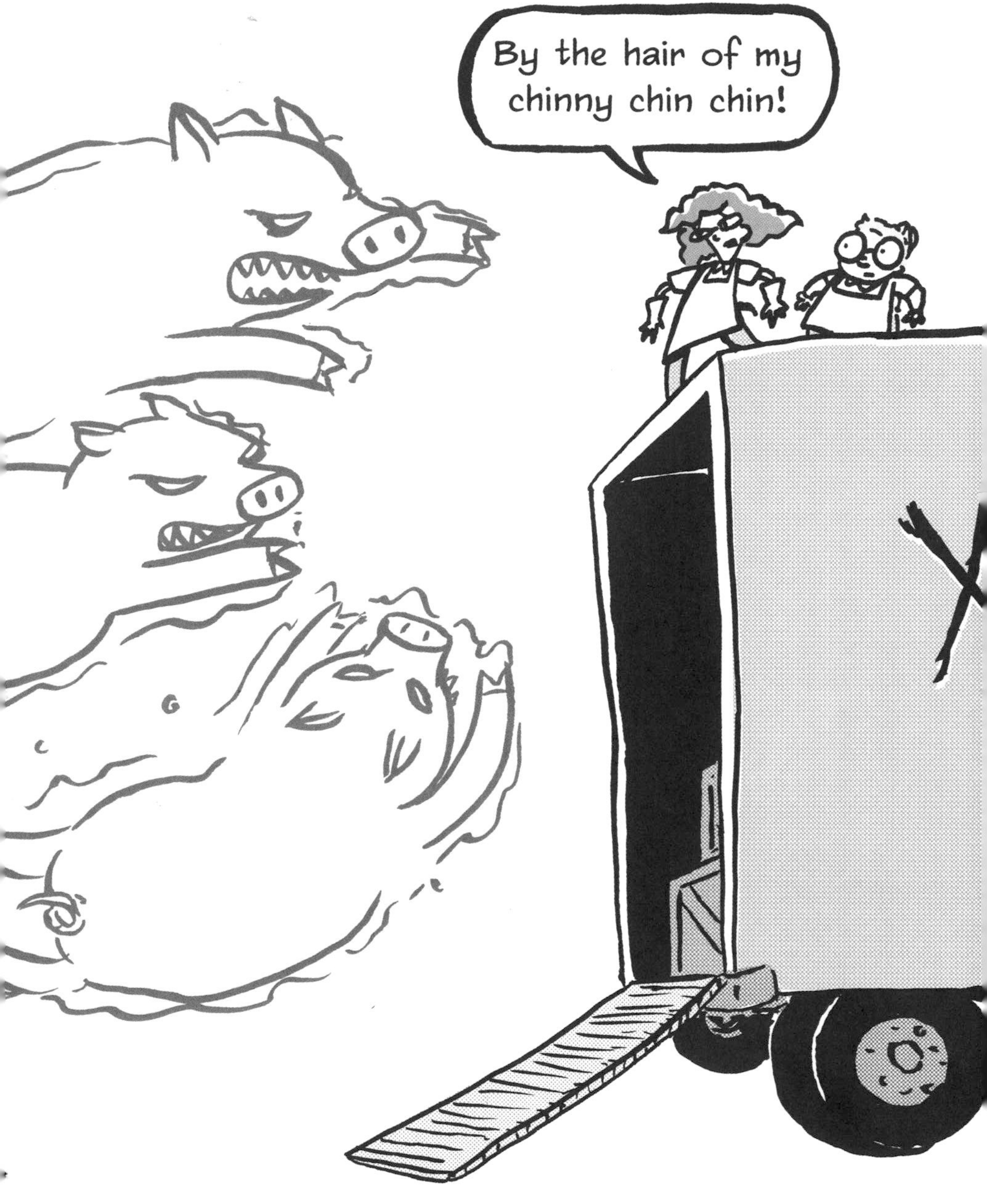
By the hair of my chinny chin chin!

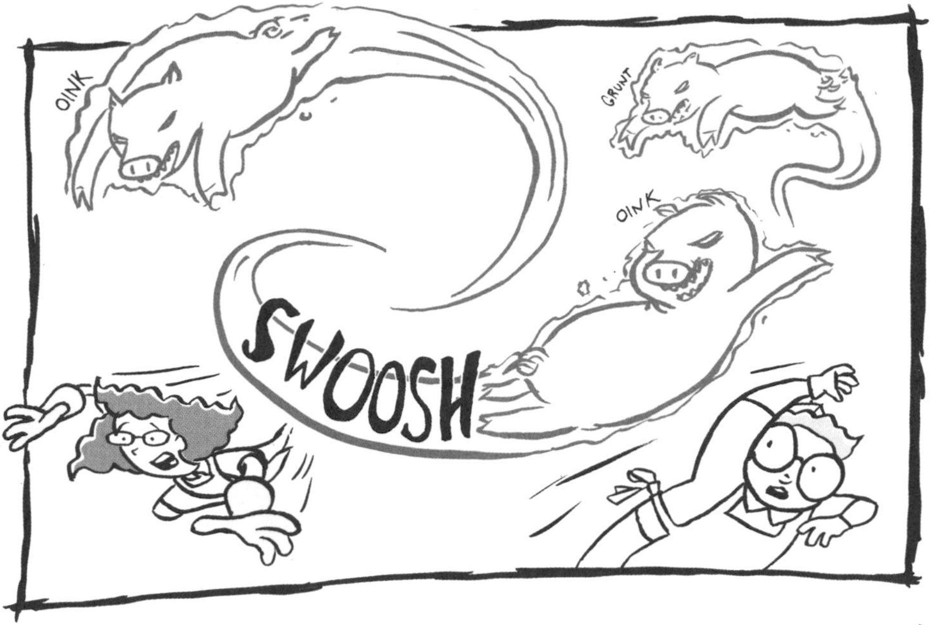
OINK
GRUNT
OINK
SWOOSH

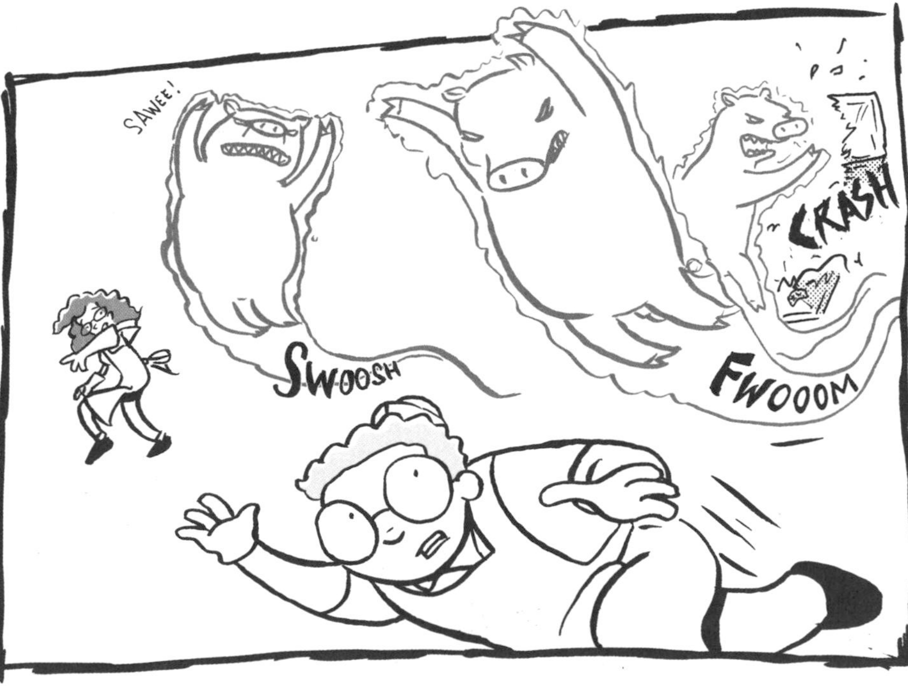
SAWEEE!
CRASH
SWOOSH
FWOOOM

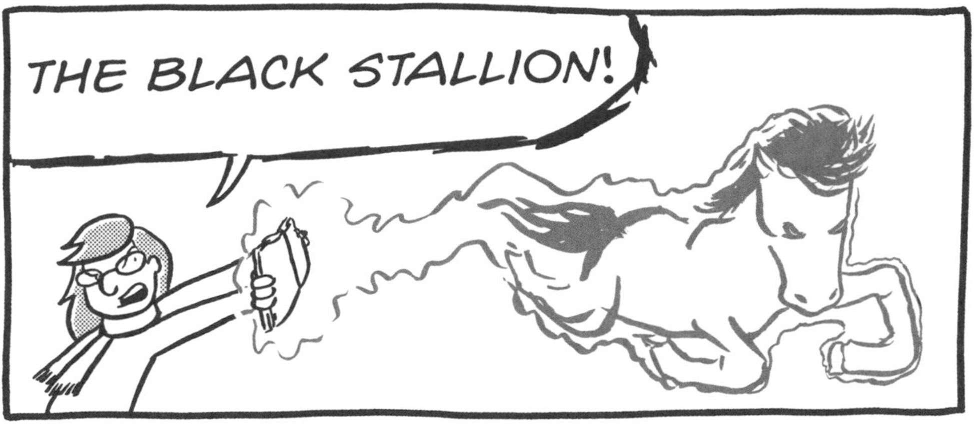
THE BLACK STALLION!
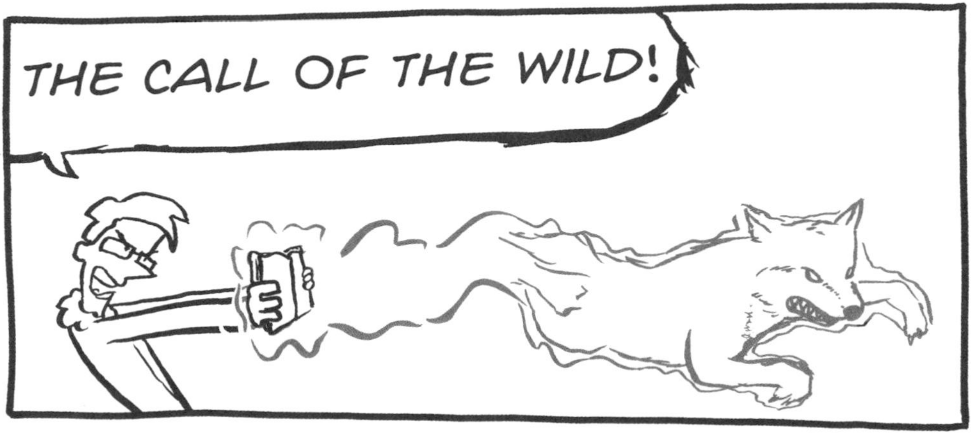
THE CALL OF THE WILD!
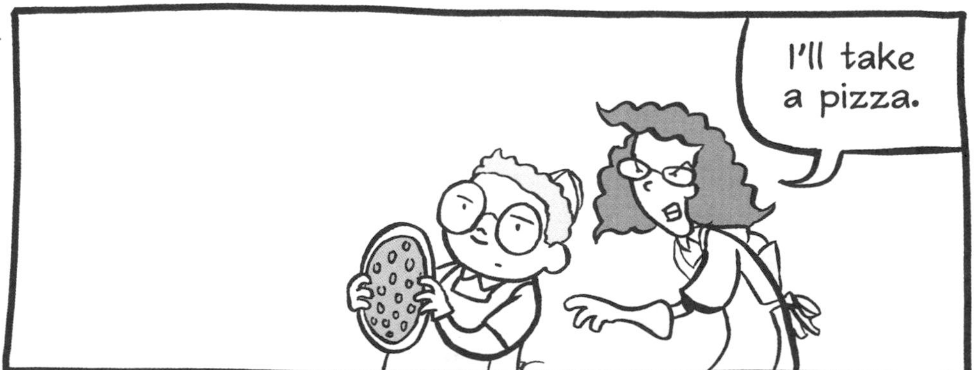
I'll take a pizza.

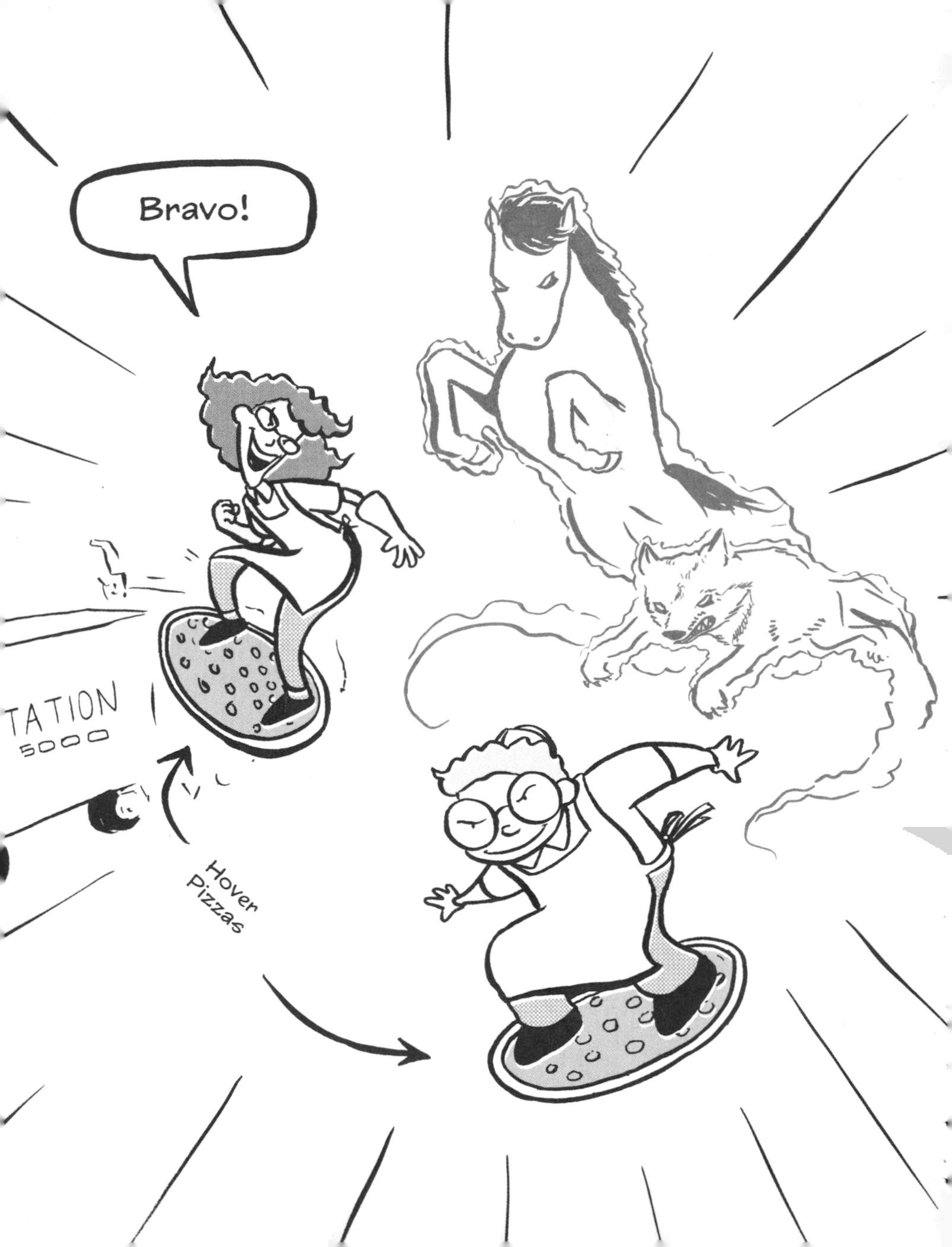
Bravo!
TATION
5000
Hover Pizzas

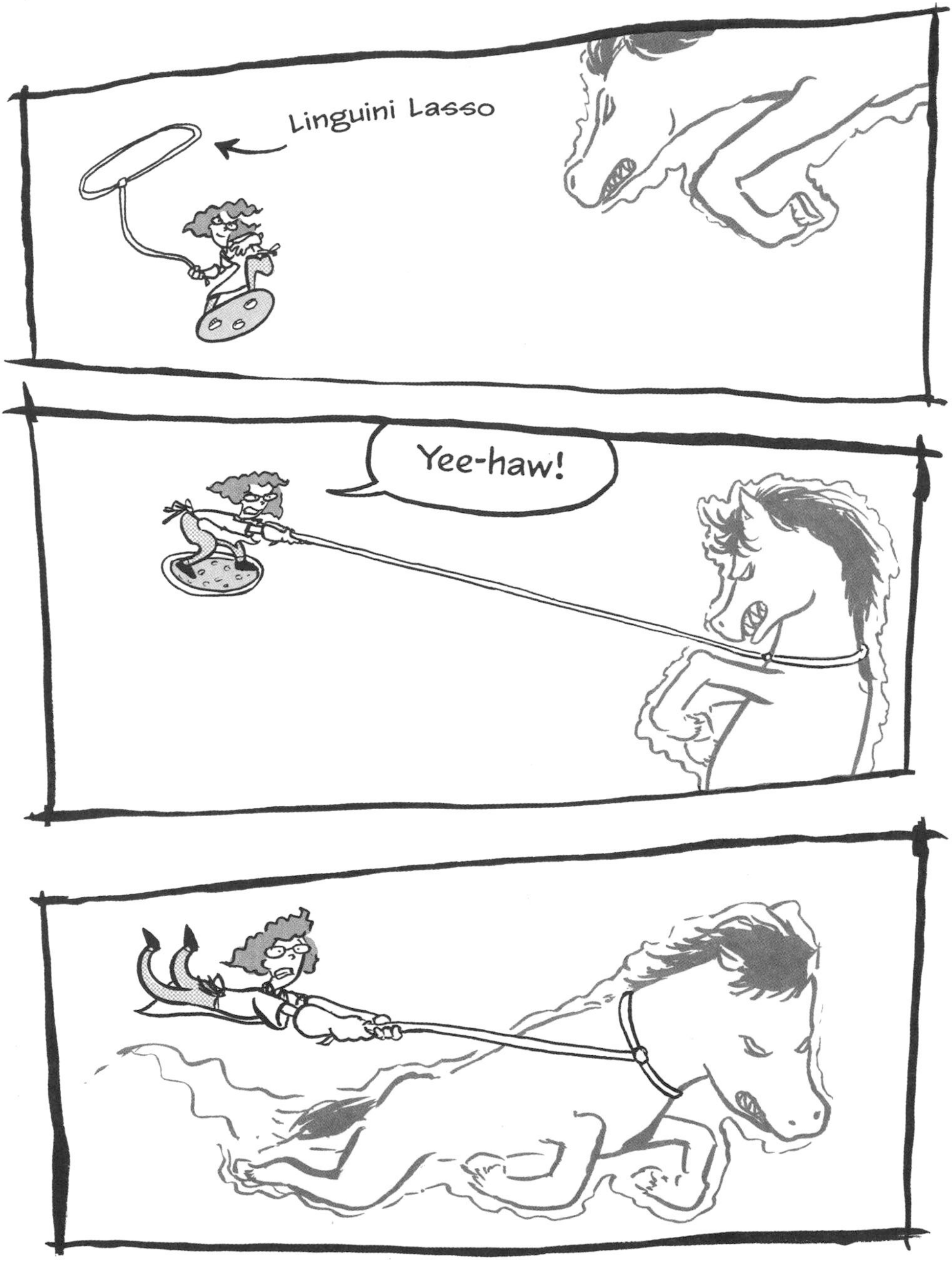
Linguini Lasso
Yee-haw!

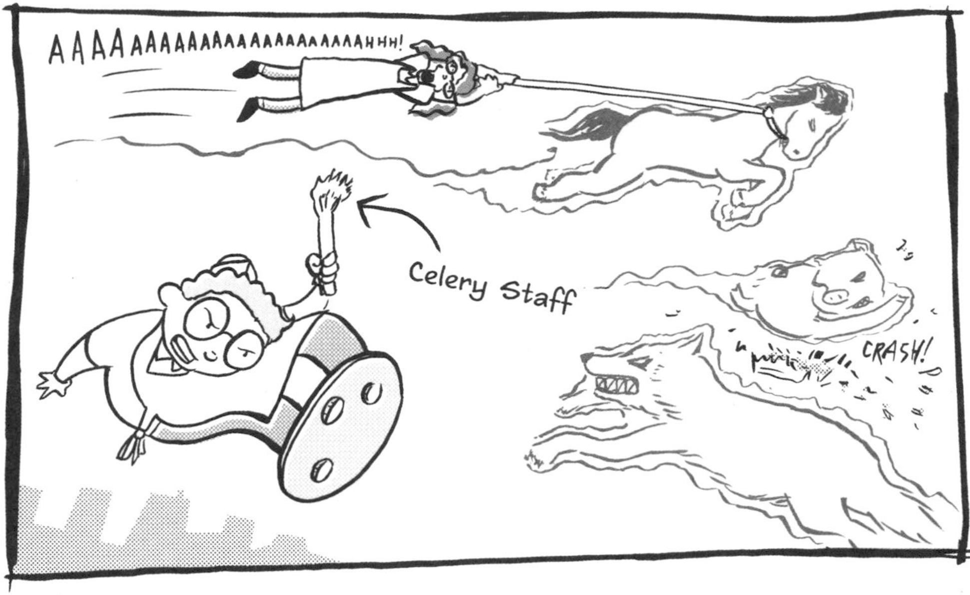
AAAAAAAAAAAAAAAAAAAAAAAAAHHH!
Celery Staff
CRASH!
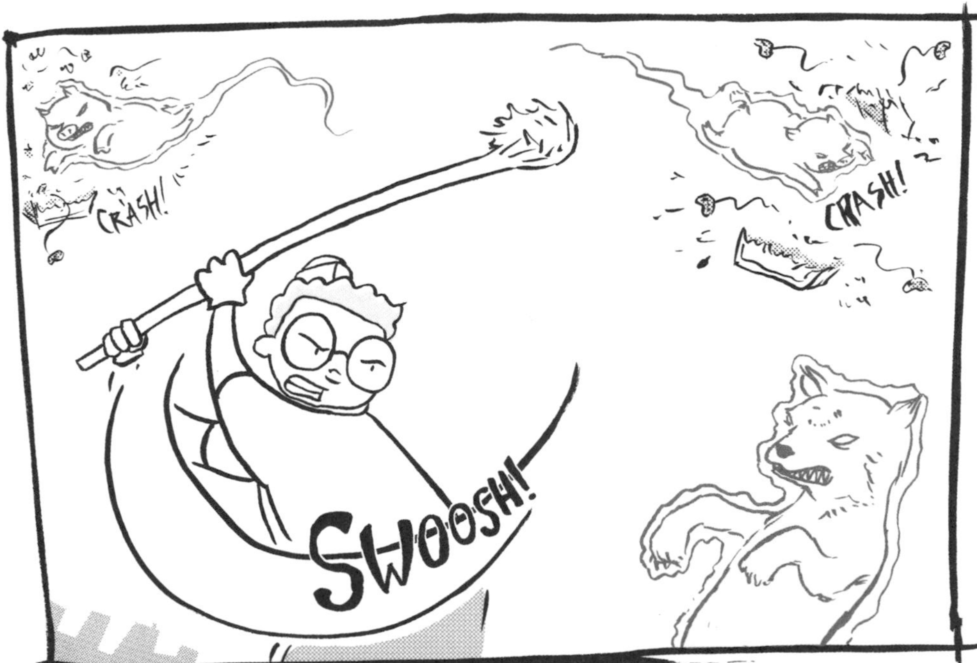
CRASH!
CRASH!
SWOOSH!

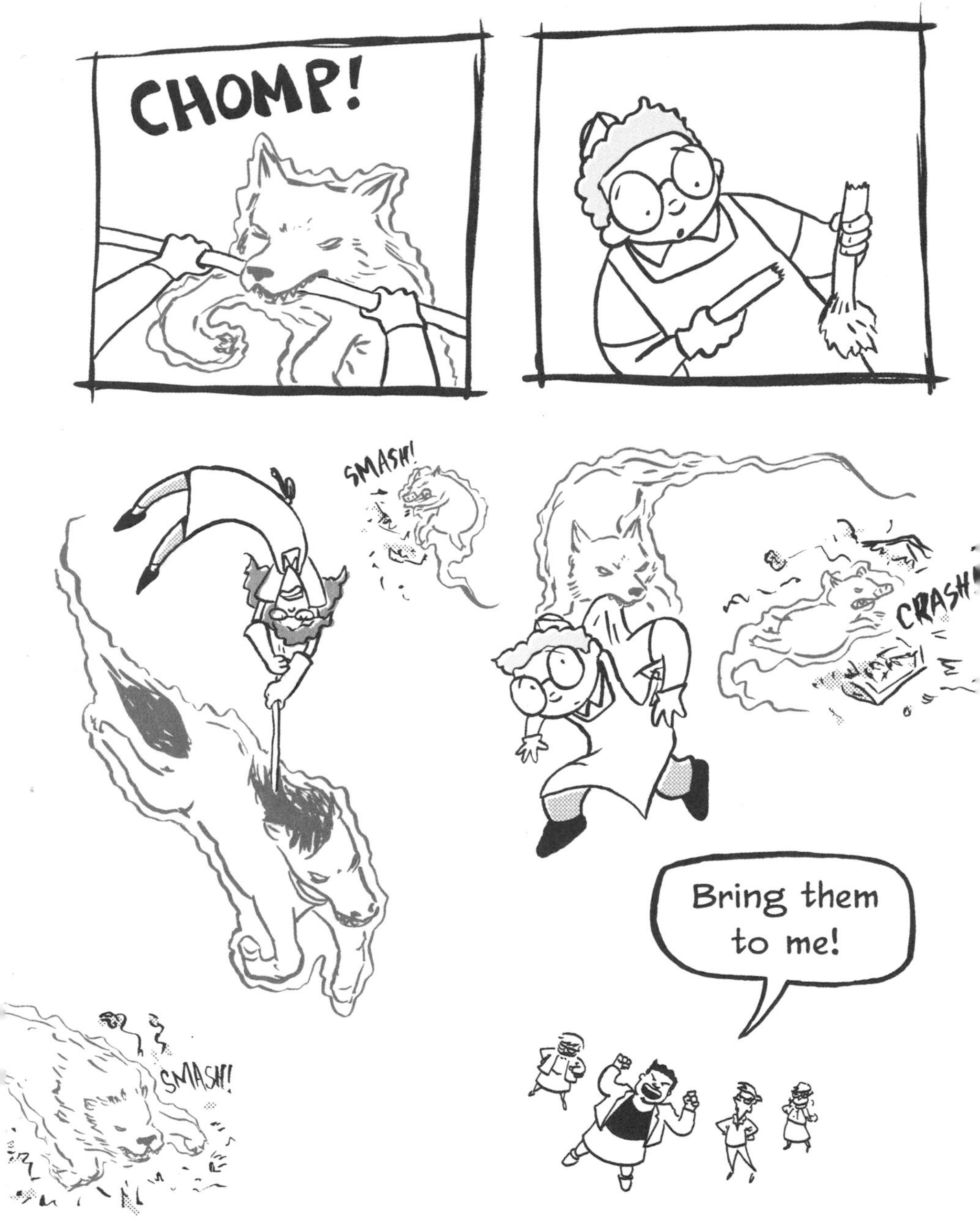
CHOMP!
SMASH!
CRASH!
Bring them to me!
SMASH!

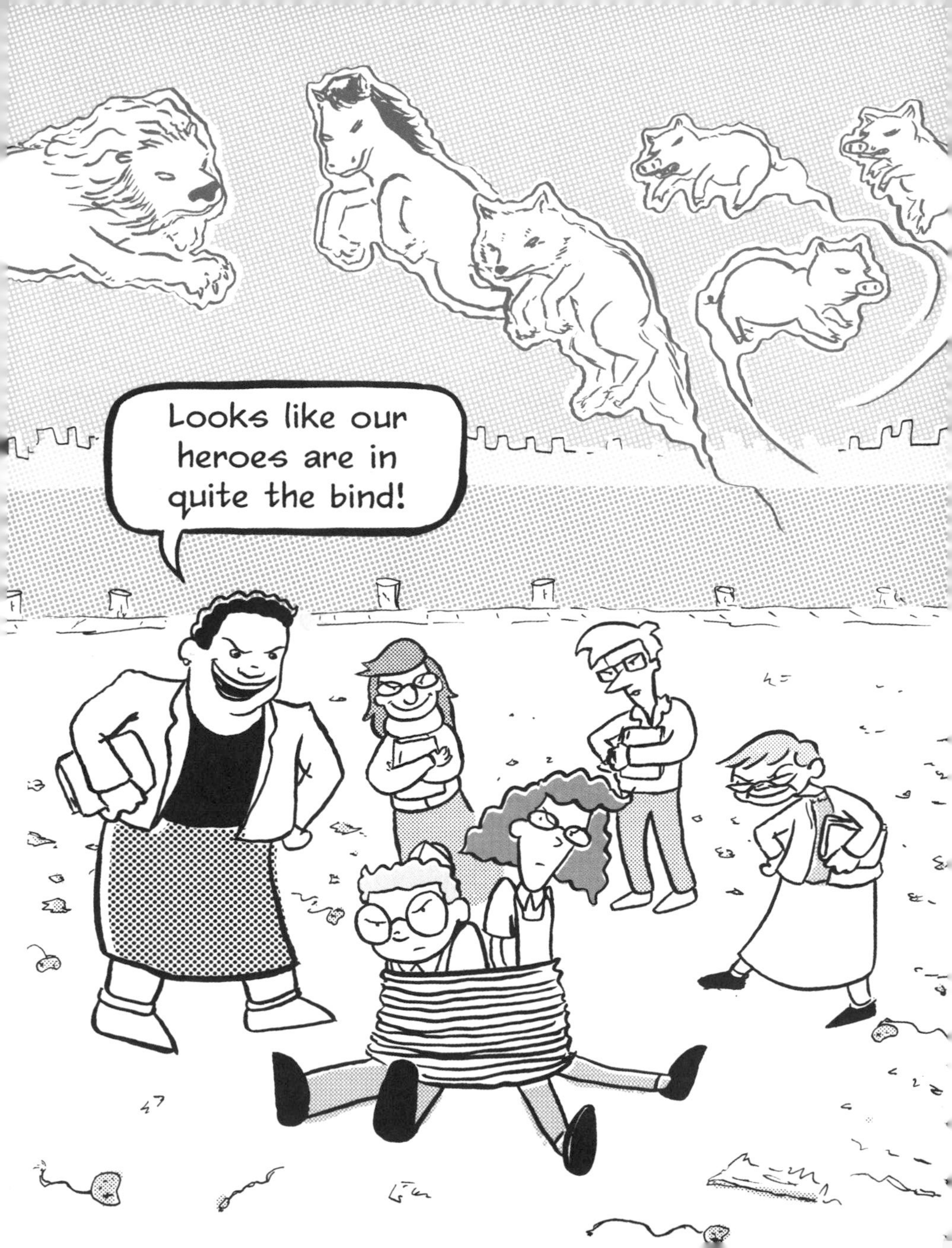
Looks like our heroes are in quite the bind!

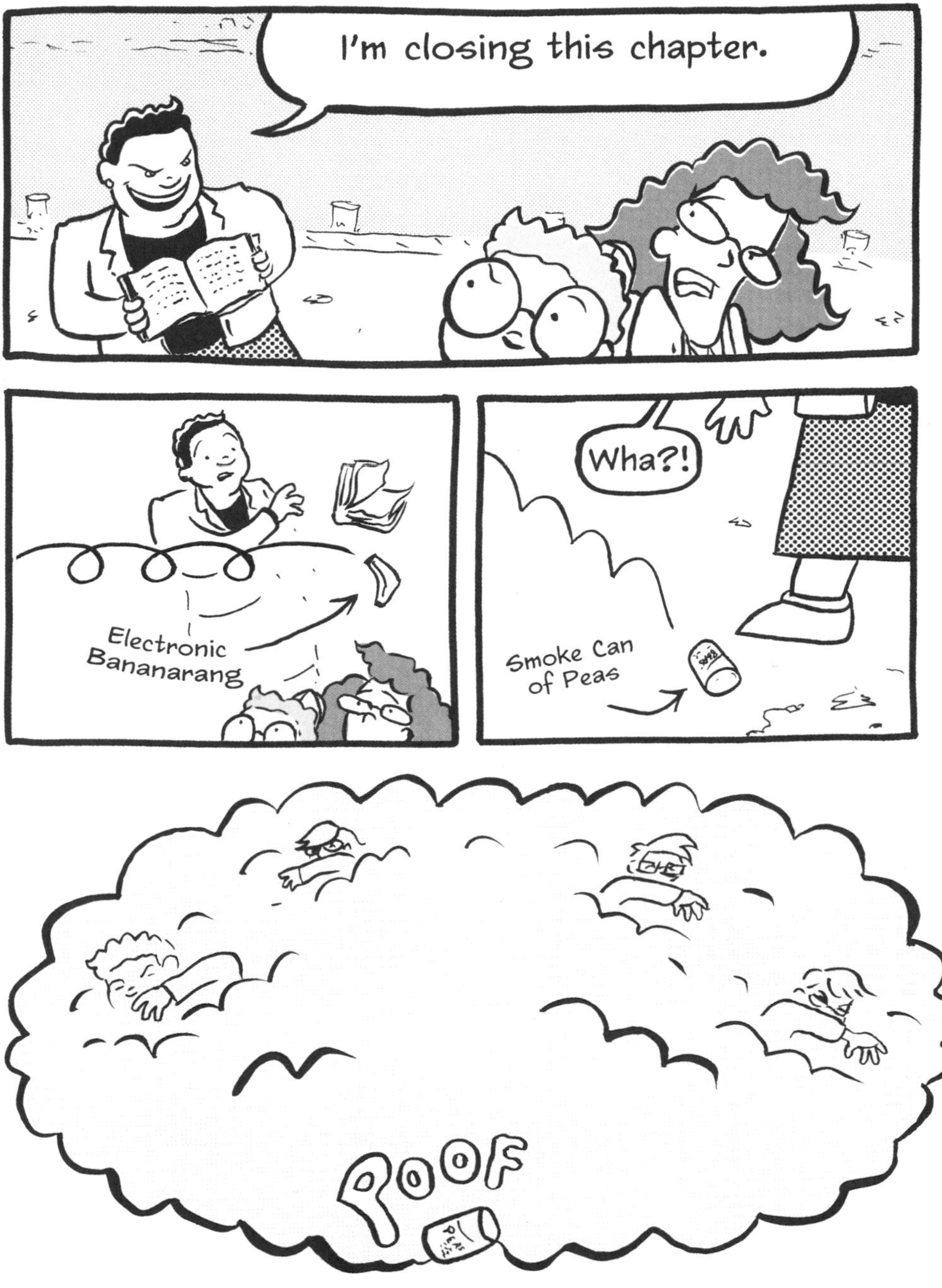

I'm closing this chapter.
Electronic Bananarang
Wha?!
Smoke Can of Peas
POOF

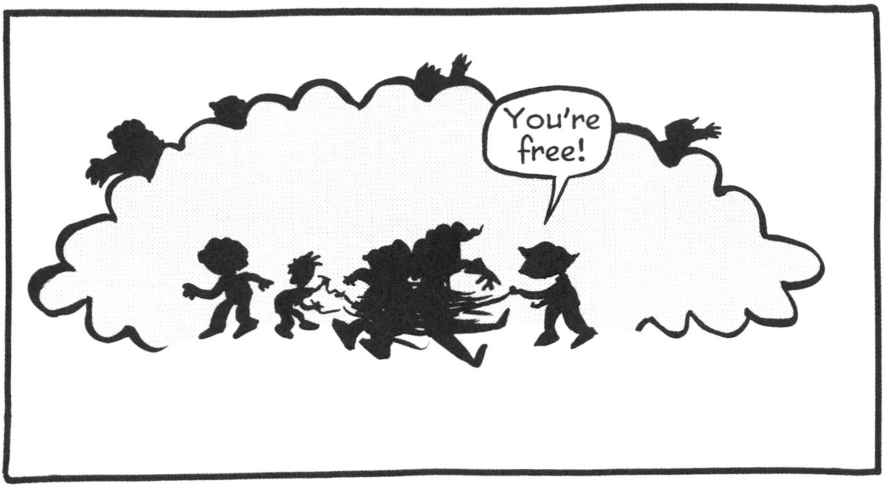
You're free!

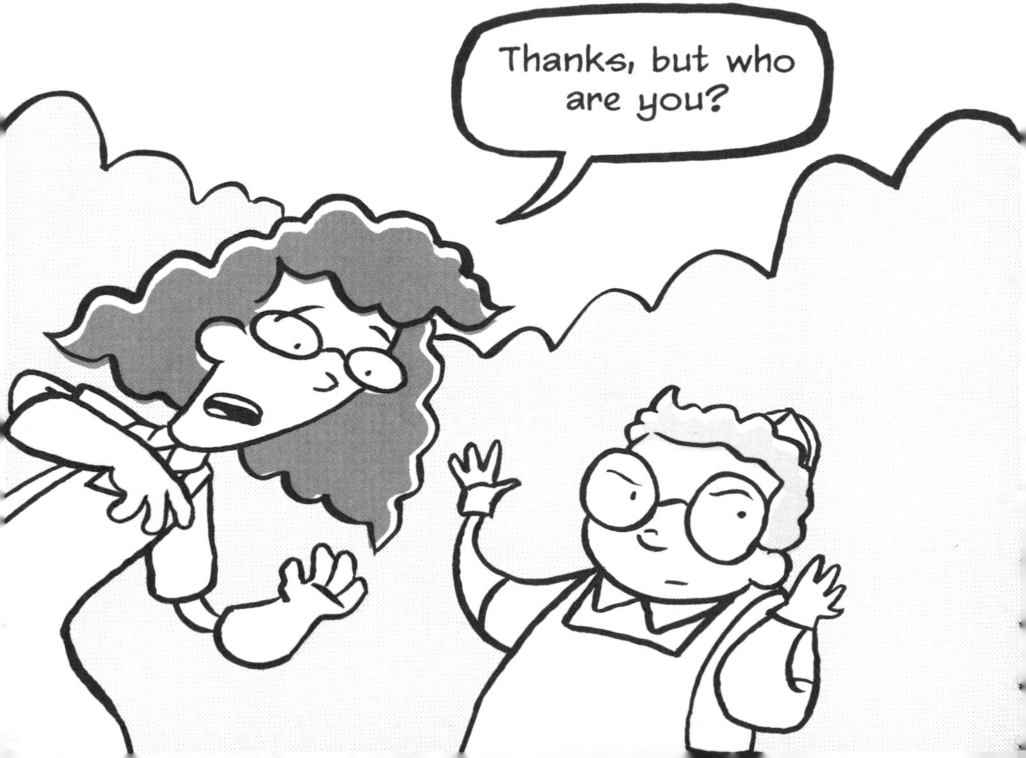
Thanks, but who are you?

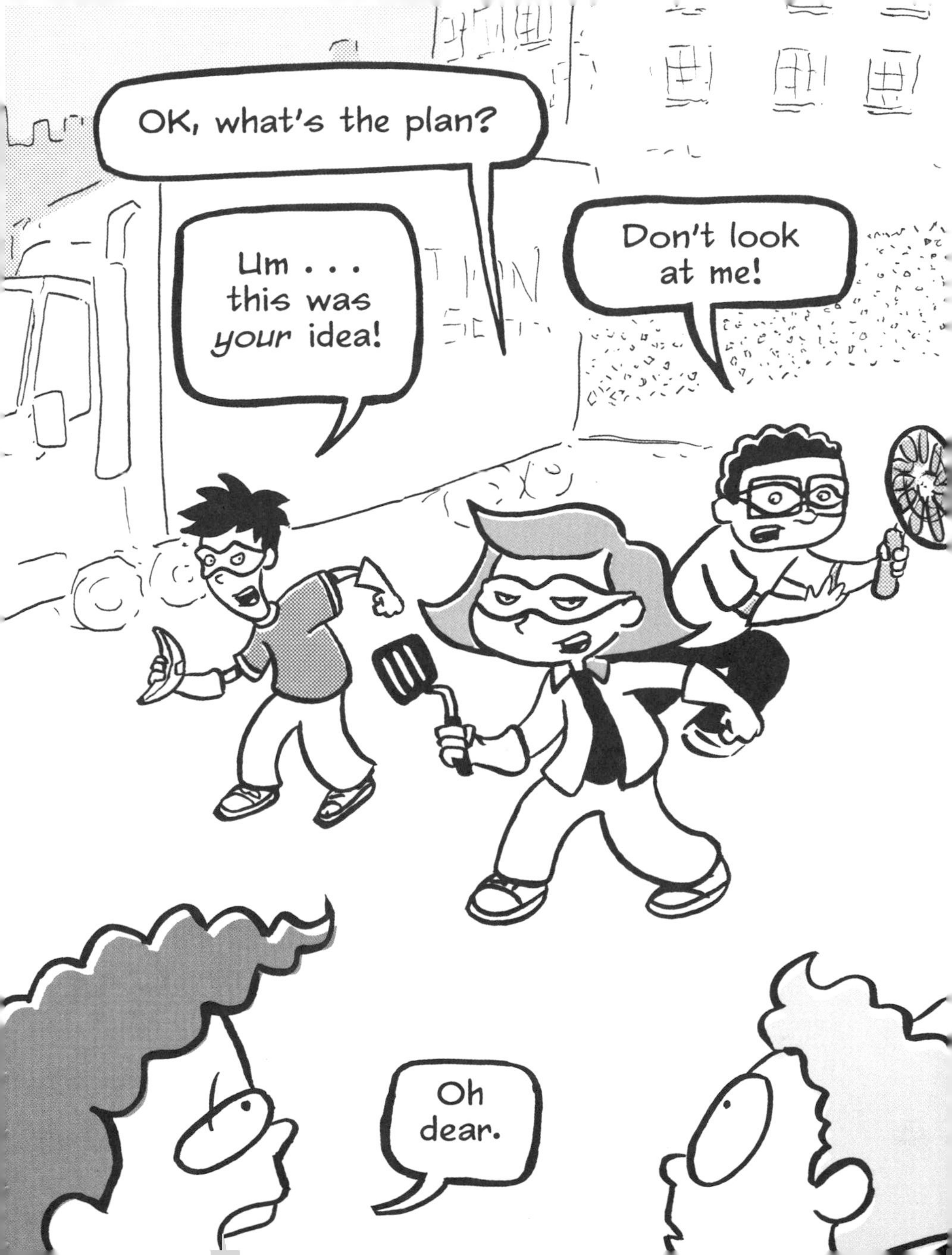
OK, what's the plan?
Um . . . this was *your* idea!
Don't look at me!
Oh dear.

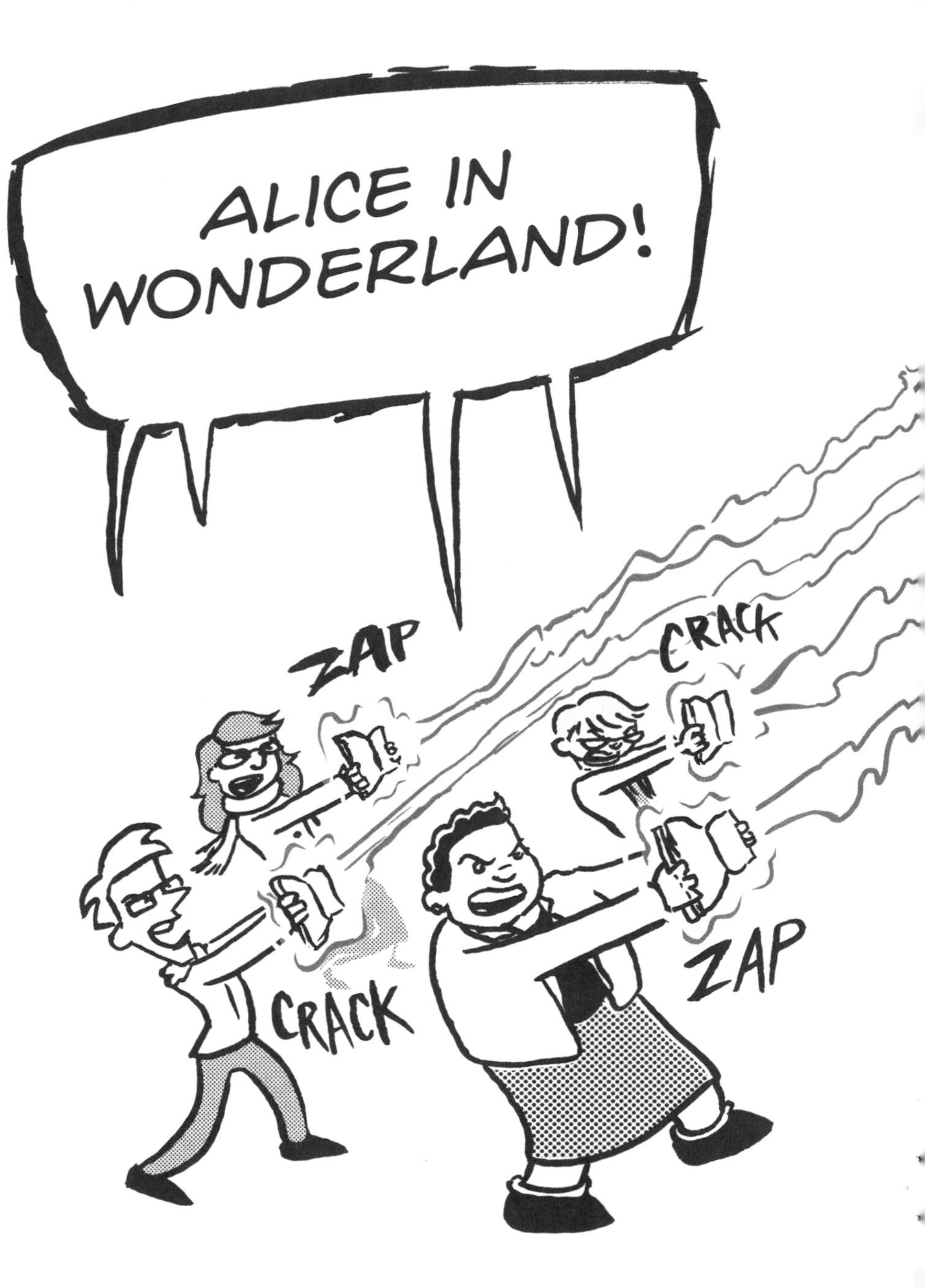
ALICE IN WONDERLAND!
ZAP
CRACK
CRACK
ZAP

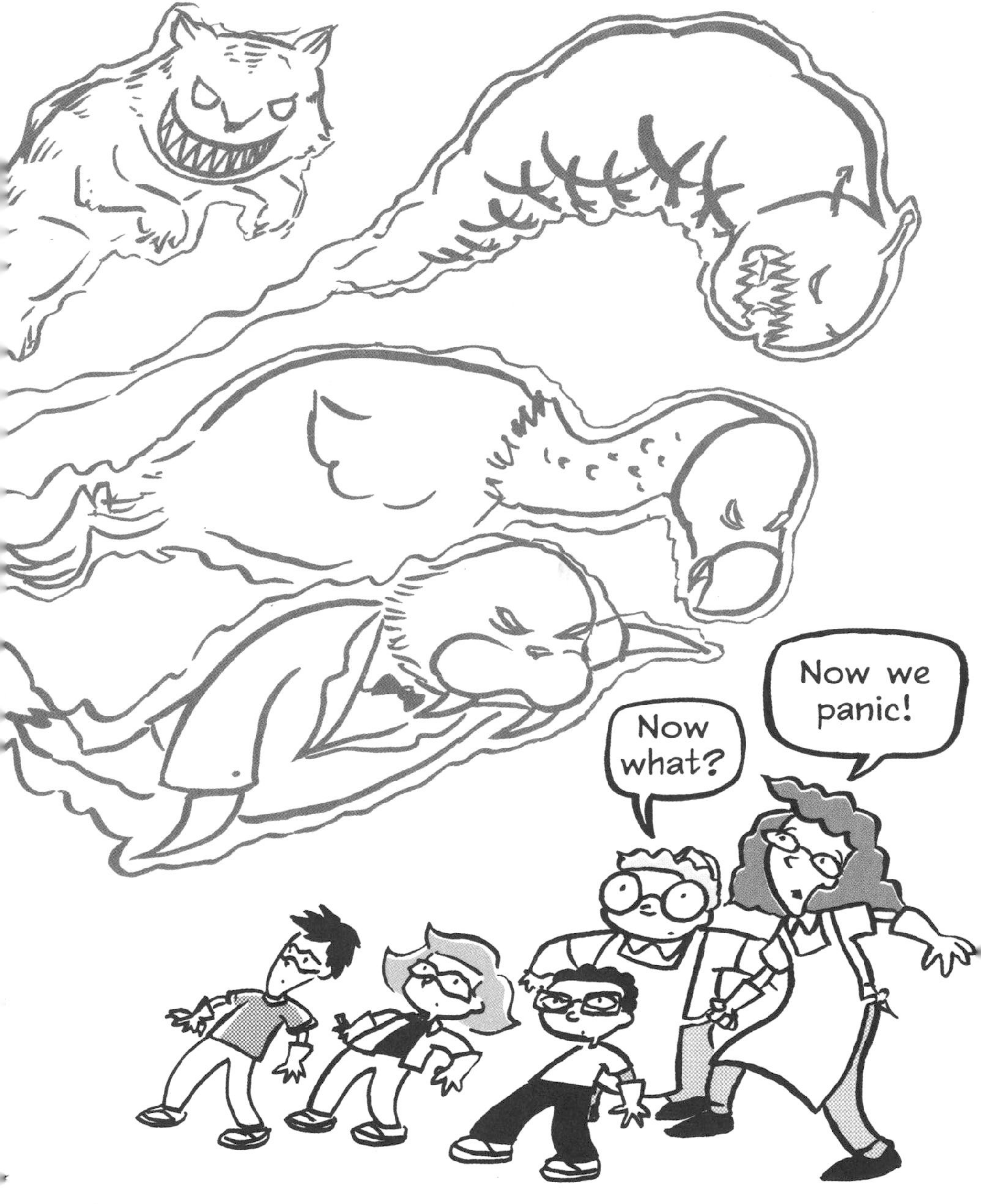
Now what?
Now we panic!

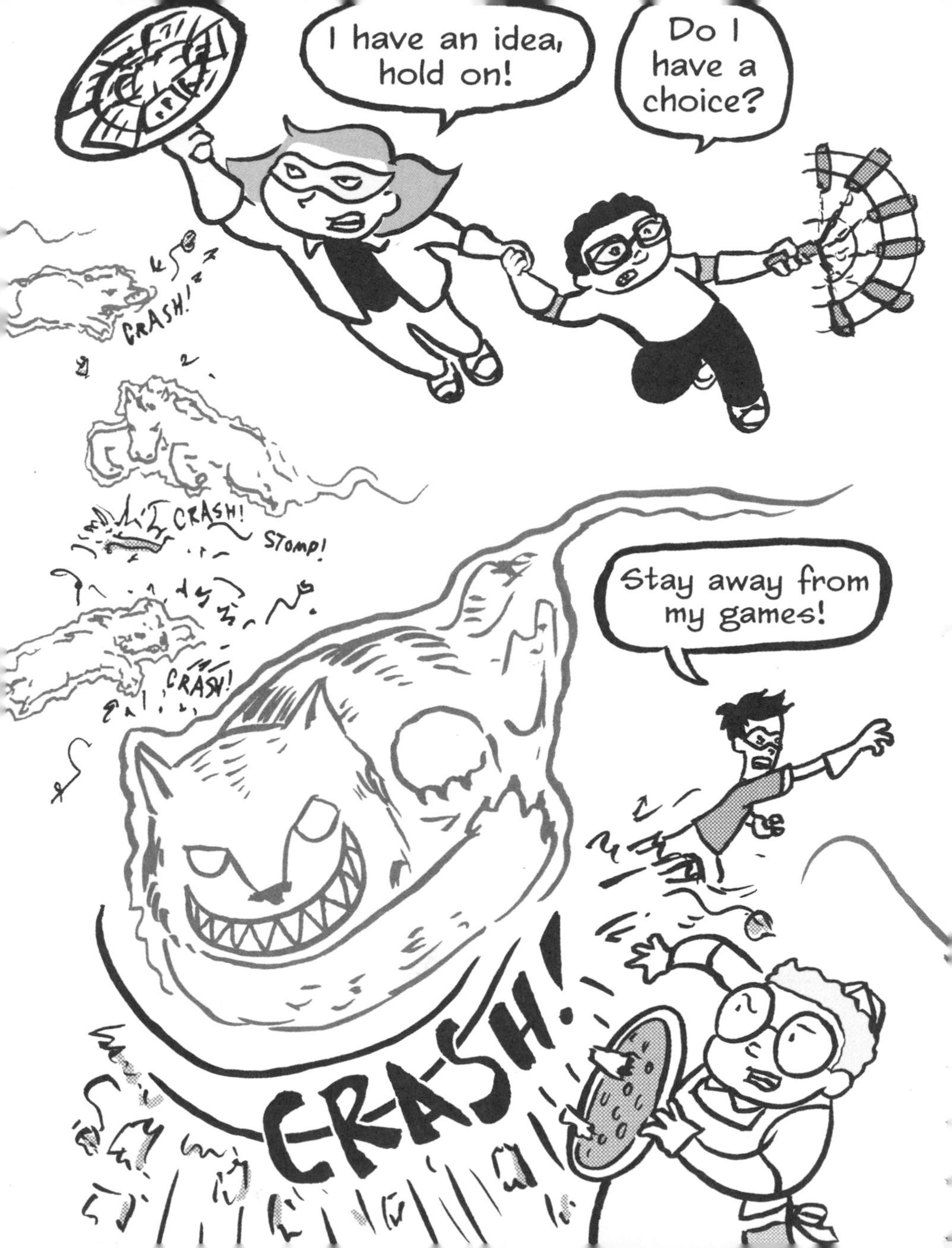
I have an idea, hold on!
Do I have a choice?
CRASH!
CRASH!
STOMP!
Stay away from my games!
CRASH!
CRASH!

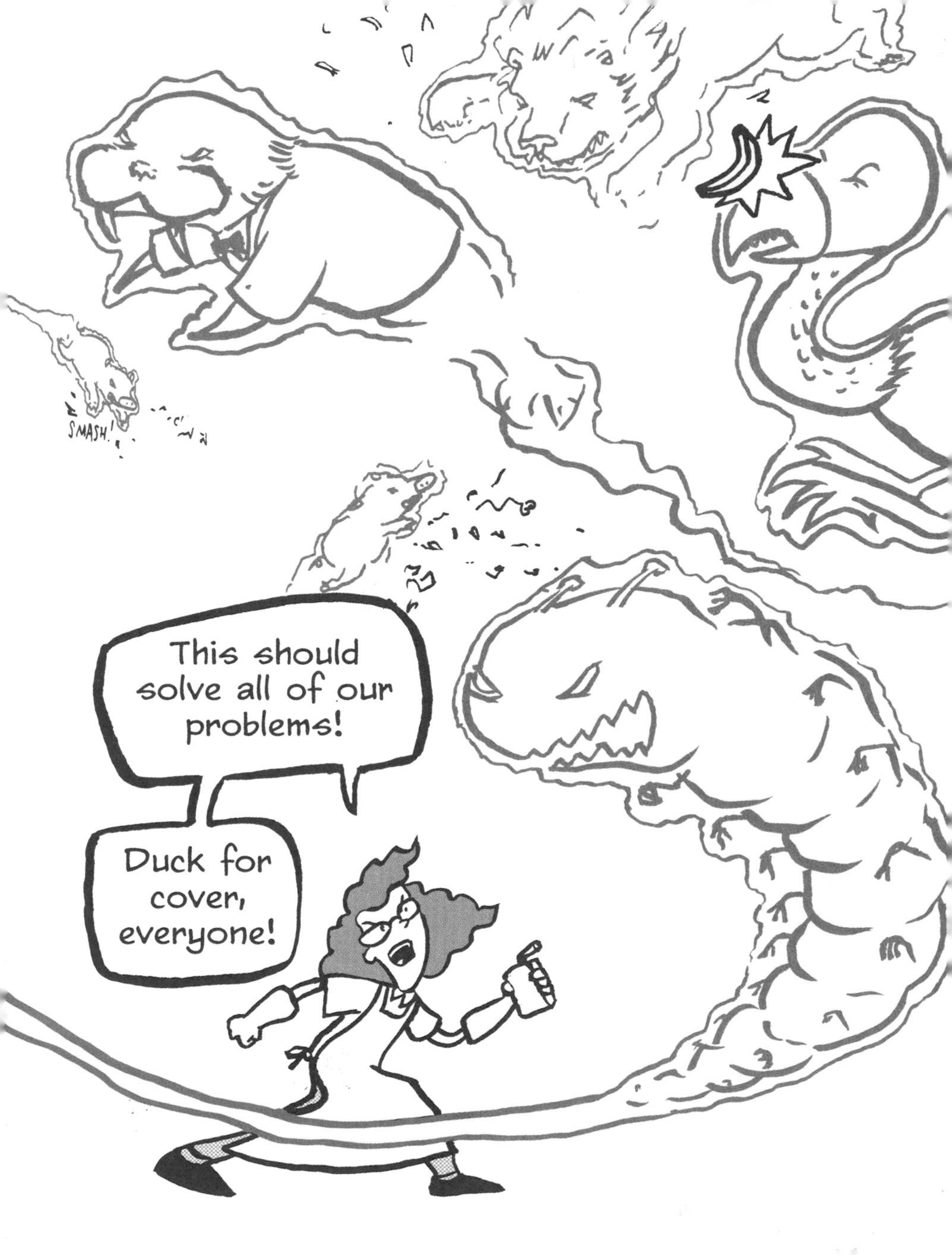
SMASH!
This should solve all of our problems!
Duck for cover, everyone!

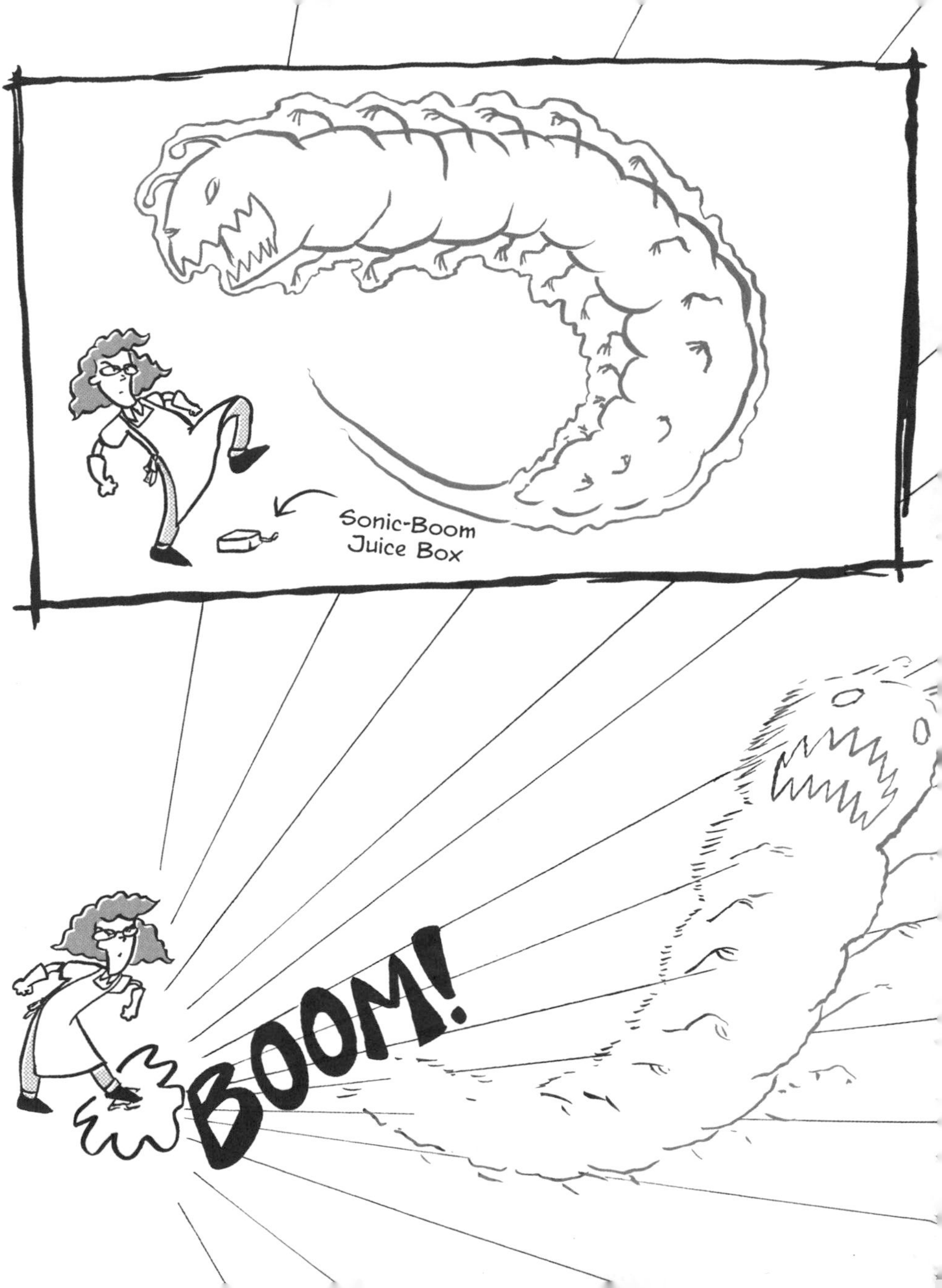
Sonic-Boom
Juice Box
BOOM!

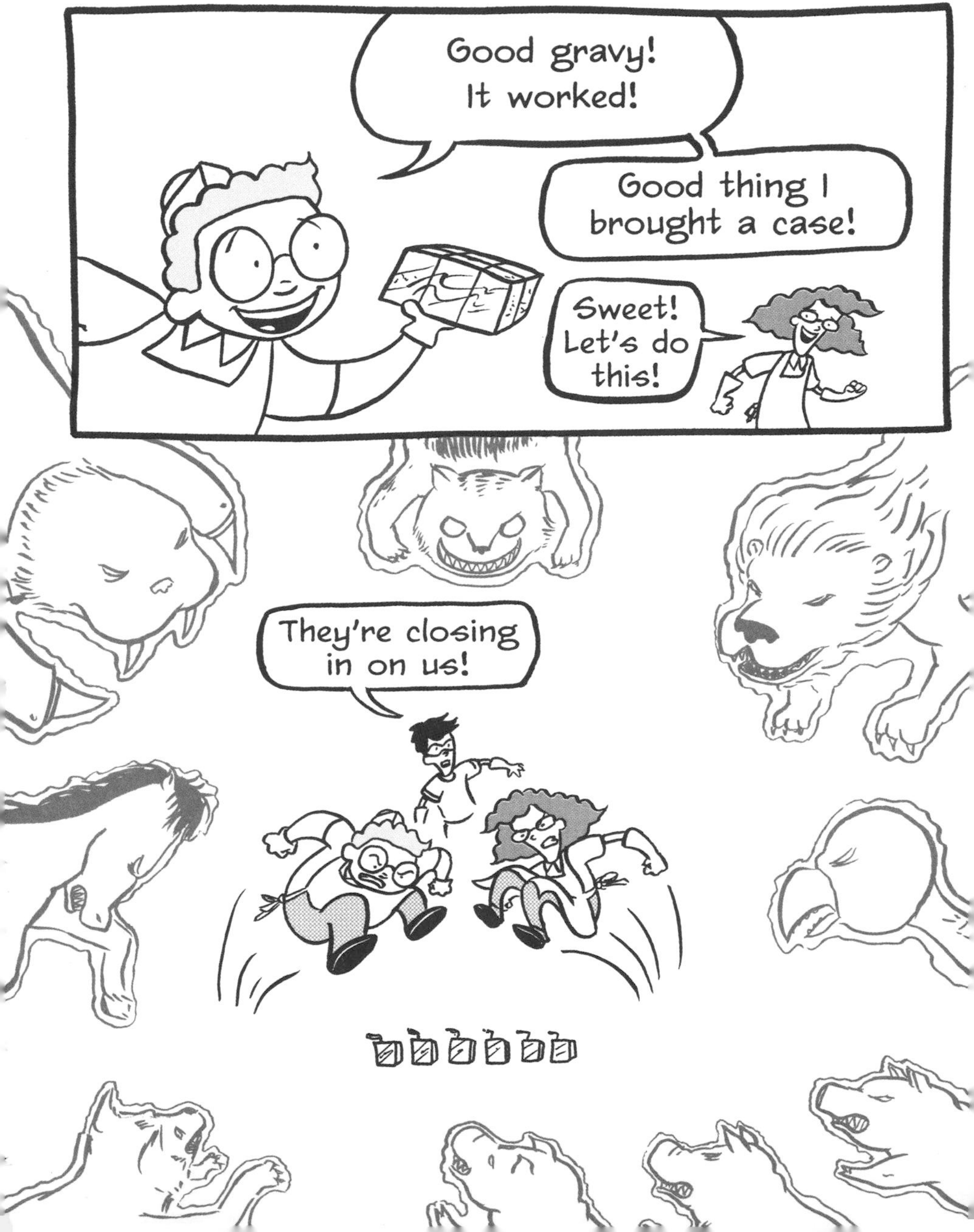
Good gravy! It worked!
Good thing I brought a case!
Sweet! Let's do this!
They're closing in on us!

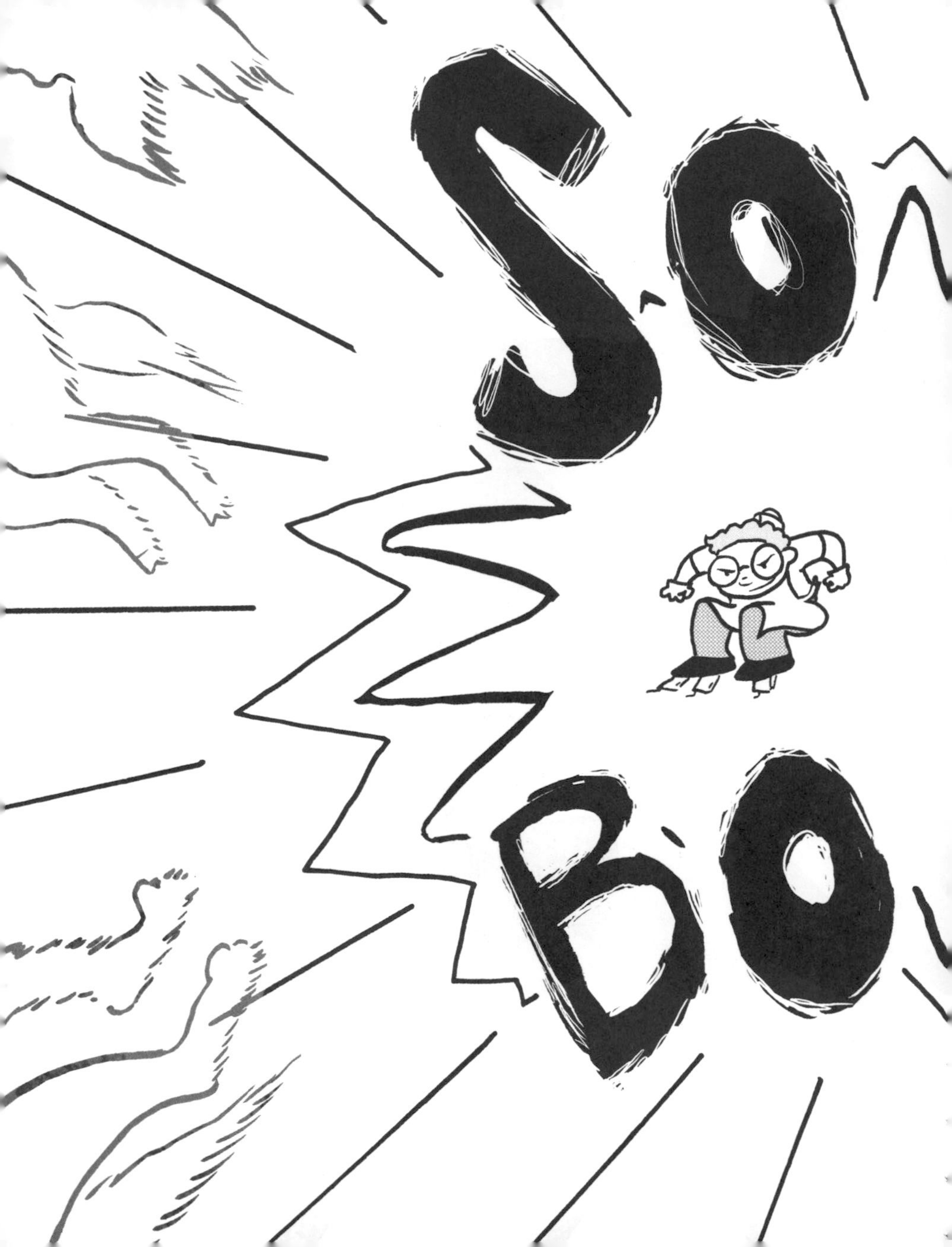
SO
BO

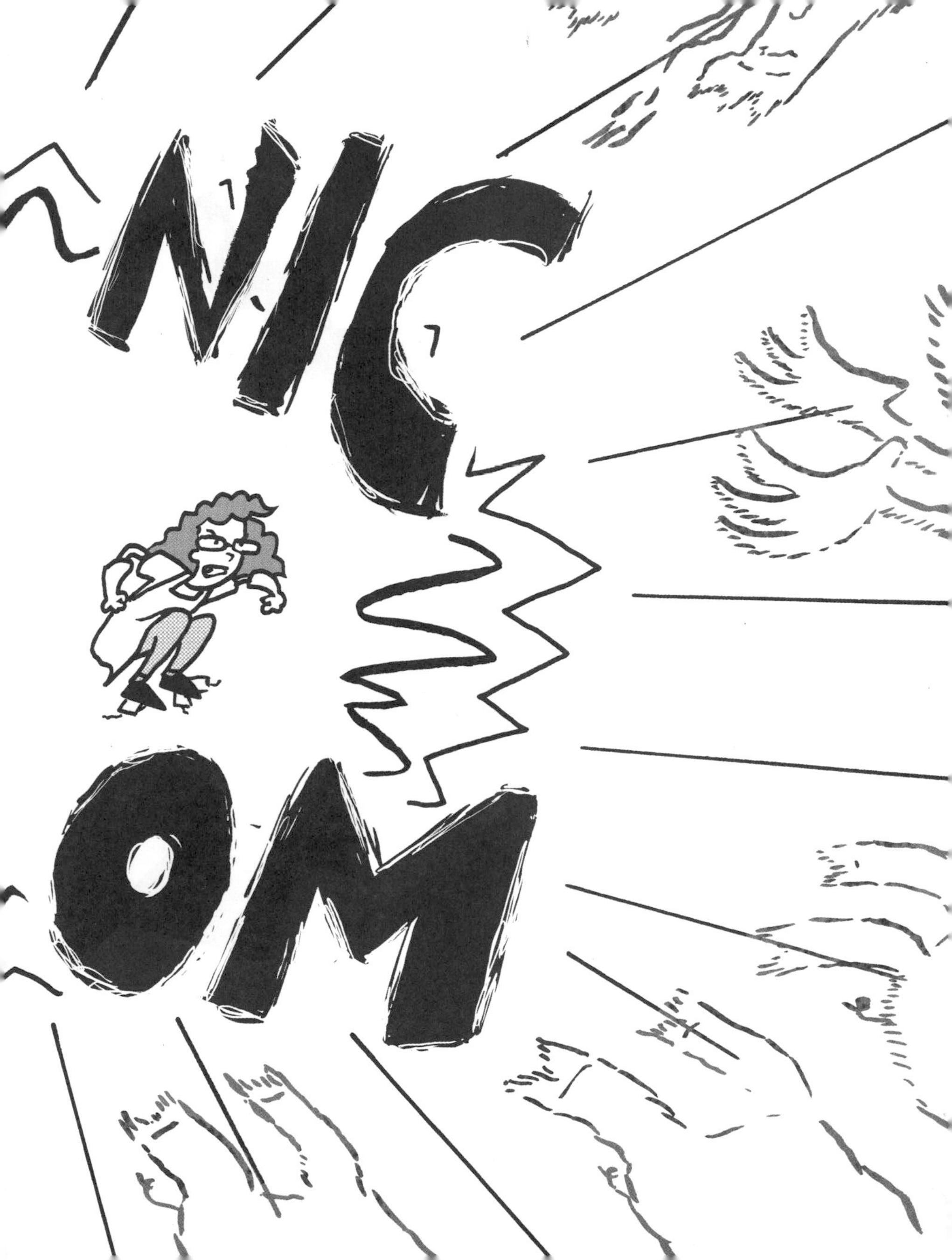

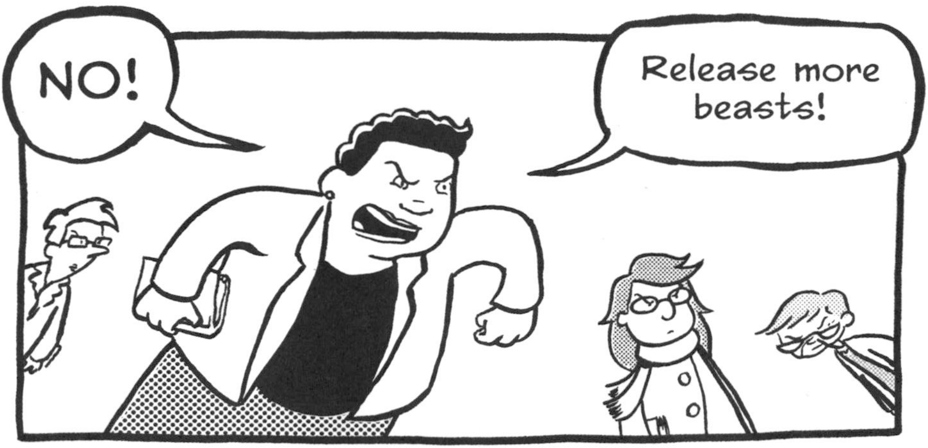
NO!
Release more beasts!

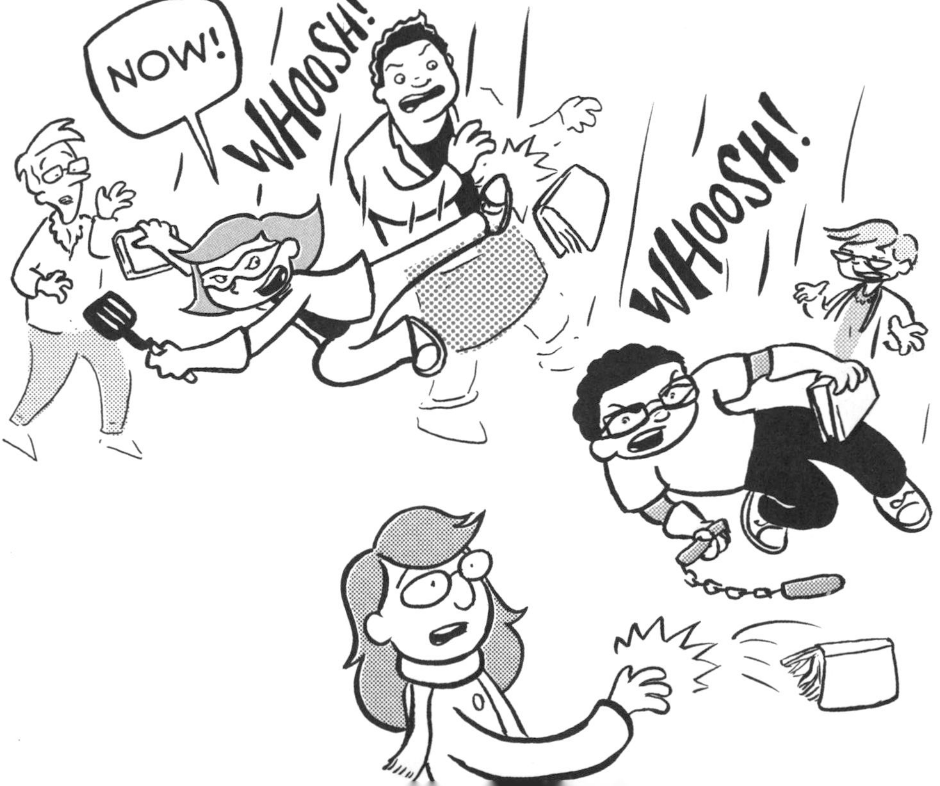
NOW!
WHOOSH!
WHOOSH!

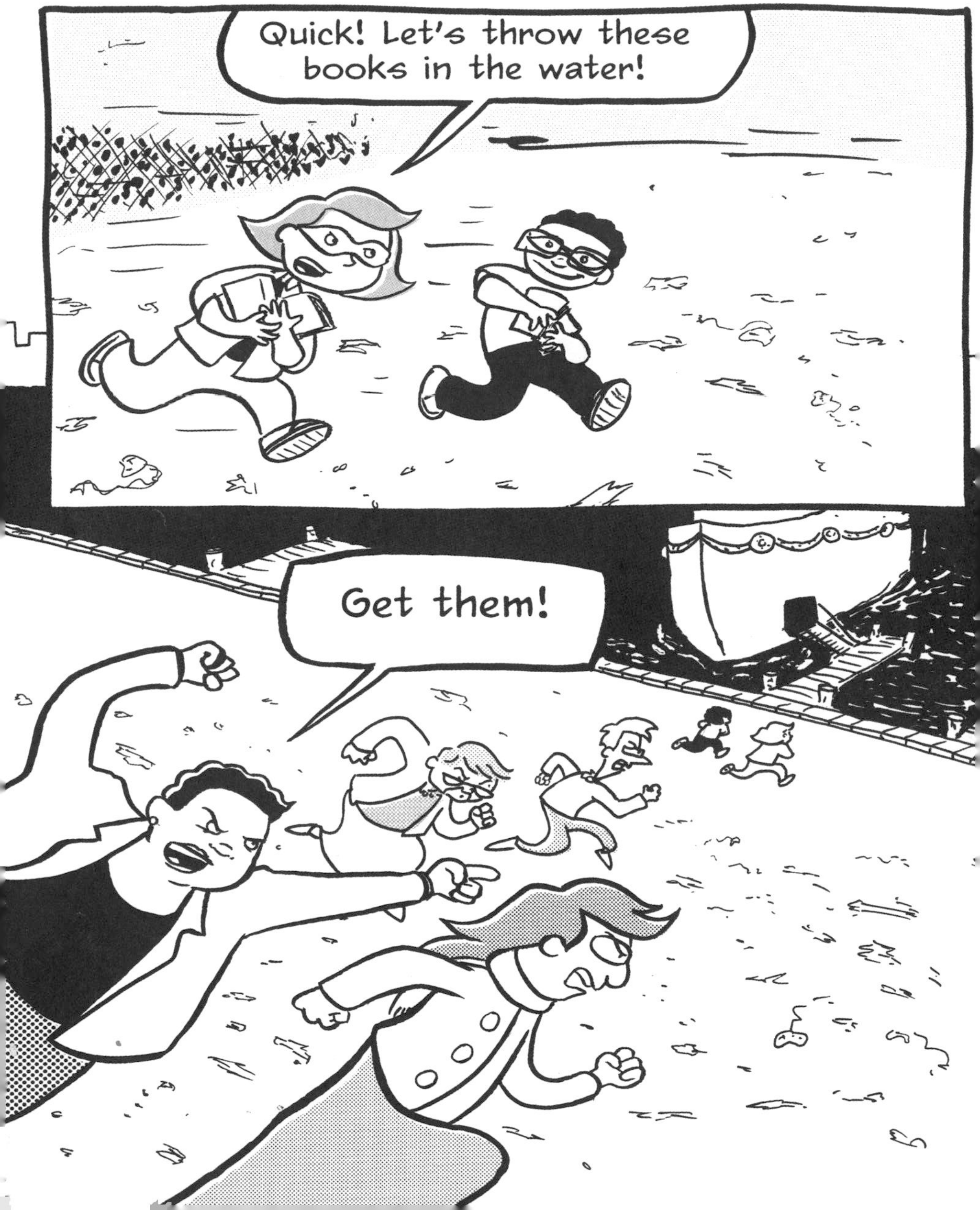
Quick! Let's throw these books in the water!
Get them!

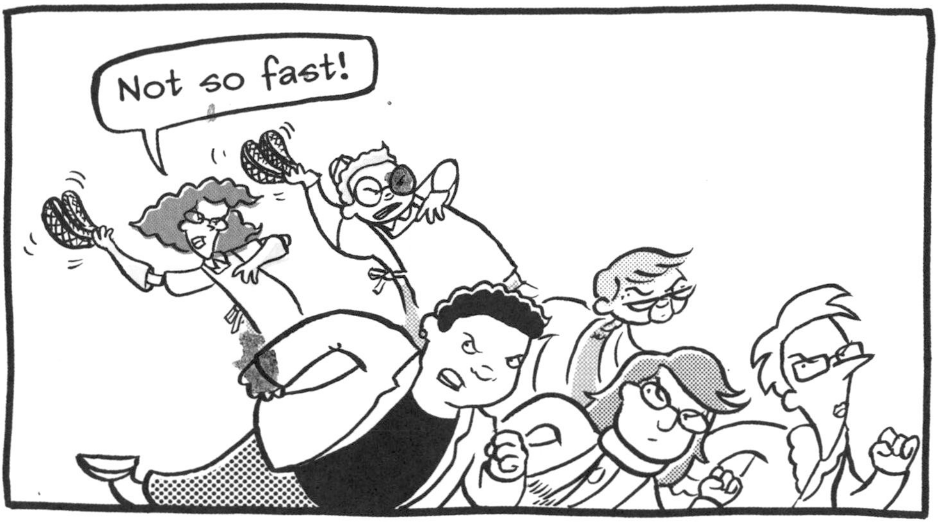
Not so fast!

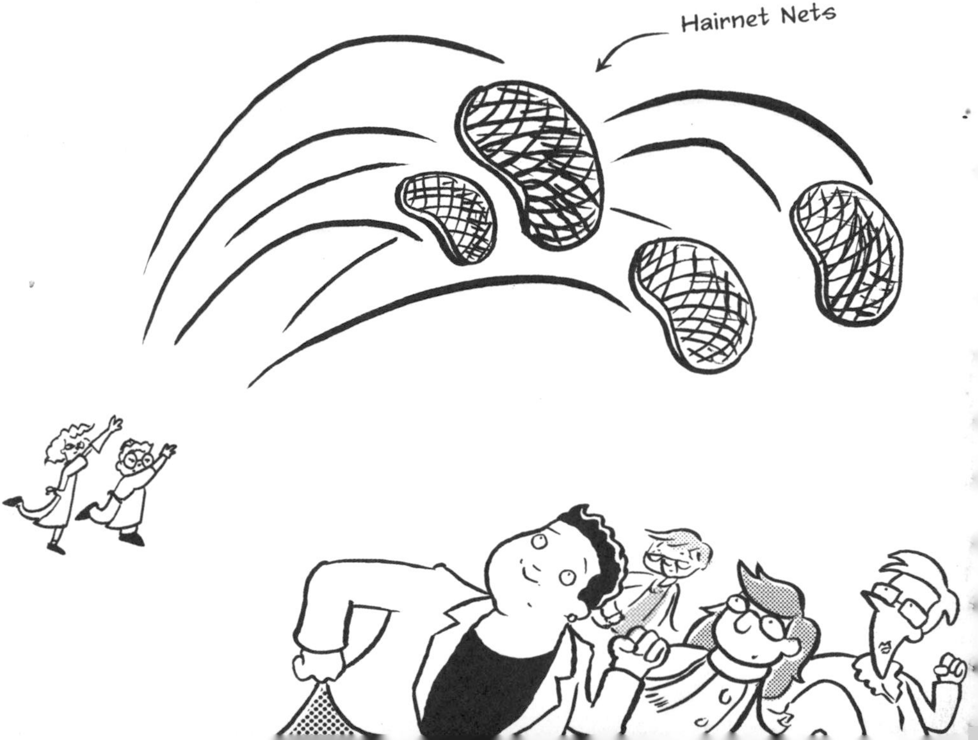
Hairnet Nets

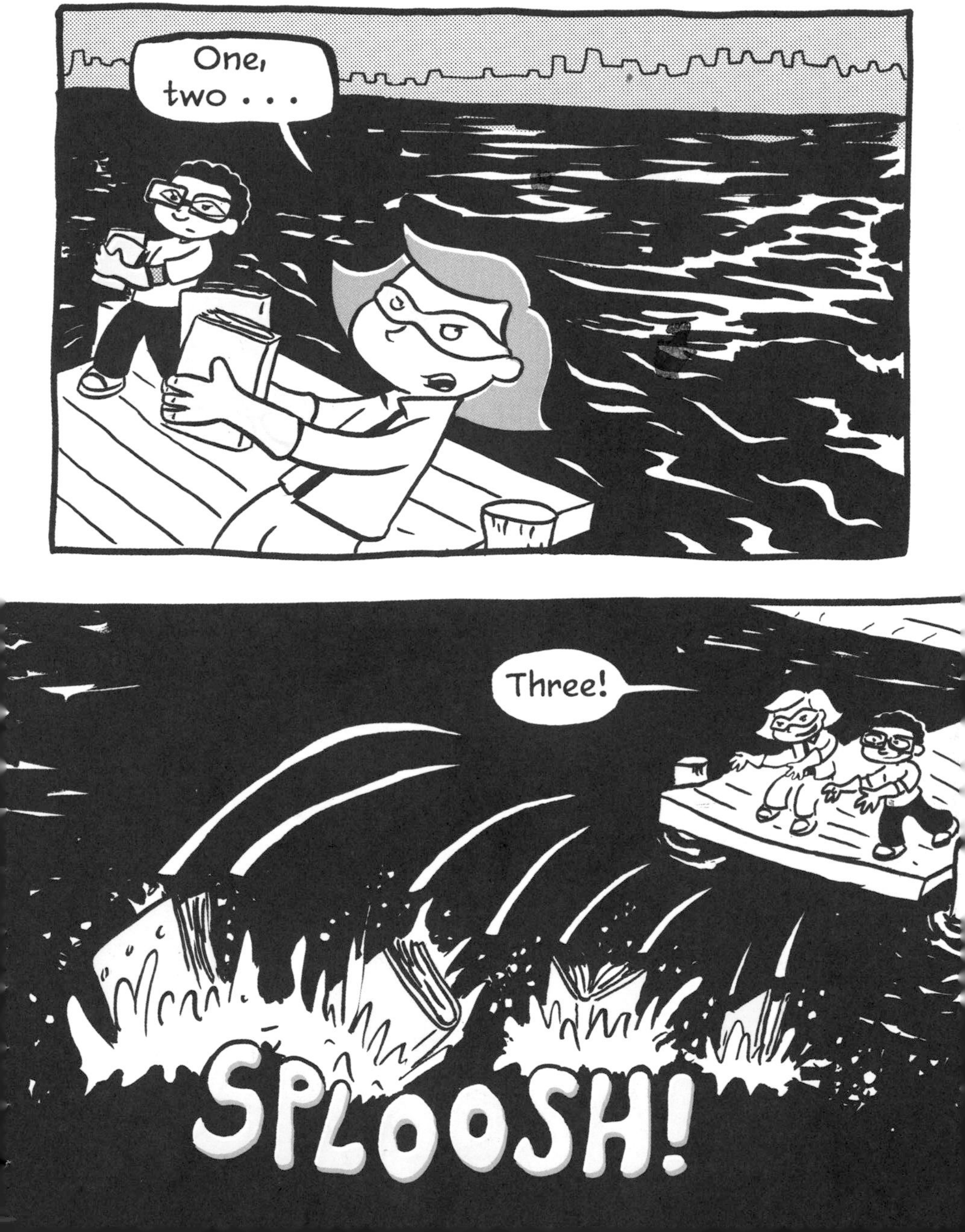
One, two . . .
Three!
SPLOOSH!

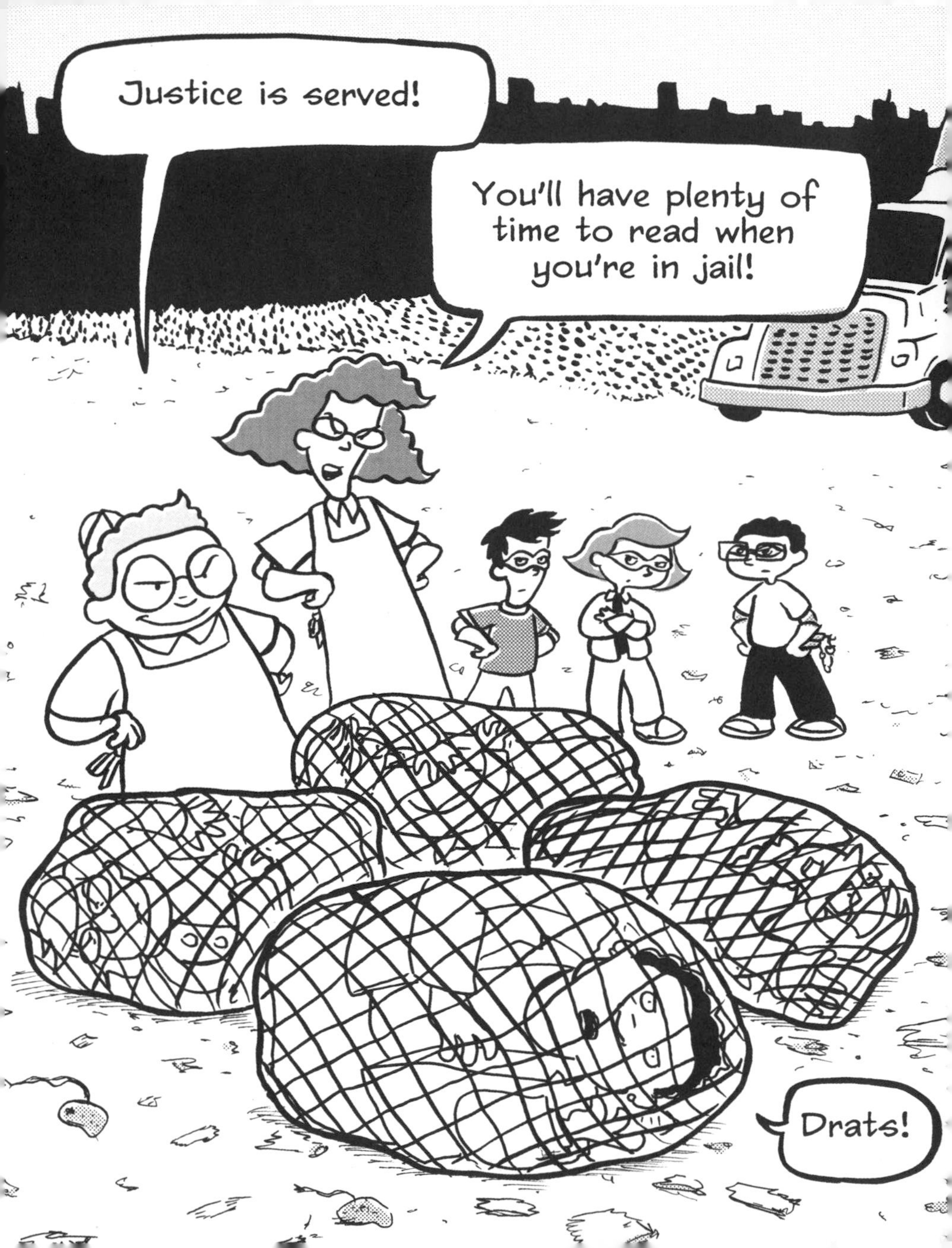
Justice is served!
You'll have plenty of time to read when you're in jail!
Drats!

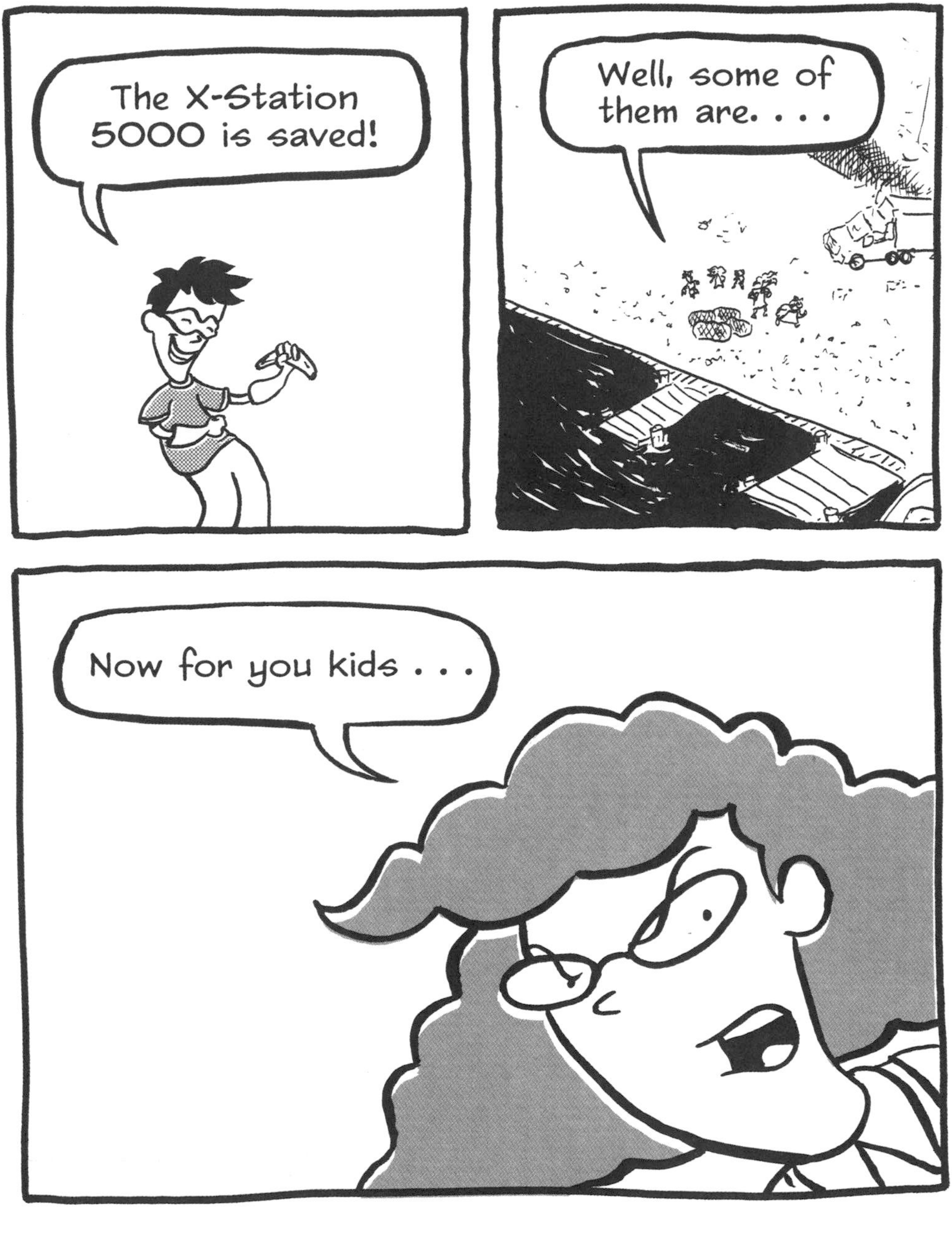
The X-Station 5000 is saved!
Well, some of them are. . . .
Now for you kids . . .

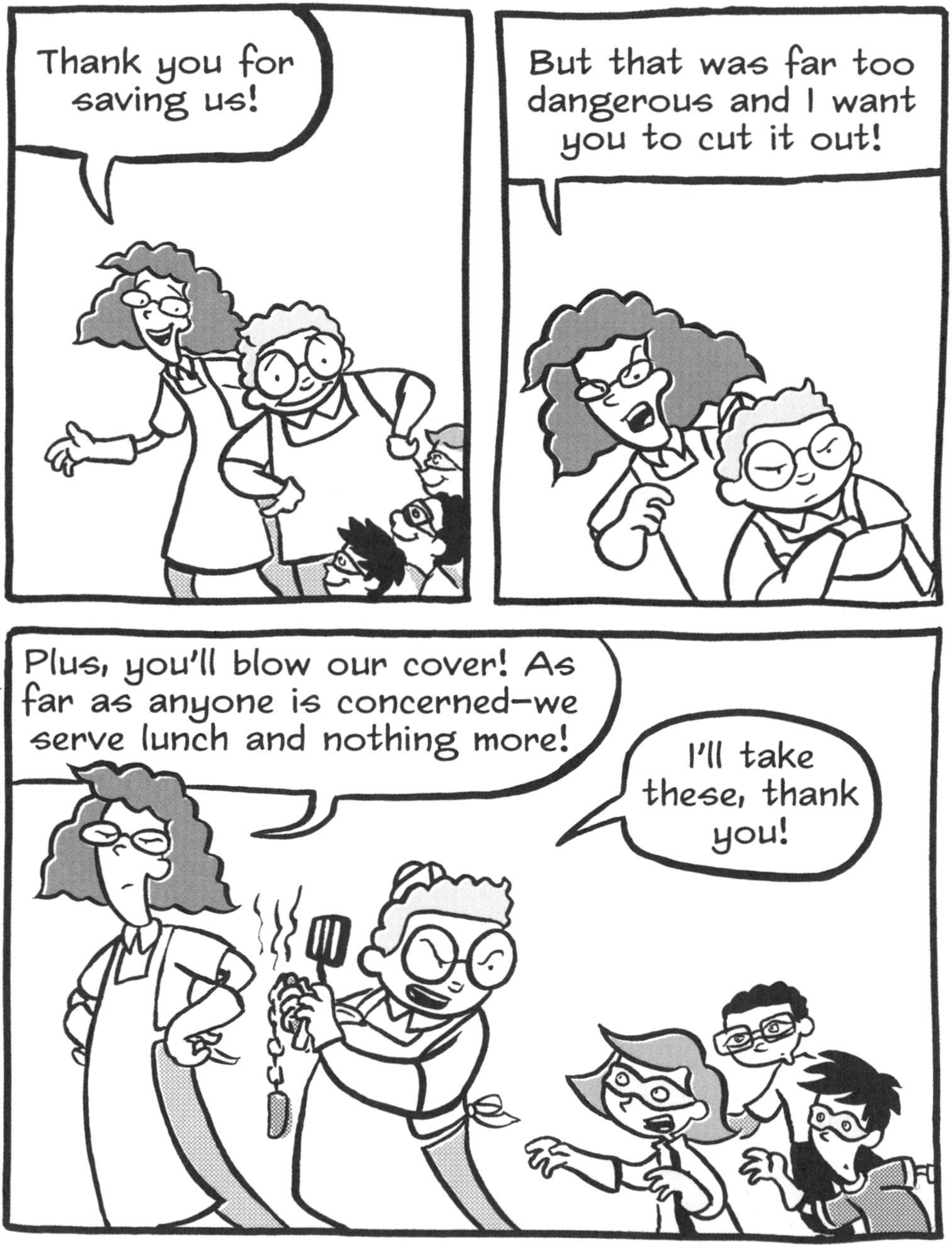

Thank you for saving us!
But that was far too dangerous and I want you to cut it out!
Plus, you'll blow our cover! As far as anyone is concerned—we serve lunch and nothing more!
I'll take these, thank you!

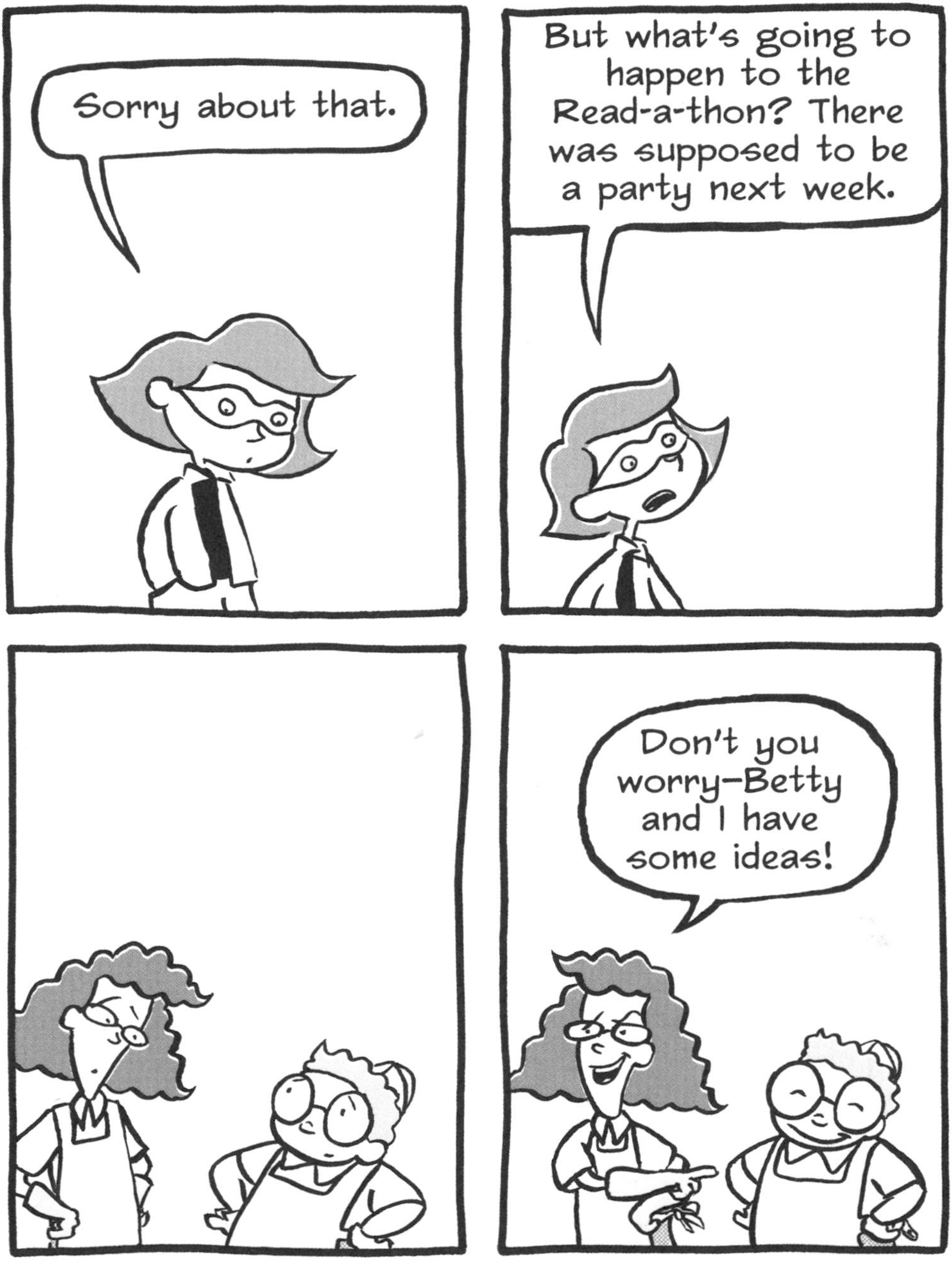
Sorry about that.
But what's going to happen to the Read-a-thon? There was supposed to be a party next week.
Don't you worry—Betty and I have some ideas!

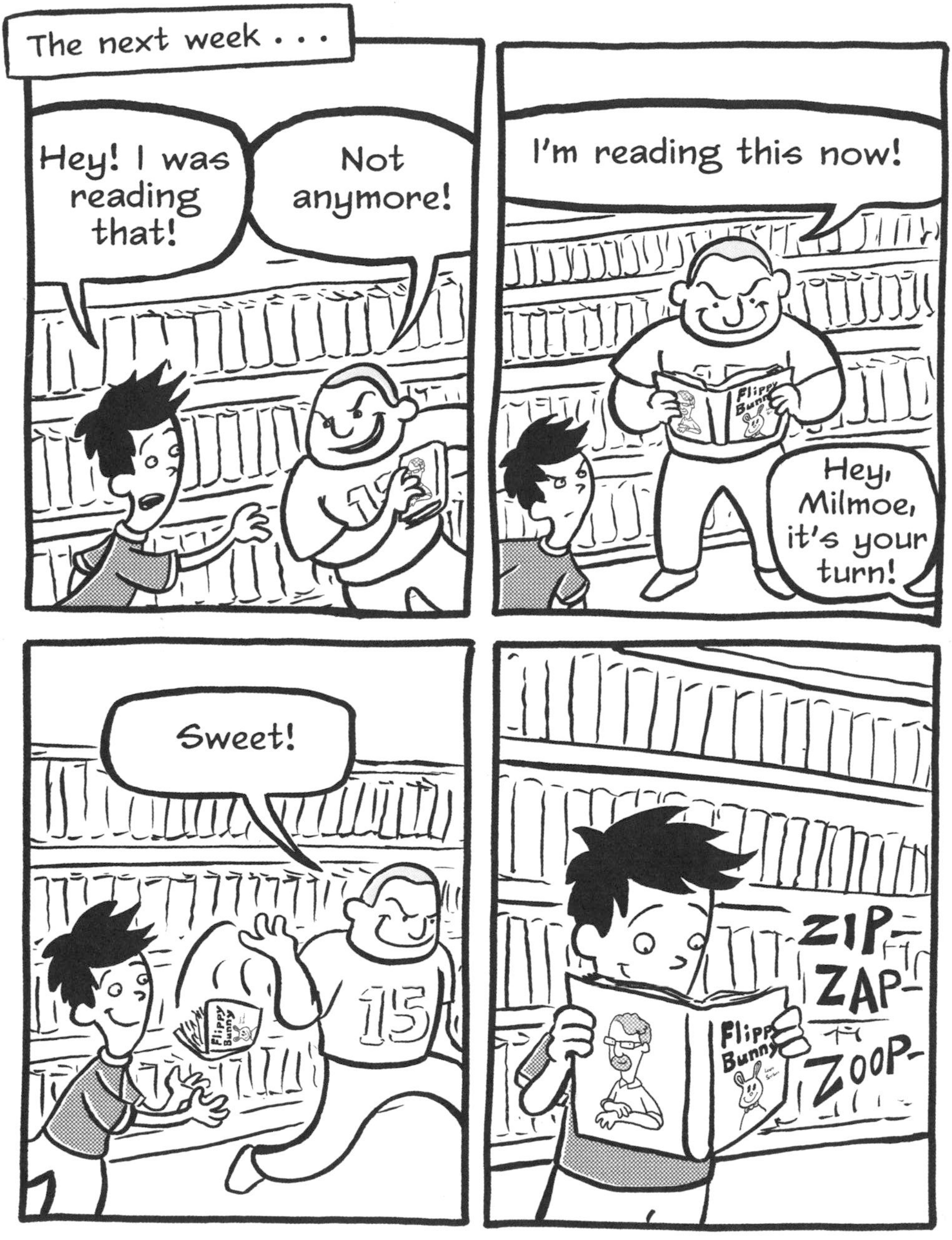
The next week . . .
Hey! I was reading that!
Not anymore!
I'm reading this now!
Hey, Milmoe, it's your turn!
Sweet!
Flippy Bunny
15
ZIP
ZAP
ZOOP

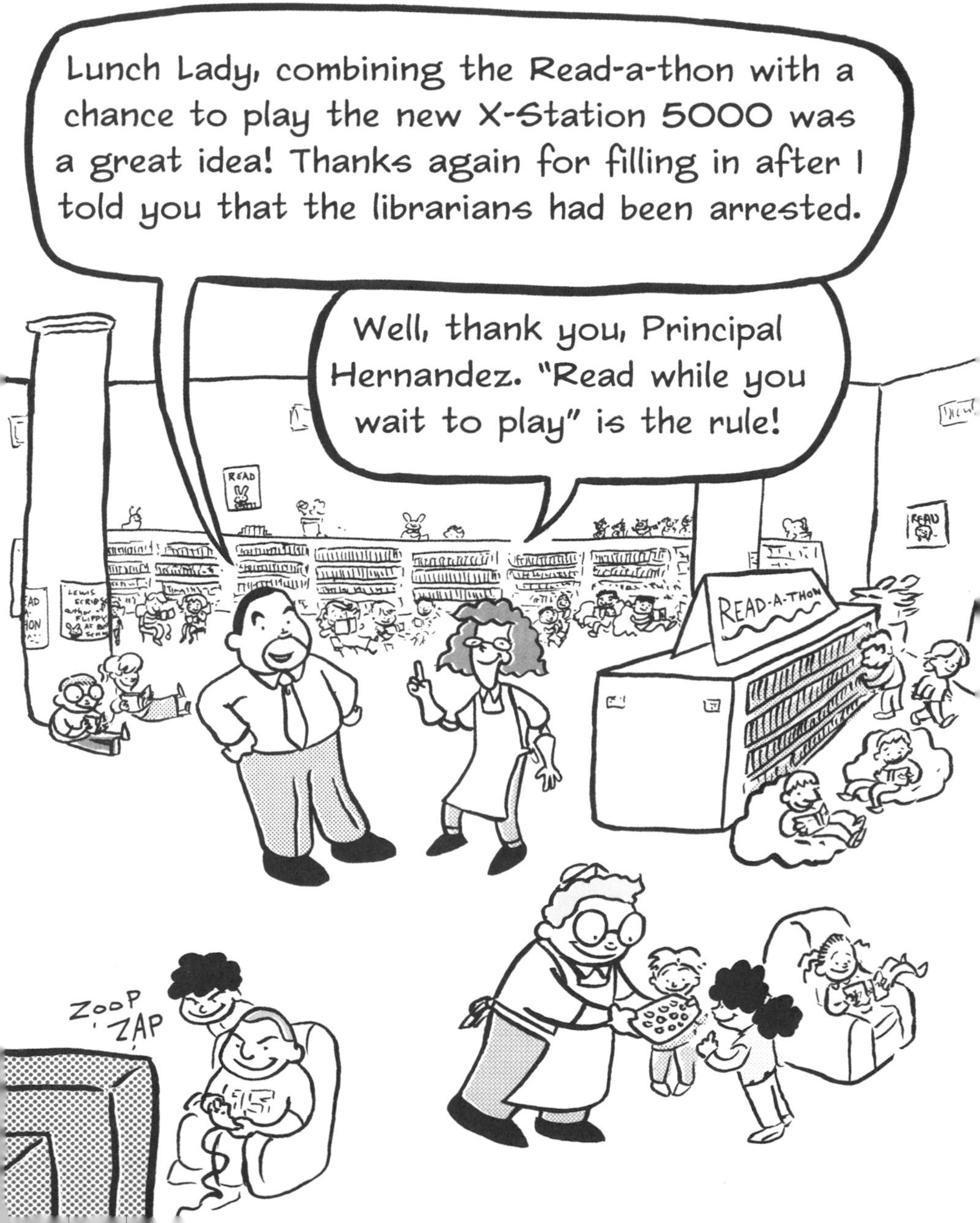
Lunch Lady, combining the Read-a-thon with a chance to play the new X-Station 5000 was a great idea! Thanks again for filling in after I told you that the librarians had been arrested.
Well, thank you, Principal Hernandez. "Read while you wait to play" is the rule!
READ
READ-A-THON
ZOOP
ZAP

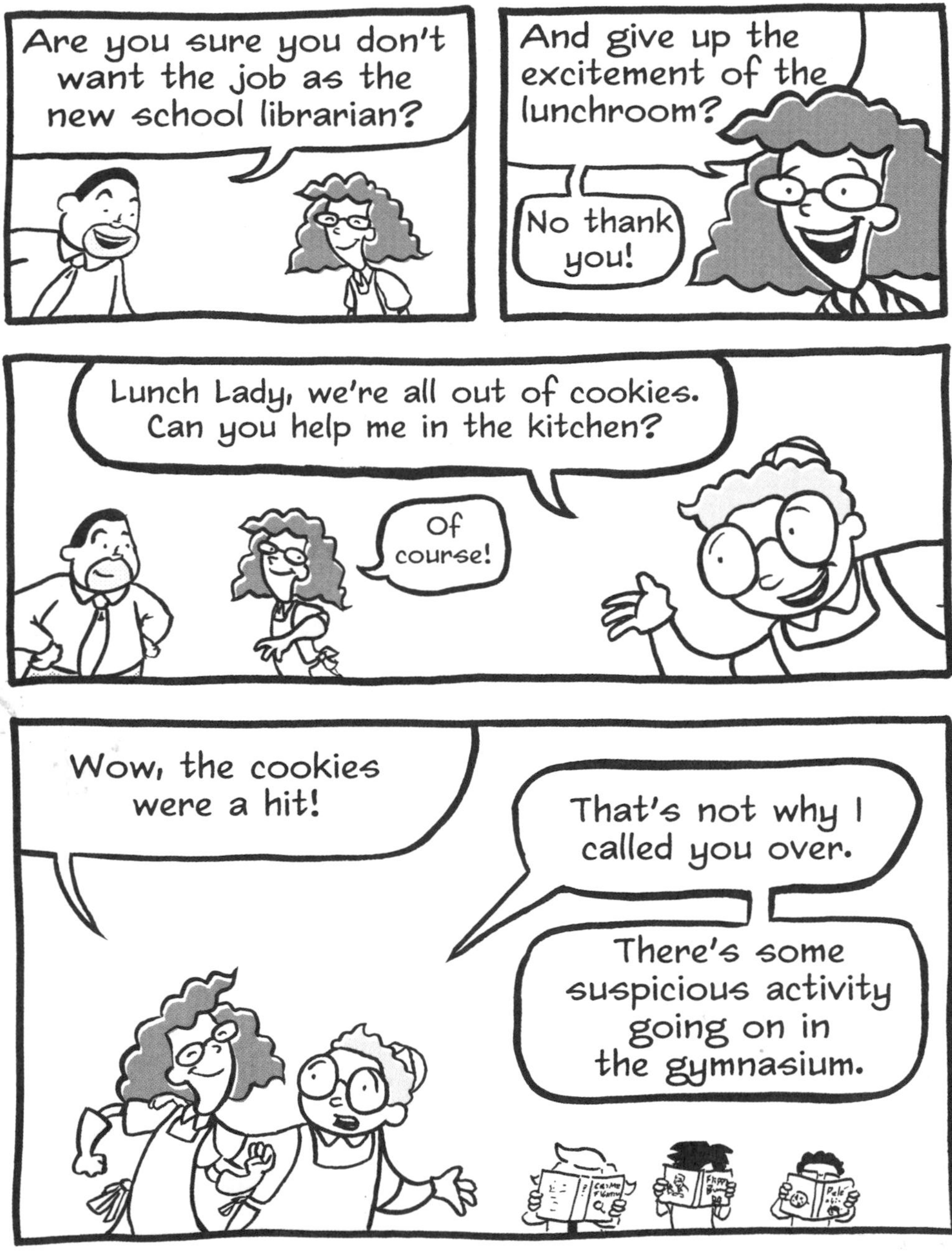
Are you sure you don't want the job as the new school librarian?
And give up the excitement of the lunchroom?
No thank you!
Lunch Lady, we're all out of cookies. Can you help me in the kitchen?
Of course!
Wow, the cookies were a hit!
That's not why I called you over.
There's some suspicious activity going on in the gymnasium.

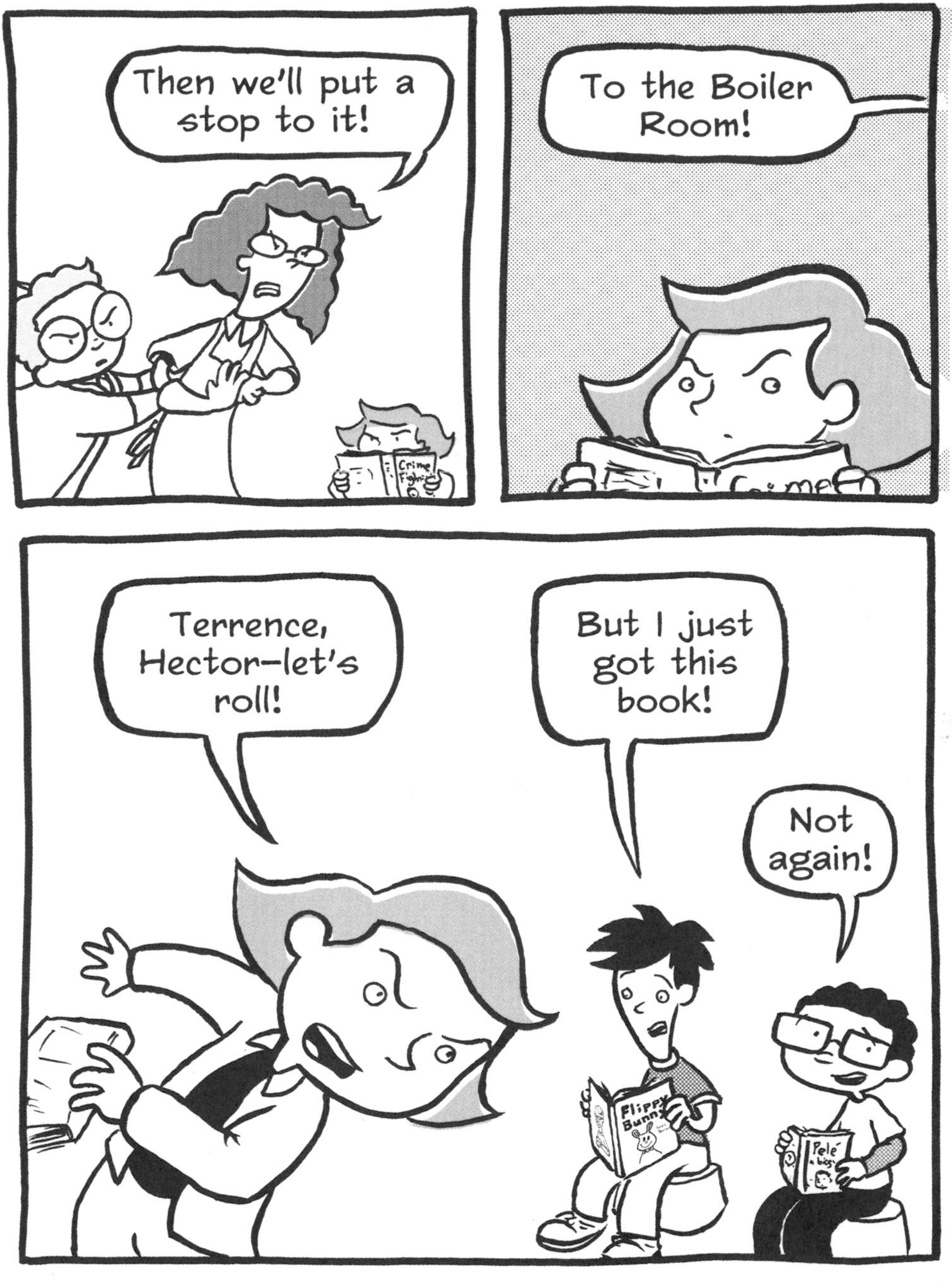
Then we'll put a stop to it!
To the Boiler Room!
Terrence, Hector—let's roll!
But I just got this book!
Not again!

For Mrs. Krosoczka and Ralph Macchio
–J.J.K.

THIS IS A BORZOI BOOK PUBLISHED BY ALFRED A. KNOPF

Visit us on the Web! www.randomhouse.com/kids

Educators and librarians, for a variety of teaching tools,
visit us at www.randomhouse.com/teachers

Library of Congress Cataloging-in-Publication Data
Krosoczka, Jarrett.
Lunch Lady and the League of Librarians / Jarrett J. Krosoczka. — 1st ed.
p. cm.
Summary: The school lunch lady, a secret crime fighter, sets out to stop a group
of librarians bent on destroying a shipment of video games while a group of students
known as the Breakfast Bunch provides backup.
ISBN 978-0-375-84684-7 (trade pbk.) — ISBN 978-0-375-94684-4 (lib. bdg.)
1. Graphic novels. [1. Graphic novels. 2. Librarians—Fiction. 3. Books and reading—Fiction.
4. School lunchrooms, cafeterias, etc.—Fiction. 5. Schools—Fiction.] I. Title.
PZ7.7.K76Lul 2009   [Fic]—dc22   2008043117

The text of this book is set in 11-point Hedge Backwards Lower.

MANUFACTURED IN MALAYSIA
July 2009
10 9 8 7 6 5

First Edition